THE C

"Run!" Melelki cried, gripping her knife tightly. And they did.

There were more howls from behind them. Melelki glanced back, trying to see through watering eyes. They had run through a milling mass of goblins. Most of the creatures simply looked on, confused and surprised, but some were beginning to follow.

The road before them was rocky but clear. They pushed themselves and ran faster. Behind, Melelki could hear a stampede of small footsteps.

"Don't wait for me," she got out between breaths. "Go! Keep running," she yelled fiercely at Tamun. "Get to Teedmar. You understand?"

"Mama!"

"Say it!"

"I will!"

Melelki yanked her hand out of Tamun's grasp, stopped suddenly, and whirled to face the oncoming horde, hoping that Tamun was still running.

Look for
MAGIC: The Gathering

From HarperPrism

*coming soon

MAGIC
The Gathering™

AND PEACE
SHALL SLEEP

Sonia Orin Lyris

HarperPrism
An Imprint of HarperPaperbacks

This is a work of fiction. The characters, incidents, and dialogues are products of the author's imagination and are not to be construed as real. Any resemblance to actual events or persons, living or dead, is entirely coincidental.

HarperPaperbacks   *A Division of* HarperCollins*Publishers*
10 East 53rd Street, New York, N.Y. 10022

Cover illustration by Gerry Grace

First printing: July 1996

Printed in the United States of America

HarperPrism is an imprint of HarperPaperbacks. HarperPaperbacks, HarperPrism, and colophon are trademarks of HarperCollins*Publishers*.

❖ 10 9 8 7 6 5 4 3 2 1

For Devin, with love.
schlurp

ACKNOWLEDGMENTS

I understand that some authors write alone. I don't. I rummage through the minds of the people I know, seeking out ideas and plot twists to turn into stories. Then I cajole many of those same hapless people into reading my early drafts.

To show my appreciation to these kind souls I name characters after them (or promise not to), lavish them with praise, and occasionally even listen to their comments. I'd like to take a moment to thank some of the people who have been generous enough to give me their time, expertise, and encouragement on this novel.

Heartfelt thanks to my first readers: liesl, Elizabeth Lawhead Bourne, Martitia M. Dell, John E. Johnston III, and Glenn A. Slate. (A nod also to Shannon Slate, whose fault it is that I got hooked on MAGIC™ in the first place. Boy, do I owe you.)

A very special thanks to David Kell Fox, for whom Reod Dai is named, who persistently and optimistically helped me sweat the story's details and heart, not just once, but many, many times over.

And lastly, there are no words that will suffice to thank my friend and partner Devin Ben-Hur, who believed in me from the very start all those years ago, knew better than I did how well I could write, and helped me find my courage even when it was hidden behind the spare batteries and science experiments in the fridge. I owe him for every word I've had published.

Sonia Orin Lyris
February 1996

AND PEACE SHALL SLEEP

PROLOGUE

MUCH IS MADE OF THE ICE AGE AS THE cause of the fall of the Sarpadian empires. While the cooling climate of Sarpadia was a factor in the struggles for resources that led to the great wars, other important factors are often overlooked. Thousands of years of racial tensions created an atmosphere of mistrust, escalating misunderstandings into differences, and differences into wars.

Records from those times indicate that there would have been more than enough food to feed all of Sarpadia's children, even at the worst of the freeze, had the empires been willing to cooperate, which, of course, they were not.

While the high courts of the land clung to their traditional struggles, the screams of battle and cries of the hungry echoed from sea to mountain, bringing another message entirely. Despite the flowery words of kings and councils, politic to the bitter end, there was never any question that when frost and famine came, every race would hold tight to what it had, keeping the best for itself, each convinced that another had more. Individuals counted for little in those final days, serving their race only as hands and feet and then, finally, as hungry, hungry mouths.

In times of such scarcity, suspicion, and hardship, there can be only one result.

So did the great wars begin, and the great empires begin to fall.

—*Sarpadian Empires Vol. I, Introduction*

We cannot expect even those who lived in the final days of Sarpadia to understand their times as well as we do now, we who have the maps of warlords and the diaries of kings.

But I must warn you, as you study these times, not to be distracted by individuals. They seem so romantic to us, these heroes and villains of the last days of the Sarpadian empires, but they were like actors in a drama that they could not escape. Examine closely and I am sure you will conclude that a single person can never truly affect the movement of empires. Even in those cases where it seems that a single man or woman was crucial to a series of events, look more deeply and you will discover that there were others who could have stepped in at a moment's notice to fill the same role.

In history there are no true heroes and no true villains. History moves people, and not the other way around.

—*Lady Ornder, introduction to Letters: A History of Sarpadia*

You are to inform the commanders that if he is found he is to be arrested on charges of high treason. Remind them of the destruction his betrayals have cost us. They have my authority to execute him on the spot rather than to again risk his escape.

No one must speak of him. See to it that his mother and father act as if he had never been born.

Erase his name from all possible records. Be thorough. I do not want him remembered.

—*Fragments of a letter found under the rubble at
Trokair. Signed "HJ." Matches handwriting samples of
King Henry Joseph I.*

*Nail the robin way up high
to hush away his many lies
Keep the traitor from our door
Stay away! Come no more!
Praise the army, praise the king
The traitor will no longer sing*

(whispered)

*Robin bring us meat and bread
And stay the demons of the dead
Robin fly high into the night
I'll say nothing of your flight
Robin fly here to your home
The king is dead, the rest are bone.*

—*Icatian children's rhyme*

CHAPTER

1

"I'd rather trade with elves than sleep with pigs, but not by much."

—Icatian trader

IT WAS A MONTH BEFORE THE FIRST DAY of winter, and Reod Dai was tired of being cold. Even in thick boots his toes ached. Someone ought to tell the Crimson Peaks that winter was supposed to be only one of the four seasons.

A weak sun shone down through gaps in the thick clouds, adding no hint of warmth to the bitter morning breezes that danced snowflakes up and around the sides of thatched stone houses. Piles of ice and crusted snow framed the village walkways and glinted off the high pines.

Reod Dai twisted one end of his heavy wool cloak up and around his shoulders to gain an extra layer and brushed newly gathered snowflakes out of his beard with covered fingers.

At the center of the cobbled square he stopped, drawn by the promise of warmth to a handful of dwarves clustered at the edge of a blazing firepit. After four days travel over snow-thick roads, his appointment could wait a few more moments. Around the fire dwarves chatted in heavy mountain dialect about logging and grain stores and who might be promised to whom by next spring. No mention at all of the unusually cold autumn.

So Reod took what satisfaction he could from dwarven noses red with chill. Last year at another village they had laughed at his hand-coverings, but this year everyone wore them, and children had cold-weather hoods and scarves. They might not mention the cold, stubborn mountain creatures that they were, but they felt it.

He exhaled, his breath smoke-thick in the morning air.

A dwarf edged away from him a little, to see him better, and the rest stared at him.

"What's that doing here?" one asked another, thinking he could not understand their dwarven dialect.

"Ta, a human here, in winter? Must be lost."

"It must be so cold. Poor fragile humans."

To further confuse matters, he had dressed in coarse clothes and acted the part of a poor trader. Now he smiled at them a little, as if sharing the joke at his own expense. They fell silent, not quite sure if he might have understood.

The flickering warmth of the fire brushed across his face. He took one last breath of warm, smoky air, and continued on into the village.

For all the harshness of this land where winter lasted more than half the year, Reod would find more hospitality here in isolated villages of the Crimson Peaks than he would in warmer human settlements to the north. In truth, this mountainous land was a haven. He doubted that the dwarves knew how fortunate they were to live in a place so remote from the strife in the warmer lands.

Children and adults stared openly at him as he walked by. It was not merely his human features, or his height—

they stood only up to his chest—or that he was human-thin, or that his night-black hair was so startling in this sea of straw-colored manes. They did see humans here in the Peaks south of the Icatian borders, rarely this time of year, but every spring humans came to trade.

No, they had all seen humans. It was not that. It was Reod's blue eyes, strange even among his own kind.

"Like robins' eggs," a boy whispered to his mother as they walked by, both turning to look at him.

Like robins' eggs. He could hood his hair, dye his skin, or change his accent, but his eyes would always be blue.

At the Brave Rabbit Inn, Reod pushed open the door, pulled it shut behind. The old dwarven man always kept a meat stew on the fire. Sometimes it was rabbit and sometimes it was better not to ask.

"It's a brave rabbit," the old dwarven man said in greeting, "who first goes into the pot. Do you want some?"

Reod eyed the bowl of meat chunks and vegetables suspiciously.

"Of course. Thanks."

At the far end of the room sat the woman he had come to meet.

If his features were an unexpected spark of light in the dimness of this village's overcast day, hers stood out like a moon on a cloudless night.

"Cold enough, Kistefar?" he asked in elven, sitting down across from her with his bowl of stew.

She turned pale green eyes on him, green as the northernmost seas.

"Yes. Cold."

Havenwood was as far north as Icatia and farther. She would be used to warmer weather and would be as miserable in this cold as he. Worse, elven-thin as she was.

The old dwarven man brought him hot wine, and Reod downed both that and the stew quickly. The cold made him hungry, always hungry.

Kistefar watched him with her impassive stare. When he finished the last bit and sat back, she bent forward, pulling from under her clothes a chain that he knew always hung around her neck when she traveled on behalf of the elder druids. Bright green flashed at him briefly then vanished again into her shirt.

He shrugged a little, hiding a sharp stab of anxiety.

"Why should I doubt you?"

She had not brought out that token since they had first spoke years ago. He already knew that she represented the interests of the elder druids. There was no need to demonstrate it again.

"Your contract is terminated," she said.

"What?"

"I am instructed to tell you to stop whatever operations you are conducting on our behalf."

"The contract has another year, Kistefar. Funds thrice yearly. *Now*, that is."

"No funds, Reod."

"But we have an agreement, a contract—"

"No funds."

"Kistefar, listen: I cannot stop now. Without funding these operations will break like glass, leaving sharp fragments everywhere."

"I am not here to negotiate. I am only a messenger."

"I cannot accept this."

Her fingers touched her chest, where the stone hung hidden. A reminder. She spoke for the elders, but how much did they rely on her to act for them? Little, he suspected.

"I do not doubt you, Kistefar. Why do your elders do this?"

"I do not know."

"What did they say?"

"'Have the human Reod Dai stop all operations. Tell him the contract is no longer in force. As of this moment we cease to supply him with funds for any such actions.'"

In his mind Reod saw the paths of alliance he had so

laboriously built over the last years, like carefully tended vines. Without his constant attention, some vines would wither and die. Others would grow out of anyone's control.

He leaned forward, met her eyes, and lowered his voice. "Do you know what I have risked these past years for your elders? Do you know how many times I have crossed into orc and goblin territory, gone into their caves to treat with them, not knowing if I would again see the light of day? I have crossed dangerous borders. I have made promises. Do you have any notion what will happen when those promises are broken?"

"That is not my concern."

When Reod had met with Tirraturranum weeks ago it had been all he could do to convince the goblin king to wait to test the new weapons. With succession to the goblin throne both quick and violent, the king was eager to act with his new power while he still could.

And that made the orcs nervous. Usually enemies, the leaders of both races were willing—at least for the moment—to let Reod lead them into an alliance, an idea they had never considered before. The balance was delicate. The elder druids could not have picked a worse time.

"Three months," he said. "Give me that. One more installment. I will do what I can to minimize the damage, to finish things off."

"No." She began to rise. To leave.

He struggled to swallow his frustration, to show her only calm and reason. With palms up, he put his hands out on the table. It was a gesture that crossed cultures, that meant peace, but might also mean a favor asked. The strangeness of it caught her eyes and she hesitated. He dropped into his story-telling voice, a voice with which he had held the attention of hundreds, even thousands. She sat down again.

"Imagine that you have taken a small bear into your house. Not merely into your house, Kistefar, but imagine that you have let it sleep at the foot of your bed.

Every day you feed it, every day it grows a little. Now it has grown large, very large. And then, one day, for some reason you simply stop giving it food." He held her gaze in his own a long moment. "At least let me put a chain around the beast's neck."

"It is not my decision to make."

"You have their ear, Kistefar. You must."

"I serve my elders. I have faith in their wisdom."

"Their wisdom will draw great quantities of blood."

"As your people have not?"

"We have. Certainly. But there will be far more."

"Indeed, Reod Dai? I ask you: is there a people who have spilled more blood than yours? Your kind is so generous with your words and actions, but the rest of us only wish to live in our own ways with our own words. It is said that a human only knows how to keep silent and when to stop moving when it is dead."

"I have heard it, and many other sayings not so generous. But we are not talking about humans. We are talking about orcs and goblins, who are even harder to reason with, and who have become a force capable of great damage, a force that needs careful tending. My reports should have made that clear. Did your elders receive them?"

"They did."

"These creatures will soon be more than an irritation. Do the elders intend me to leave them so strong? Surely not, Kistefar. They must let me make sure that the creatures cannot do great harm."

"Again, no."

He shut his eyes. The strength of the goblin mobs and orc bands was little now to what it could be in a month or more if the alliance held without his involvement.

"It will take me weeks to get to Havenwood. Must I go there to talk to them myself? Even in that short time goblins and orcs will act unchecked. But the elders must be made to see their decision for the folly it is."

"You will not be welcome in Havenwood."

Reod felt the chill outside creep into his stomach.

"I see."

"You are to stop all acts based on this contract. There will be no more funds—"

"You repeat yourself," he said sharply, his patience fraying.

"My elders also wish me to emphasize that—" Her tone quieted. "That it would be unwise for you to discuss the terms of the contract with anyone else."

"I see."

She stood quickly, her posture tense. "I am only a messenger, Reod."

He stood with her. "Those who die at goblin and orc hands will not much care who you are."

"I am not responsible for what goblins and orcs do."

"Your leaders have built a monster they will not control. Who should take the blame?"

"Some would say that it is you who have built the monster."

"At whose direction? Tell your elders that they are making a wretched mistake."

"I will relay your words."

"Tell them I am not pleased."

"I do not believe they thought you would be otherwise."

"Make sure they know that I will not soon forget this."

"No one will forget, Reod Dai. Remember that when you consider what words you might say and to whom."

Reod struggled to keep his face clear as he gave her a small, restrained bow, which she returned.

"Safe travel to you, Kistefar."

"And to you, Reod Dai."

She hefted her pack and left the inn.

"The honor of elves," Reod said softly to himself, to see how the words tasted. Bitter.

Did the elders really think they could break the contract and rely on threats to buy his silence? In all his years of fulfilling contracts he had never been treated so poorly, not even by goblins and orcs, who at least understood the risk of not keeping their promises. Reod could not afford to let this breach go by unquestioned and without consequence.

His original plan took him from this village back to the orc generals and goblin king, to then proceed with the careful business of arranging their first mutual target. But without the coin and weapons today's meeting was supposed to have given him, they would not be impressed. He could not go there with empty hands. His plans would have to change.

A month hence, near winter's first day, deep in the Crimson Peaks, there would be waiting for him the most powerful weapons in his arsenal. The weapons would be available only there, and only then. Now, without his funds, he could not afford to purchase them.

But he would have to find a way.

South it was, then, and directly, with a few favors called in along the way. South, to where it was even colder.

With that sour thought, he gestured to the old man to bring him more hot wine and food.

CHAPTER

2

"Do not rely on humans. A goat is more trustworthy."

—Dwarven proverb

MELELKI FORCED HERSELF AWAKE, BLINKING weariness out of her eyes, and pushed herself out of the warm blankets. She struggled to her feet, dressed, and stamped outside the tiny cabin into the winter sun.

"Daylight to you," she said, greeting her daughters.

"Daylight, Mama," Tamun said, sounding entirely too cheerful. She stood by the clothesline near a basket of wet clothes.

Melelki sat down on the step next to her other daughter. Sekena groaned. With her own arms and back aching Melelki knew that the fifteen-year-old would be feeling even worse from the long night's hard labor.

High, icy rocks and long drops, all by lamplight. It was good that they were all competent climbers. And dangerous though it was in darkness, it was still far better than risking running into a men's mining group during the day. The miners would not appreciate what the women were bringing down from the mountain.

Hard work, indeed. But for this year, at least, the work and danger were past. Now they had sixteen eggs in the basement, and that meant gold. Melelki smiled.

Among the clothes Tamun was pinning to the line were sheets of linen so thin that tree-splintered sunlight shone through them onto the flat, small stones on the ground. The linen was for stretching across a frame and sewing pictures into, though lately they had not been doing much of that. In winter they would. When it was too cold to do much else.

But Tamun, getting up so early after the work they had done last night—she must hardly have slept at all. No sleep, after carrying far more than her share of sixteen eggs down the steep mountain trail, from the high cradle to the cabin. And still so much spirit?

There was, unfortunately, only one explanation.

Melelki put an arm around her youngest daughter. "You were so strong last night."

"Thank you, Mama."

She tilted her head close to Sekena's, enough to mix their thick dwarf-streaked straw colored strands, and whispered, "Look at Tamun. See the blush? The color under her eyes? The red on her ears? Notice how little sleep she wants? First heat, that's what it is."

"No," Sekena gave back in whispered shock. "She's too young."

Melelki snorted softly. "Ta! You're the one to ask, eh, child? Fifteen years and you're an elder wisewoman?"

Sekena blushed and scowled. "She's too young," she said, her insistent voice tinged with fear.

"If you're going to talk about me," Tamun said from the line, "speak up so I can hear you."

Her mother sighed. "You look to me to be going into first heat."

Tamun's hands froze on the line. She looked distant. "That would explain—well, a number of things. But I'm only nineteen."

"Ta, a woman's time of power doesn't come to every woman in the same way or time, my eldest flower.

Rare as early as you, but also rare as late as twenty-five, as with my sister Belkena some years back. Remember the year we had the big earthquake, with her pregnant? She's got three now, two girls, and can barely take a breath for all the talking she does about them."

"Hope it never comes to me at *all*," murmured Sekena.

Her mother cuffed her lightly on the head. "Ta. Then what will you do, steal Belkena's extras? I can have children no better than the stones can, so you'll get no more from me. Take it when it comes, because you'll only have a few years of heat. Don't wish for idiot things."

"But I don't want—"

"Hush," Melelki said, putting an arm around her daughter's broad shoulders. "It's fun, you'll see. You'll be as strong as the strongest of the men. Not that they would be able to resist your charms anyway. But then they'll come all the time. They'll bring gifts. Jewels and pretty things forged—"

"Swords?"

"Perhaps, if that's what you want. And then. Well . . ." She smiled a little. "You'll see."

"I'm strong enough to carry dragon eggs, Mama. Isn't that strong enough?"

"Hush," Melelki said quickly. "Only talk about that inside, child. I've told you that. Someone could be coming up the path. Even the trees—"

"Mama, in the years we've been—"

"Magic can hear," Melelki insisted.

"But that's silly—"

"I said *hush*," Melelki said, her voice turning as sharp as the needles the three of them used to sew picture into the fine linen. With that she stood, brushed down her trousers, and went to help Tamun hang clothes.

"We've got a lot of sewing to do for the fine ladies in the big houses in Kalitas next spring. Isn't that right?"

"Yes, Mama," Tamun said enthusiastically.

"Ta." Sekena exhaled, threw her hands wide in disgust, and went into the house.

Tamun snorted and softly said, "Does she want to go back to dyed fingers and bloody pin-sticks? Not me. And this year, with the gold, we could even move back to Tigaden. Don't you think, Mama? Seems that it gets colder up here every winter."

"Oh, it's not so bad. And the village isn't that far."

"Most of a day there and back, Mama."

"Ah, there is that, especially now, with you—"

Her daughter blushed a little, frowned, stared at the ground.

Maybe it would be a good time to go back to live with family and friends and not have to walk nearly a day to get to the market. Of course, here they had a lot of privacy, and that was nice, too.

And here they were closer to the mountaintop. Closer to the cradle. She thought again of the gold the eggs would bring. Last year and the year before it had seemed so much, but somehow there was always less left than she had expected. It wasn't that they spent too much. No, it was the price of things. At market this year everything had cost many times what it should.

Or maybe it was that they didn't work as hard on their sewing, knowing that the eggs would be there the next winter.

They had become used to living in a clean place, without rats and bugs and crawling slime. Their poorer days seemed long ago. Then Melelki's only luxury had been the mountain, which she would climb just because she wanted to. The mountain was a sort of question, and every time she climbed it she found a different answer.

It was fine luck the autumn day she had found the cradle, fine luck and a strange scent that caught her attention, leading her up and up, past outcroppings and long drops onto sharp stones, to a small opening between two high peaks of ice-crusted rock.

And there it had been: a cache of large white eggs, bright and sparkling, hinting of rainbow colors under the sun's touch. Like goose eggs, they were, but much, much larger, each longer than her arm. She knew that there was only one thing they could be.

Dragon eggs.

Some would have turned and fled, fearful not just of the hatchlings but of the parents. It was said the adults could destroy whole villages with an exhale of fire.

But to leave now would mean that she would always wonder, and there was nothing worse than that. It would keep her up at night, wishing she had taken a closer look.

So she walked around the eggs, heart crashing inside her, but eyes and hands too fascinated to leave until she had run her fingers over all the hard shells.

Dragons would come out of these. Dragons.

She had seen them before, but only from a distance, during harvest. Every now and then one would come, flying so far away it looked like a bird, except that it wasn't the right shape for a bird. Then everyone would stop whatever they were doing, point and yell. At night there would be tales of dragons feeding on virgins and lining their nests with babies.

Melelki grinned at the eggs. There were no babies here. Maybe it wasn't true about the virgins, either.

Her mind moved in new directions as her eyes flickered over the sparkling eggs. She and her daughters were mud-poor. She had heard once that humans and elves made jewelry from dragon shells and sometimes even weapons. What might a whole egg be worth?

And who would buy it?

Weeks earlier, an arrogant, thin human with blue eyes and stringy black hair had come to the village, spending money, buying up weapons from the high-house smith. For the human soldiers, he said, fighting orcs to the north.

Melelki was sure that no dwarf in Tigaden would have the faintest notion of where to sell a dragon egg.

And dangerous as the hatchling whelps were, asking would only have the whole village fussing at her. So the day after she made her find, she swallowed her distrust of humans and went to the Squat Duck where the human was said to be staying. There she spent much to buy him too much hot wine, which she had heard was all that humans drank. Then she had asked him what he knew about dragons.

"I recommend avoiding them," he said.

"Well, what if someone were to find some—" she shrugged, "—some of the eggs? Would they be able to sell them? Usually we sell our cloth pictures, but if—"

His look had changed. He leaned forward, his voice much lower.

"Take care discussing such things. Items like those are worth much. Dangerous, too."

"Dangerous? Because of the whelps?"

"Yes."

When her eldest had still been a child, a dragon hatchling with a broken wing had somehow wandered into the village and tried to eat sausages off a marketer's cart. A fivecount of dwarves tried to tackle the whelp and it bloodied them all. Dwarven men, of course, braver than they were smart, had attacked barehanded. Only when the women came and thrust spears and swords into the little beast did it stop moving.

Everyone had been surprised that something so small could be so nasty. There had been a great deal of tale-telling that night to go with dragon whelp stew. She still remembered its odd taste.

The human was still watching her carefully. "I've never heard of them laying this far north before," he said slowly. "They like the cold. But I suppose it's possible."

She glared at him. "It is. But what about the parents?"

He sat back, took another swallow of wine as he stared at her, then continued. "The females lay in the high, southernmost mountains. They kick around ice and snow and boulders to make a nest, but that's it. They're lousy parents. Too horny to stick around. The females drop their eggs, then fly back to the warm lands where the males are. There they screw until the next time they have to lay."

She smirked at his crude words. "Do all humans speak dwarven language so well?"

"I doubt it."

"So the parents don't guard the eggs at all?" That would be a relief.

"No need to. The shells are as hard as metal, and the hatchlings can take care of themselves."

"What do the hatchlings eat?"

"Children and virgins."

He watched her a moment, then laughed. She scowled.

"Nothing bigger than they are, if they can help it," he said. "They're about the size of a large village mutt. They'll attack if they're scared, but they don't like to attack anything big. They'll eat almost anything. They prefer meat, but they'll eat grass, leaves, pine cones, fallen branches, even rotting trees. Garbage. Anything. Just like orcs."

"The females only lay once a year?" Dwarven women could become pregnant almost twice a year.

He nodded. "Once a year, every year, but only during their few years of estrus. Just like your kind."

She thought about his words, thought about them again, and decided she didn't like them.

"Dragons," she said, "are beasts. Is that what you think we are?"

He was so thin. She was sure she could break him in half if she wanted to. Just grab and twist and pull, and he would pop like dry wood.

His eyes darted around the room to see who might be listening, then back at her. "I didn't mean it that way."

Humans, she thought disgustedly. But she was fascinated by his words.

"What do the adults do after they breed?"

"Vanish. There are legends of older dragons, past

breeding age, and much stronger. But we don't know for certain, because dragons are so reclusive, and those who seek them out usually don't come back. The whelps hatch mean and they get meaner every year. You don't want to be there when they break out of their eggs." At that he leaned closer, his voice soft again. "You really don't. I am interested in your—pictures. Embroideries. I'll take as many as you can get your hands on. How many, and when?"

Melelki blinked in confusion, then realized that he meant the eggs. She thought of the one egg she had managed to take back with her, stashed in the forest near their cabin. She had almost run into a group of men on the mining route on her way back from the cradle. They would have to move the eggs at night. In her mind she was already weaving transport slings.

"How much?" she asked.

"Two gold each."

She caught her breath. He said it easily, as if he spoke such numbers every day.

Fourteen eggs. That was a lot of gold. More than a year's labor for her family.

So she and the human had agreed on where and when to meet, she with her eggs, and he with his wagon.

And his gold. So much gold.

Then she and her daughters had gone up to the cradle. After the first night of climbing and pulling and lowering, the three of them were so sore they could barely move. Then the human had given them gold for the eggs, and that had almost made the sore muscles vanish. They had been able to pay off their debts and buy new winter clothes. In the spring they built a little cabin halfway up the mountain.

Closer to the eggs. Would they be there the next year? They were, and this year, too. For two years they sold the human their sparkling, rainbow-tinted dragon eggs, and they lived better than they ever had before.

And now—

Tamun snapped a wet rectangle of fabric out onto the breeze and then hung it on the line. Melelki thought about her offspring, Sekena hinting at her adult size, Tamun warrior-strong and quickly becoming quite distractible.

The eggs lay in the cellar, carefully surrounded by thick straw, only because the three of them could not bear to put such expensive and dangerous things on hard brick.

The eggs would be hatching in a few weeks, judging by the mottling that grew thicker as the eggs got close to their time. But it was all guesswork, for they had never seen one hatch. There was no room for mistakes where dragons were concerned.

And so, tired as she was, she readied herself for a hike into the village. There, if she were lucky, she would find the blue-eyed human already arrived at the Squat Duck. If he was not there, she would leave a message for him, telling him to come and buy their pictures. *Embroideries.*

He would come with his wagon and gold, and take away the growing eggs. Before they hatched.

But the blue-eyed human was not there. He had left her a message: meet him at the traveler's station along the isolated high mountain trail the next day.

So she hiked back home and the next morning she woke at dawn, put on an oil-soaked cloak, and wrapped herself against the slushy, falling rain, and hiked along the ice-encrusted mountain trail. Hours later she opened a creaking wooden door, stepped into the small traveler's station, and shook the water off her cloak.

The room stank of wet human. He sat on the wooden bed in the middle, long, dark hair falling over his shoulders, into his bearded face, and across those startling blue eyes. Melelki nodded at him.

"Wet out there," he said.

She frowned, confused. Of course it was wet. It was

raining. It was early winter and it was supposed to be wet. Maybe it was a human joke.

"Yes," she said. Then, "I have the . . . embroideries for you."

They didn't talk about actual eggs anymore, even miles away from the village, in case someone might be listening. But "embroideries" was such a human word. She knew some human words, but they were a struggle to use. They were such long, slippery things, and they always meant more than one thing. Why couldn't they just say "pictures" and be done with it?

Of course, they weren't talking about pictures at all, but dragon eggs.

"How much?" he asked.

She stifled her tension beneath an impatient exhale. "Same as always."

He waited, eyebrows raised in question.

"Two gold for each," she said, irritated. Perhaps he would like her to do the Spring-Whistle-Toe dance for him, too?

"I don't think so."

"What? That's how much you always pay."

"Not this time. My employer thinks that your price is too high. He offers you less."

She felt panic rising inside her. How could he offer less?

"Last year—"

"Last year is last year."

"And the last two years!"

"The past is past."

"How much less?"

"Two gold for as many as you have."

She was stunned. "Human-crazy. That's absurd."

"That's the offer."

"But—*why*?"

"I don't know. Maybe he doesn't need them anymore. Maybe he's found another source."

"I don't believe you."

He shrugged. "I'm only a messenger."

Something about the way he said that made her suspicious. But then, he was a human, and all his words made her suspicious.

She thought fast. What did his employer do with the eggs? She had wondered that before and had decided that his employer must be a wizard. Who else would want dragon eggs? Who else would know what to do with them once they hatched?

But what would the wizard do with that many dragons, year after year? It must be the battles to the north, the ones that kept the dwarven village forging weapons, that hired so many dwarves as mercenaries. Who knew what a wizard might do with dragon eggs? Maybe he did have enough of them, after all.

But then, why would Blue-eyes be here talking with her at all?

No, he wanted them; he just thought he could get them for less. And if he wanted them, then he needed them. He just didn't want to pay for them.

She snorted her amusement. "I could make far more than you offer by just selling the shells." She didn't care who overheard now. Maybe someone would make her a better offer.

His eyes met hers, locked. That blue, that unnatural blue, like living ice. That must be it: humans had ice in their eyes, ice in their minds. Ice didn't think.

"Go ahead," he said. "And good luck with the whelps when they hatch."

She shuddered inside. Melelki did not like the idea of sixteen hatchlings, all hungry at once. Not at all.

Could it really be that she had competition? It was hard to imagine anyone else's luck, nose, and climbing ability could be as good as hers had been that first time. But who knew?

She decided. "Ta, too bad," she said as if she were only mildly disappointed. She ignored the nagging fear inside that said he was more used to these games than she and could probably see right through her pretense. "I guess I'll have to sell my cradle to someone else."

He chuckled. His amusement made her feel very cold. It shook her resolve a little, so she fueled it with anger at his cheating bluff, at his making her come all the way here to be told this.

She shook the last bit of water off her cloak and onto the floor, even though the cloak would get wet again as soon as she went out. Then she twirled it onto her shoulders, fastened the laces, and glanced back at him.

He seemed thoughtful. Maybe he was reconsidering. With a human, who knew?

"The offer still stands," he said, fixing her again with that ice-cold stare.

"Two gold to take them *all* away?" She laughed, letting her anger overwhelm her fear and sore temptation.

They would find another way.

She turned and left, closing the door hard enough to shake the small shack.

Melelki thought dark thoughts about the human as she trudged through the muddy, ice-ringed puddles on the trail home. Part of her wanted to go back and tell him yes, she would take the two gold for all the eggs if he would only come with his cart and take them all away.

She had that part of her under control, though. She had a valuable cache—sixteen dragon eggs! Surely someone would want them and would pay at least as well as he had. She would have to buy her own cart, of course, and without raising questions. They could pull it themselves. Couldn't they? She wasn't sure.

Then she would need to find another buyer, and quick, because the whelps would hatch in just a couple of weeks, and—

And there was no time for all that.

She was an idiot. All these years, assuming that Ice-eyes would want the eggs, would pay for them forever, instead of—what? Instead of finding another buyer. Instead of finding out what they were good for.

So much for dwarven curiosity, she thought viciously. Where was that curiosity last year, or the year before, when the weather was good, when she could have gone wandering to the north and the east, to see what the blue-eyed human did with the eggs he bought from her? She could even have asked at the Kalitas market last spring festival, where someone might have known more than she did. Instead she had spent the year climbing around on the mountain, sitting around with her daughters, telling tales, weaving baskets, and sleeping late. And occasionally sewing pictures.

Never again. From now on she would find out everything.

But first she had to get rid of the eggs. Before they hatched.

And not to him. Not to that arrogant, blue-eyed, smelly human. Not for two gold, not for four. Not even if she had no other choice but to take them back to the cradle before they hatched.

She exhaled slowly, her breath visible in the cold air.

That was exactly what they would have to do. Take them back up the mountain and put them back in the cradle. There just wasn't the time for anything else. Not this year.

That was a bitter thought; it was getting to be winter and everyone got stingy at market during the cold months, and everything was too expensive anyway. She was glad she had some money saved from previous years, but it wasn't much. It would see them through until spring, if they were very careful, and then they would have to find something else to do for money. Maybe they could sell the pictures again. At least their house was well built and would hold against the snow and cold. They would simply huddle down and sleep a lot.

She thought wistfully of an enormous cauldron, of hard boiling every single dragon egg. The dragon stew hadn't tasted so bad. At least they would eat well all winter. Then she sighed. The shells were probably too thick, or it would spark them all to hatch at once, or some other terrible thing.

She did not relish the thought of climbing back up the mountain, dragging each egg along in a sling, hoisting them up the slippery edges of the high crags where she had gotten them from.

Then again, she wouldn't have to return them to exactly the same place, would she? Just far enough away from the cabin to be safe. And away from the mines. If whelps got loose in the mines—

Far away.

She stamped her frustration into the puddles of mud, ignoring her cold feet, the wet rain on her face, which was turning to snowflakes, and the memory of Ice-eyes laughing at her.

Sekena stood in the dark, tiny basement, the sixteen eggs shining in the lamp's flickering light. The eggs crowded the straw-covered floor. Upstairs Mama and Tamun slept deeply. There was not even a mumble as Sekena slipped out of the shared bed and crept downstairs.

They had decided to take the eggs back to the cradle. None of them were happy about it, but Mama was right, and there was no other choice.

The storm had other ideas, though. They couldn't go up the mountain in this night's driving snow, so they would wait until the storm passed. Maybe tomorrow.

Sekena was disappointed. It wasn't just the work, the awful, cold numbing, arm-aching labor of climbing the mountain all over again, but to put the eggs back . . . ! How strange that the human wouldn't pay this time. Humans.

In any case, with the eggs soon going back to the mountain cradle, Sekena could no longer fight the urge. Hands trembling, she crouched down and ran her fingers over one of the mottled, iridescent shells.

Smooth as glass and hard like iron. In some places, Mama said, they made jewelry and weapons out of the brilliant white shards of dragon eggs.

Weapons made of dragon shells. She wanted to see those.

Mama had said that it would be just like humans to make jewelry out of eggs that someone else had gotten for them. It made them feel brave, she said, as if they had been there when the egg hatched, as if they had faced the whelp. None of them had, of course. Who would want to be there when a whelp hatched?

Sekena would. She thought about it in the daytime, dreamt about it at night, wondering how the whelps would look. She hadn't seen the dragon whelp in the village years ago, but had heard all about it, and wanted to hear about it again and again.

To see it, though, that would be something else. Something better.

She never slept well when there were eggs in the basement. She would lie awake while the others slept and fight the temptation to come down and try to break one open. Sometimes she grabbed her edge of the bed, hoping that her sister and mother would wake up in time to stop her if she couldn't stop herself. But why worry so? She would not be able to break open the eggs herself, would she? Still, some part of her was desperate to try.

It was the dwarven blood, of course, the strange curiosity that drove her kind. The same curiosity led Mama to poke about up in the high crags of the mountains where she found the cradle, and pushed Tamun to explore the forest floor, collecting the dead animals that she then cut open, dried, and added to her bone collection.

Sekena looked at the marvelous sparkling eggs and inhaled the wild scent of them, deliberately making the temptation as cruel as possible. Curiosity burned inside her like a forge fire, but she fought it down. She was no child to be thrown about like a leaf in a storm.

She was nearly an adult. So she would stand here, burning all the way through with desire, and not touch a single egg.

Mama would be proud of her, if she knew. But Sekena would never tell her. This was Sekena's own battle, her private triumph. This was the sort of dwarf she would be.

In recent days she had watched Tamun's feverish actions. Sekena was filled with dread. Her sister talked of going to the villages, of houses, men, and children. Tamun would be a fine mother, certainly, but Sekena didn't want to spend her life like that, running around after her brood.

The thought made her shudder. No, that was not the life for her. Nor would she stay in the village, doing whatever odd work she could and living with her mother. She had a secret: when she reached her heat, she would become a dwarven mercenary. They took women when they were in heat because they were stronger than the men, but only if they promised not to get pregnant. She could make that promise. No matter how her passion drove her, she would never let it control her.

And so she stood there, testing herself, her fingers aching to touch the eggs, to take a hammer to them and see just how strong the shells were.

Today she proved herself with the eggs, but some day it would be with a fine dwarven sword in battle. She could see it clearly in her mind. Light armor, that would favor her speed. And the sword—she could feel the grip, the weight of it swinging, the *chunk* as it sank into a squealing orc. The ugly creature would go down, its dark blood feeding the land.

So vivid was her vision, so clear the sounds, that she barely noticed the new sound in the cellar. She blinked when she heard it again.

Breath left her. It was a ripping, crunching sound. There, on a far egg, was something she thought she would never see.

A crack.

She took the stairs three at a time.

Melelki led them downstairs, each of them holding a lamp. There it was, in the far corner: an egg with a small, jagged line through it.

In the dim light Melelki checked the rest of the eggs, stepping slowly and carefully around them, aware that her children were watching her, counting on her to be strong. Inside she struggled to think more about that which made her curious than that which terrified her.

Like dragon eggs hatching.

The mottling on the cracked egg was much thicker than on any of the others, and thicker than it had been when she had last checked, the day before. The darker splotches of iridescence were supposed to mean the eggs were closer to hatching. Only the cracked one seemed heavily mottled. It was a small relief.

For long moments the three of them stood in silence, listening, watching, and waiting. Then the sound came again, a muffled, crunching sound. The sound of something alive, trying to get out.

"Up," Melelki said. They climbed the stairs into the house.

"I'll barricade the door to the basement," Tamun said.

Melelki nodded. "Sekena, pack us food and bring cloaks and lamps to the door."

Sekena ran for the kitchen.

With both of them gone, Melelki allowed herself a deep breath and a ragged exhale. The eggs were not supposed to hatch for weeks. How long would it take the whelp to break through the shell? She didn't know. Was there anything they could do to prevent it? She didn't know.

Should they try to kill it?

A memory visited: bloodied dwarven villagers.

No. She and her daughters would simply not get in

its way if—or when—it hatched. The human told her that they did not attack unless they were frightened, and that they did not hunt animals larger than themselves. As long as they did not get in its way, the three of them should not be in any danger.

A human. She was trusting their lives to the words of a human.

She hoped he had been telling her the truth.

Darkness. Urge. Hunger to break free.

Out, out, sang the song of his blood, *the beating of his heart. He bit and kicked and howled at the dark, hard world that tried to keep him in.*

Determination was hot inside him. He fought, struggled, stretched. Sounds came. Good sounds, rewarding sounds.

Free sounds.

The sounds cut the smoothness that was his world. It cracked, his world. Cracked again. Became sharp-edged.

He had broken it.

He was free. Cold, hungry, and free.

He lay on the sharpness, exhausted, gasping, as the sweetness of escape washed over him.

Free.

When some strength returned to him, he looked around, then up. He opened his mouth to taste the air. There was darkness and the world was close. Too close.

Something was wrong and missing. Where was the sky? Where was the breeze? Need cut through him. Discontent returned, washing through him, sparking him to anger.

These things were supposed to be here.

Fury kindled a fire inside him.

Somewhere was the sky and the breeze. His sky and breeze. He would find them.

Out, out, sang the song of his blood.

Up, up.
He began to climb.

The sun had just risen when the sounds began to come
from the basement. Melelki felt a chill all the way
through. The whelp had broken free of the egg, that
was certain, and now it sounded as if it were breaking
the very stones and beams that held up the house.

"Out," Melelki told her daughters. They all grabbed
packs and lamps and cloaks and piled out into the
thick new snow, making tracks toward the trees where
they stopped to look back.

"Do you think it's safe here?" Sekena asked.

"I don't know."

"We can't just leave," Tamun said.

"No."

It was curiosity and fear and something else that
kept them from fleeing down the road to the village.
They had built that cabin with their own hands. It was
theirs. And in the basement were eggs. Their eggs.
How could they leave?

As they waited, the sun came up in a deep blue sky
with no sign of clouds.

"At least the weather's good," Sekena said softly.
But in the light of day they could all see that the trail
up the mountain was so thick with snow that passage
would still be impossible. There would be no returning
the eggs today.

If it even mattered.

The house shook as the whelp bashed around inside,
over and over. Such a lot of power for such a small
creature, Melelki thought.

The sill that supported the north side of the house
shook then snapped in half. Melelki felt it like a blow
to her own body. Should she take her children down
the trail? She could not leave. Not just yet.

Tamun clenched and unclenched her fists. "Mama—"

Melelki put a hand on her older daughter's shoulder,

feeling tense muscles fired with the power of her full heat. She had come into it fast, probably spurred by the events of the last day. Melelki patted her gently, trying to keep them all calm.

The house trembled again. Then there was a repeating slamming sound.

Sekena nudged her and pointed away from the cabin, far to the right, where a figure hiked out from the trees.

"Ta, by the Moon," Melelki hissed. It was the blue-eyed human. He was looking at the shaking house. Fury surged in her. She struggled to fight it down, lost.

"Human scum," Melelki yelled at him, unable to stop herself. "You said they would not attack. Look!"

Another beam snapped. The entire end of the cabin sagged. There were tearing sounds coming from the inside, like a giant rubbing together trees and rocks.

Tamun's eyes were wide and furious. Melelki gripped her shoulder tightly.

"It's destroying our home!"

"Ta," she said to Tamun. "I know, Flower, I know."

"What does it want? Food?" Tamun sputtered. "What? Stupid beast."

The human was as close to the house as they were now. He answered. "It's trying to get out."

Tamun's face was red. "Get *out*?"

"Yes," he said. "It wants to get out. To get up onto something, then throw itself off. That's how they learn to fly."

Some part of Melelki's mind stored the information for later. Right now, though—

"Make it stop," Tamun told him harshly.

He laughed once, a short laugh. "Make a dragon whelp stop?"

A window shutter splintered open. A green nose poked out.

"There it is," Sekena whispered, more fascination in her voice than fear.

The nose disappeared. More crashing sounds issued from the cabin. Melelki winced.

"You must know how," Tamun insisted.

"Not without—" He stopped and shook his head.

"What are you doing here?" Melelki asked.

"I thought you might have reconsidered my offer."

"Ta," Melelki hissed. "Did you make the egg hatch just to convince us?"

"No," he said. "No. It hatched early. It's rare, but it happens."

"We can't let it finish," Tamun said through clenched teeth.

"We'll have nowhere to live," Sekena said. Then more softly, "we've got money saved, right, Mama?"

"A little, my flower. A little."

They would be begging from their friends and relatives in the village to survive this winter, and winter's mercies were usually small ones.

The roof of the cabin trembled, buckled, and fell in with a loud crash. Pieces of wood flew out from the collapsed walls, plowing up little puffs of snow.

Tamun yelled, a deep, long yell, like a battle cry. Melelki and Sekena both grabbed her at once, but she shook them away effortlessly and took off at a dead run toward the cabin.

Melelki started after her.

"No, Mama!" Sekena grabbed her arm, pulling her back, her face twisted in pained determination.

"It'll kill her," Melelki howled, struggling against her younger daughter's surprising strength. Sekena pulled her down into the snow, where they wrestled for a furious moment. Then they stopped, turning to watch Tamun.

The human was yelling at Tamun to get back, that she was stupid and other things that at any other time Melelki would have found outrageously insulting. At that moment, however, she agreed entirely.

He reached down, picked up a handful of snow and dug deeper for a handful of dirt, then hurled them both into the air after Tamun.

Crazy. Human-crazy.

Just as crazy to store dragon eggs in the basement? Dwarf-crazy. And now Melelki would pay for her insanity.

Tamun was halfway to the cabin, halfway to an impossible confrontation with a dragon whelp that would simply kill her. Halfway might as well be all the way, because it was too late to do anything now. Except watch.

Tamun was strong. Heat-driven and heat-strong. But she was no match for a dragonling. It would snap her like a dry twig.

Melelki wailed her grief. Still she watched.

It was odd how many details she noticed now, and all at once: Sekena's fingers still pressed hard and white into her arm to keep her from following Tamun into death; Tamun's hushed, hurried steps in the snow; the human chanting as he threw more handfuls of snow and dirt at the remains of their cabin.

They were odd, the details that made this scene stretch into a very long, horrible moment. She could not believe that in heartbeats her eldest daughter, her Tamun, her flower, would soon be unmoving meat. Alive in one moment, dead in the next. How could such a thing be? If she could somehow freeze her daughter, freeze the whelp, freeze the whole world—if only, if only, if only—

Then thunder fell upon them. The earth shook hard enough to entangle Melelki and Sekena and roll them a few steps away. A silence came, followed by a ringing in her ears. Melelki struggled back to her feet, but Sekena had rolled over faster and was already standing, already running toward the cabin.

The cabin was completely flattened into rubble, every piece of timber and stone charred black and scattered outward. Tamun lay in the snow, halfway there, a bundled heap. Melelki ran toward her, but Sekena and the human arrived first. The human knelt on the ground next to Tamun. Melelki gripped his shoulder, tossed him backward, and dropped down next to her daughter.

The irritating creature was back again in a moment. She growled at him, deep and guttural.

"I'm trying to help her, you stupid woman!"

"Touch her and I'll kill you," Melelki said in one breath.

"Curse you, I just saved her!"

The words meant nothing, not now, not with Tamun lying there. Melelki bent down to listen at her daughter's mouth, holding her own breath until Tamun's breath sounded clear in her ear. With it, a deep, vast relief washed over her.

"She breathes," Melelki said, swallowing a sob.

The human sat back on his haunches. "I'd like to tell you that she'll be fine, but if you won't let me near her—"

"To hell with you," Melelki said softly, stroking her daughter's streaked hair gently.

"I guess it's too much to expect a little gratitude from a dwarven woman."

"*Gratitude?*"

"The dragon whelp is dead." He said each word slowly, clearly, as if she were a stupid child.

Indeed, the words barely made sense. She looked over at their flattened cabin. Sekena had gone to it and was now walking around, toeing pieces of charred wood with her boot.

"Where did the whelp go?" Sekena called back.

"It's here," the human said. "Sort of. In small bits. Very small bits." He looked at Melelki again, seemingly annoyed. "Do you want me to look at her or not?"

Grudgingly she motioned him closer. He dropped down next to Tamun, touched her neck, pulled back an eyelid.

Melelki thought through the last few minutes, then thought them through again.

"You're the wizard," she said. "You're the one who uses the dragon eggs."

"Yes."

A chill worked its way down her spine.

"What kind of wizard are you?"

"Elemental," he said. "Not—not the other kind."

She exhaled slowly. "A mud wizard," she said, relieved. Not the sort who could plow under whole villages with a word, or summon hordes of zombies with a gesture. That was good.

"Mud wizard," he echoed sardonically. "But wizard enough to turn a dragon whelp into a piece of thunder. She'll be all right. What did you call her?"

"Tamun."

He bent down over her. "Tamun," he said softly, and then again. Tamun opened her eyes.

"Praise land and sky," Melelki exhaled.

"Did I kill it?" Tamun asked, struggling to sit up, brushing away the human's attempts to help her.

He laughed once, a short laugh. "In a way."

"It's dead? Then the cabin—"

"No," Melelki said, "Flower, the cabin's gone."

"Gone?" Her tone was pained. "The eggs—"

From the ruin came Sekena's voice. "I found one," she said, picking up a large piece of wood and hurling it to the side. "Here's another. The whole house came down on them and they're not even *scratched*."

"Dragon eggs," the human said, nodding. "The one that hatched was early, but the rest are probably still a couple of weeks away. Check them for thick spots. Mottling. Check for—"

"You," Melelki said, her anger rekindling. "You foul, stinking human parasite—"

He exhaled and stood, scowling at her. "Even an orc would consider thanks, woman."

"Thanks? For offering us nothing for our cradle, for leaving us to this—this monster?"

He turned away, brushing the snow off his cloak. "Thanks for your daughter's life, maybe. But not from a dwarven woman. Of course not. Heartless, selfish bitch. You'll make a good parent for those whelps."

She stood, came around him to block his way, staring up into those cold, blue eyes.

"Ta, you're one to say, trying to cheat us and leave us to a hatchling's fury!"

"At least I would have taken the eggs away. Then this wouldn't—" He waved his hand, made a frustrated sound and a dismissive gesture. He tried to walk around her, but she moved to block him. His eyes narrowed.

"You ought to be a little afraid, woman. Even a mud-wizard is dangerous."

"Ta, but you ought to pay for what you ask for."

"I can't pay you with what I don't have," he said through clenched teeth.

"Don't have?"

"Money. Gold. I don't have it."

"But—why not?"

"Inquisitive creature, aren't you?" He smirked humorlessly. "I'm not here to discuss my fortunes."

Tamun was standing just behind him. "The eggs," she said.

He turned, took a half step back, momentarily startled at how close she was.

She fixed him with her brown eyes. "What did you do with the eggs last year and the year before?"

For a moment he returned her stare, then he glanced at the cabin where Sekena was throwing more pieces of wood around to uncover the remains of the basement. "That."

"That?"

"I pump mud magic into the whelps. If I get it right, they explode."

"But why?" Tamun asked.

"Why should I tell you?"

Tamun reached up her hand and put it on his chest. He flinched, as if uncertain of whether to stop her or not. He looked down at her hand for a moment, then back at her.

"What's this?"

"Why do you want the eggs?" Tamun asked again.

"The eggs," he said slowly, "they're weapons. I—" He stopped, swallowed. An amused smile flickered across his face, then vanished. "What are you doing?"

Melelki had seen that expression before, the one the human now had on his face. Where had she seen it?

On the faces of dwarven men, that was where.

Oh.

"Tamun," she whispered. "No. Not a *human*."

Sekena quietly joined them.

"The eggs," Tamun prompted, ignoring her mother's plea.

For a moment the human's face showed struggle, then he shut his eyes.

"There are battles to the east," he said. "You may have heard. Orcs and goblins on the Icatian border. And Havenwood—"

"Havenwood?"

He shook his head, smiled again. "You're doing something to me. Very clever."

"What about Havenwood?"

One of his hands, shaking, came up and hovered over hers. For a moment Melelki thought he would pull hers away. Instead he pressed her hand against him.

"Havenwood hired me to cause trouble on the Icatian border. I have been teaching orcs and goblins to fight humans."

Melelki and her eldest daughter exchanged quick glances.

Sekena was staring at her feet with a look of intense concentration. "But you're Icatian, aren't you?"

"Yes."

"Why do the elves want this?"

"I think—I'm not sure—it's because—" He shut his eyes tightly, his breath coming harder, his hand still on Tamun's. "The elves want humans busy fighting to the south instead of coming farther north into Havenwood."

"The elves had you start a war for them," Sekena said.

He opened his eyes. "Yes."

"Then why did they stop paying you?"

His tone was bitter. "I don't know. Perhaps because I succeeded too well."

Melelki snorted. "Ta, I'm not surprised. Elves hate to get their hands dirty, don't they? But they love to have their big shows. Now it makes sense, why they've been buying up so many weapons and armor from the forges, hiring dwarves to guard their borders. Disgusting creatures."

"Then what—" Sekena asked "—what did you want *these* eggs for, if the elves have stopped paying you?"

Another smile crept over the human's face. "I want to give the Havenwood elves a chance to change their minds. If that fails, I want to show them what their coin has bought."

Tamun returned his smile with one of her own, bright teeth showing. "Ah! Wonderful. We will come with you."

Melelki turned to her daughter. "What?"

Sekena grinned. "Yes, of course."

"Are you crazy?" Melelki demanded. "Is this mud magic at work, stirring your minds into garbage soup? We have nothing. *Nothing*, you hear? Maybe a few gold coins, somewhere under the rubble that used to be our home. Maybe. Probably not."

"Yes, Mama, exactly," Tamun said. "Rubble, fifteen dragon eggs, and two weeks. That's our whole fortune now. So let's go visit those elves. I wonder how they will like the sort of entertainment we can offer them." She let her hand fall from the human's chest. His hand followed hers as if it had a mind of its own. Their fingers entwined.

Sekena's face was alight with anticipation. "Maybe we'll see some fighting."

"Or maybe they'll buy the eggs from us."

"Travel at the start of winter?" Melelki demanded. "Has the cold frozen both your minds?"

"We'll be moving fast, Mama. We'll stay warm. And besides, we've only got two weeks before they hatch, then we'll be done."

Melelki had a feeling that it would take longer.

"If we get cold we can start a fire," Tamun continued. "Or the human can blow up one of the whelps."

"I don't remember inviting you all along," the human said.

Melelki considered. It wasn't as if they could bring their cabin back by wishing for it. Rebuilding would have to wait until spring. They could go down to the village of Tigaden, but then they would have to leave the eggs, and she still hated to give them up.

As for the human, well, they could trust him more than most humans, with Tamun's touch on him.

Besides, hadn't she resolved to find out everything she could about dragons?

"No," the human said. "Two gold to take the eggs away. Not all of you as well."

"All or none," Melelki told him.

He looked at her, then Sekena, and longest at Tamun, who brushed thick strands of streaked hair back from her glowing face. He looked away, looked back, his free hand clenched into a fist, his other still entangled with Tamun's.

"What are you doing to me, woman?"

She laughed.

"Tamun—" Melelki said in warning, then cut herself off, shaking her head a little. There was nothing for it, not when a dwarven woman went into her time of power and made decisions. But a human? It made her feel funny to think about.

Sekena rubbed her hands together. "Let's get going. I want to see one of these dragonlings. All I've seen so far is a nose. Besides, all this standing around talking is making me cold.

"*You* cold?" he murmured.

"So, human—" Sekena began.

"I have a name."

"Yes? So say it."

His eyes were still on Tamun.

"Reod. Reod Dai."

"A strange name," Melelki said.

Reod snorted, glared at them. "There are no songs sung about dwarven tolerance."

"Reod Dai," Sekena said, pronouncing the words carefully. "Where is your wagon?"

"Down the trail."

"There's still a price to figure," Melelki said. "For our eggs."

Reod's mouth dropped open. "You astound me, woman."

"Ta, you won't get them for nothing."

"Let's go and fetch my wagon," he said, shivering. "If you insist, we can haggle on the way."

"Mama," Tamun said, "Sekena and I will stay here and bring up the eggs from under the house."

Her eldest daughter's look told her that while they were there they would also be searching for the stash of gold coins, while Reod Dai was away.

Reod Dai gave Tamun a look that was part worry and part something else. In return she gave him a reassuring smile and at the same time gently disconnected his hand from hers.

"Come on," Melelki said to him, doing her best to keep her amusement hidden. A dwarf with a human? Who would have thought it? She shook her head.

She and the human walked away from the house and down the trail. The sun was climbing higher, adding a little warmth to the day.

"Price," she reminded him.

"Price," he snorted. "What price? I have nothing to give you."

"I'll take the two gold, and—"

"*And?*"

"And I expect all the protection you and your mud magic can give us, every step of the way. And—"

He laughed. "There's more?"

"And if we manage to make any money on the eggs, we take three-fourths of it."

"Three-fourths? I don't think so. A quarter at most."

"Half."

He sighed. "Half. All right. You were never so difficult to bargain with before."

"I've learned. From you, human. Reod Dai. Or do you still think dwarves are as dumb as dragons?"

"You mistook my meaning, woman. And from what I understand, an adult dragon is hardly a simple-minded creature."

"You are hard to make sense of, human."

"When you speak my language as well as I speak yours, we'll talk about who makes more sense."

"With a human's slippery tongue nothing stays still long enough to be understood."

"Do you think dwarven words are so much more clear?"

"I do. But you may ask me about any word that you do not understand."

"I understand dwarven well enough, if not dwarves themselves. Perhaps I could ask you about Tamun."

She chuckled. "Perhaps you could."

CHAPTER

3

"May you be strong and valiant, to defeat the enemies of the pure."

—Leitbur's Prayer

THEY DECIDED TO SKIRT TIGADEN, TAKING a slightly longer road. There were too many dwarves who knew them in the village, and with a cart of dragon eggs in tow, there was no reason to invite questions. They camped in the snow, huddling together for warmth, and pulling dead branches down from the trees for the fire they kept burning all night long.

A day went by, and then another. Next would come the foothills and the town of Kalitas, still days ahead on the snow-thick road. Sekena remembered the Kalitas market from last year's spring festival where she had seen things she would never see in Tigaden: dancing dogs with painted faces, birds that flew and dove at their trainer's direction while trailing colored strands of silk, and elves and humans who came to trade with the good weather. It was in Kalitas that Sekena had first been exposed to strange races that were not dwarven. She glanced over at Reod.

The three of them had gone to Kalitas every spring. They would stay at the women's house where the Kalitan dwarves always made them feel welcome even though they came from deep in the mountains and had few new stories to offer. Wealthier travelers and humans and elves stayed instead at the wondrous three-story inn that was said to have warm baths that came from an underground spring all year round, even in winter.

It was true, Reod said as they hiked alongside the cart. He looked cold with his hands buried deep in the folds of his clothes. They would stay at the inn, he said, with the great fire in the center and soft beds and hot wine. He had a friend there who owed him a favor, who would happily pay it off with a night's lodging for Reod and his guests.

As they walked, Sekena stayed next to the wagon, near the eggs. Reod walked up at the front, near the ox, to gain some small warmth from the creature, and Tamun walked next to him. It was strange to see her with the tall, thin human.

Mama walked with Sekena, to keep an eye on Reod and Tamun and make sure they didn't have too much time alone together, no doubt. It had become a tense game between them over the last days, with Reod trying to gain a few moments alone with Tamun, and Mama insisting on accompanying her daughter everywhere she went, even to collect wood and to make water behind the trees. This morning, when Tamun went off into the trees, Mama followed, and Reod got that annoyed expression on his face again. Sekena chuckled.

"What's so funny?" Reod demanded.

Sekena nodded toward Tamun and Mama. "You."

"She is of proper age, is she not?"

"Of course. She is in her time."

He nodded. "That is what I understood. Then why does your mother so diligently guard her from me?"

"Mama guards you from her, not the other way around."

Reod scowled and shook his head. "Spare me the logic of dwarves."

"She is in her time," Sekena repeated slowly.

"So you have said."

It was clear from his expression that he did not understand. How could he know so much about some things, yet be so ignorant of others?

"She is in her time of power," Sekena tried. "She is stronger than you. Stronger even than the best of dwarven men."

He frowned. Did he not believe her?

"Is it not the same with humans?" she asked.

"No."

Sekena leaned back against a tree, digging a small trench in the snow with her booted toe. "Then what happens to female humans when they go into their time?"

"Females of my kind don't go into heat."

"No heat? But then, how do the men know when to court them?"

"They are always ready."

"Always ready? Which is it, always in a heat or never?"

"It is not quite either."

"Are they never stronger than the men?"

"No."

"But then—how do they choose the man they want and keep the rest away?"

Just then Tamun and Mama had walked back into the camp area, and Reod became distracted by Tamun again. Sekena never got her answer.

Now as they all hiked along the road to Kalitas, she puzzled over what it must be like to be human. She decided that she would not like it. As uncertain as she was about coming into her own time of power, she was quite certain that being in heat all the time would be far worse. When would you have time to do anything else?

As they walked Sekena watched her mother's eyes

on the strange pair before them. Mama was always trying to sort things out, trying to figure out how things might go and how to make them come out right. It was her mother who had taught Sekena to wonder and think about the world.

As she did constantly about the eggs. Sometimes she would put a hand on the cart's wood siding as they walked, and sometimes, when no one was looking, she would sneak a hand under the heavy oil tarp and brush the hard shells with her fingertips. She couldn't explain why she did it exactly. It just felt good.

Today wasn't quite as cold as yesterday, though the human would probably disagree. He was constantly wrapping himself in layers. At night he spent most of his time tending the fire, sending the dwarves out for more wood while he huddled down around the flames, and Tamun would sleep next to him. To keep him warm, of course. During the days the two of them walked together, brushing each other's hands. But that wasn't for warmth.

At least not the same sort, Sekena thought. And that was strange. She looked back at the cart and the dragon eggs, which were even stranger. Her mother gave her an inquisitive look. Sekena shook her head a little and gave Mama a reassuring smile.

This morning Reod had said that they were making good time through the mountains. The three of them had little trouble with the steep roads or steadying the ox and cart around high cliffs. But Reod seemed to fall out of breath easily, and he always seemed cold. Did they really have a great empire to the north, these fragile humans? Did they really take on orc raiders so easily and send them back in defeat?

Orcs had been spotted wandering in the usually safe dwarven lands, Reod had told them.

"What if we run into orcs?" Sekena asked, breaking the silence.

"I'll deal with it," Reod said.

He never seemed to want to tell her anything interesting.

"But if we do find orcs," Sekena persisted, "would it not be better if we faced them with weapons?"

"What do you know how to wield?"

"I could learn. I want to learn."

"You pick them up and swing them, yes?" Melelki added. "That doesn't sound so hard."

Reod glanced back at them, smiling. "Weapons are heavy to carry, and they invite squabbles. We're better off without them."

Sekena looked at him. "Even you?"

He held his hands out. "Do you see weapons here?"

"They're hidden," she guessed.

He snorted. "What sort of weapon could I hide under my cloak that would be of any use?"

Sekena considered a moment, for she had been wondering that very same thing. She fingered the sharp dragon egg shard in her pocket which she had found in the wreckage of their cabin next to the shattered rocks that used to be their home.

It had stunned her then, that the rocks were nearly crushed into powder by the blast but the dragon shell remained unscratched. She had found the edges of the piece of shell very sharp. The flat of the shell was smooth, like a new coin, but the edge was like a knife.

As for the human, she was sure he had weapons he had not shown them. Did he think them such fools? She stepped up her pace until she walked alongside him, then pulled out the shard.

"This, perhaps?"

He chuckled. "Perhaps you could blind your enemy with the shiny side, eh?"

"Ta," she said angrily, embarrassed, putting the shard away. "It's sharp enough to cut flesh."

"Perhaps. If you get close enough. If the enemy doesn't move. But for a real opponent you must have a real weapon."

"I'll use a sword, then. I'm strong enough."

"Then you'd better check behind each tree as we go by. You never know where you might find one."

She snorted her disgust at him and dropped back to walk with her mother.

"Humans," Melelki said softly, consolingly, as if that explained everything.

The next day the sun won the battle with the clouds and the clouds scampered off. The sky was such a bright blue that Sekena wondered if it had been a day like this, many years ago, when a bit of the sky had broken off and fallen to the ground and Reod's mother had picked it up, causing Reod's eyes to become their strange color.

She had slipped into a sort of trance as she walked, watching her feet and the cart's wheel turning against the rutted road of dirt and snow.

"Sekena," her mother hissed. Her head snapped up. Away in the cool blue sky where her mother pointed, framed by white-clad mountains and tall evergreens, was a small, black shape.

Tamun and Reod were talking quietly together, holding hands, distracted.

"What is it?" she whispered back. "A dragon?"

Mama shook her head. "Not this time of year, I don't think. Doesn't look right, besides." They squinted up at it. Melelki made a thoughtful sound and they continued to watch.

"Look," Sekena said, more loudly. The other two glanced up, saw where she pointed. Reod stopped the ox and wrapped the reins around Tamun's hand. "A precaution," he said quickly. "Get under the cover of trees. That way. All of you. Go."

"What is it?" Melelki asked, unmoving.

"You wanted me to look after you, yes? Go."

Sekena found his tone surprisingly compelling, but Mama still hadn't moved, so neither did she. Tamun pressed her lips together and took a step closer to her mother.

"It doesn't look like a bird to me at all," she said to Mama.

"No," Melelki answered. "It's not the right shape."

"Is that a tail on the end?" Sekena asked.

Reod exhaled through teeth. "It's a *kite*."

"A kite?" Tamun asked. "Like a toy, with cloth and sticks and string—that sort of kite?"

"Yes, except that it's larger. Large enough to carry a goblin. That's what you see there, wriggling in the middle."

Sekena squinted eagerly, trying to make out a figure against the strange kite. None of them had seen a goblin before.

"How does it work?" she asked.

"It's guided from the ground," Reod said, his manner suddenly relaxed. "Usually by something much smarter than a goblin, which leaves open a good many options. Most likely orcs. At least, that's what I suggested when I last consulted with the goblin king."

"*You* suggested?"

"Alone," he continued, ignoring the question, "I doubt I would have much trouble talking a group of orcs out of rolling me into a small, damp ball and taking me home as a trophy, but three female dwarves, with intimate knowledge of how the forges at Gurn Keep work, that's another matter."

"But we don't know anything like that."

"They won't believe you. Not for a number of very painful hours, not until they've answered all those nagging little questions in the back of their small minds about dwarven women, which answers, I suspect, would be considerably more fun for them to discover than for you."

"Oh," Melelki said.

"Trees," he said, his voice again sharp, his easy manner gone, replaced with a look that startled Sekena. "Now."

Tamun pulled to get the ox moving. Melelki added her strength to the cart and off they went under the cover of the trees.

From the other direction came cries.

"They've seen us," he said.

"I'll wait behind that rock in case you need help," Sekena said.

Reod's gaze flickered to Tamun.

"Another time, child. Get back with your mother and sister."

Sekena felt her face warm. Reod was walking away, toward the kite, already moving to do whatever strange thing he would do to protect them.

Suddenly Sekena felt awfully foolish and terribly young. She ducked into the trees after her mother and sister.

Reod dashed across the road and up the rocky rise toward the brush. He pressed aside branches as he jumped over rocks and between patches of snow.

Leaving Tamun was the right thing to do, and he knew it, but he didn't like it. It was safer to stay between the kite and the dwarves and deal with whatever might be at the ground-end of the kite before it reached the women.

Safer for the women, that was. Foolishly risky for him. What had possessed him to take three untrained dwarven women with him on a trip through such unstable territory?

Tamun.

From the first moment he had looked into her golden brown eyes after the exploding whelp had knocked her flat, a sense of ease had washed over him. There was something about her exotic face and streaked hair that made his pulse quicken, and at her touch he felt his worries soften, as if he had taken a swallow of the king's best wine. He found himself asking her questions so that he could hear her voice again.

Why had he not even begun to counter her simple seduction spell? It would have been easy to do, easy to walk away. But he had not wanted to, still did not want to.

And they had all fallen into the path of something he was sure he could handle alone. But now, instead, he had three stubborn, untrained dwarves to protect.

One of them was Tamun.

A high, gravelly voice came to him on the cold breeze. Goblin complaints, which was most of their simple language. Then he heard another voice, almost like an orc's voice, but not quite.

He dropped to the ground a moment, took a small handful of earth, and rubbed it across his ears. The ground under him felt right for magic, so he wasn't surprised when the spell caught.

"Dwarves, I'm sure of it," came a high goblin voice. "You big coward. Go over and get them."

"Not sure, not sure," whined the slurred orc-like voice again. "Maybe too big. Maybe hurt me."

In his travels Reod had found occasion to meet nearly every sort of creature that lived in Sarpadia. He could identify the race and even birthtown of most creatures from only language, tone, and accent. But this one . . . ? What was it?

The goblin made a short chittering sound, like a goat bleating, the sort of sound they made to their young, intended to be soothing.

"You're so much bigger. They're so weak. They're like flowers. Go step on them."

There was a cry from above, a complaint, and a hard thud, from which Reod deduced that the kite had crashed into the treetops and become stuck. The land crew must not have been paying attention, which was not surprising. When Reod had been training goblins, the biggest problem he faced was getting them to remember what they had been doing moments ago.

"What about eat?" The mystery creature asked.

"Eat them," the goblin responded.

"Eat?"

"Yes, Eat!" The chant was taken up by two other goblin voices. "Eat! Eat! Eat!"

Then the ground shook, once and again, as if a giant

were walking toward him. Reod frowned, still confused. The creature must be very large. What was it? Then he swore to himself, finally remembering where he had heard that sort of slurred tone before.

The creature was a melange—neither orc nor ogre, but a mix of both. The worst of both, as it turned out. He had heard the story of the creature's creation the last time he had feasted with the orc generals, and it had done nearly as much to ruin his appetite as the food itself.

He leapt to his feet and ran forward. He burst into a small clearing. A gray-green wall with arms and legs stood before him, its head level with the treetops.

An orgg.

The enormous creature reached up to the kite. The attached goblin hugged the top part of the tree trunk. The orgg, apparently trying to help, ripped the kite away from the goblin's back to sounds of jabbering outrage. Like pulling wings off flies, Reod thought.

Next the orgg reached for the goblin itself, who tried to bat away the enormous paws. The orgg wrapped the tiny creature in its large fist. The goblin howled, demanding to be let down.

So the orgg dropped him. The goblin lay still a moment, shook itself, then slowly got up.

Through all this, none of the goblin band had noticed Reod, who stood in plain view.

"Hungry. Dwarves. Eat," the orgg said, remembering. He took a step into the trees, toward the road.

Toward the women.

Reod forced his attention back to the goblins. "I am Reod Dai," he said in the goblin tongue.

They looked at him. "You are not," one said.

Reod walked up to the goblin who had spoken and backhanded it with all his strength, knocking it to the ground.

"Idiot. What other human would be wandering this countryside alone speaking your tongue? Who is your captain? I'll have you put in the chirurgeon's experiments."

The goblin quickly paled to a sickly gray.

"I don't have time for this," Reod said. "Call off your creature."

"Why, lord?"

"Because those dwarves are mine, and I don't want them hurt."

"Oh."

"Do it. Now."

Reod could still hear the orgg's steps, slowly flattening bushes and breaking trees as it moved toward the women. Toward Tamun. His pulse raced.

"Oh," the second one said in the same worried tone.

"Well, lord—" the other began. "He is an orgg."

"I can see that."

"The thing is, you sort of point them and they go."

"And so?"

"So we don't know how to stop him."

"Find a way."

They looked at each other, eyes wide, shrugged helplessly. "If you stand in his path, you just get—"

"Flattened," finished the other.

"Idiots," Reod snapped. "You *never* attack without being sure of your target. How many times have I told you stupid creatures that? You're going to wish you had been his goal instead. You understand?"

They nodded glumly.

With that, Reod turned and sprinted out of the clearing.

He reviewed what little he knew about this creature who was neither orc nor ogre but some of each. While the orgg had inherited the ogre's size and unpleasant character, it seemed to have gained intelligence from the very least of the ogre families. From the orc side the orgg gained such cowardice that even the orc generals, quick to praise the creature's strength, were embarrassed by its timidity.

Orggs had nothing remotely like stealth, though; Reod knew exactly where the creature was from the sound of enormous feet slamming into the earth with each slow step. Reod sprinted past it through the bushes, sorting through his options and silently swearing.

Sekena stood by the cart, fingering her dragon shell shard, frowning at the sudden, distant pounding that she was sure had something to do with Reod. She was thinking about what he had said, going over it again and again in her mind. Maybe he was right, maybe her shard wasn't a real weapon.

But it was something. And wasn't it better to use what was available? Better to have something than to have nothing?

Footsteps came suddenly through the trees at them. Sekena crouched, held the shard sharp side out, and wished for a real weapon. Curse Reod, anyway. He could have taught her if he had wanted to.

But it was Reod himself who burst out of the trees, breathing hard.

"Egg," he said breathlessly, yanking free the knots on the cart's tarp. He began to wrestle an egg up and out of the cart.

Tamun was instantly by his side.

"Let me." She lifted the egg almost effortlessly.

"On the road," he said. "Sekena, get some charq meat from my pack."

Sekena dropped to the ground, working his pack open, looking for the dried strips as the pounding got louder.

"What is it?"

"Something very big, very stupid, and very dangerous. It's called an orgg."

The three of them followed Reod to the road. There Reod knelt down over the egg, put some dirt on top, and spat. He rubbed the dirt, graying the brilliant white surface. As the women watched, a black line began to appear on the egg. A crack.

Melelki and Tamun took a step backward.

Under Reod's touch the crack deepened, lengthened.

What must have been hours of hatching passed in seconds. A pale claw and green arm reached out tentatively then vanished back inside. Reod grabbed both sides of the egg and pulled hard, murmuring furiously. The egg slowly opened with creaking and cracking, breaking apart into pieces.

Sekena held her breath. Finally she would see more of a dragon hatchling than just the nose. As she exhaled and inhaled, a flush of pleasure went through her, as if she had just woken to a warm summer's rain. There was a scent on the air, something she had never smelled before, or something she might have smelled once, in a dream. It was odd and wonderful at once.

The whelp emerged, flopping on the ground like a wet green lump, limbs tangled together, wings wrapped up tight, its little chest moving up and down.

It twitched in an attempt to right itself, then twitched again. Reod stepped back quickly, apparently unwilling to risk helping the creature any further. Without thinking, Sekena stepped forward. Reod's hand was out in front of her, asking for the charq meat. She stopped, suddenly aware again of her surroundings.

He took the meat strips from her, crouched forward, and with an outstretched hand waved the meat under the whelp's nose. Then he tossed the meat toward the slow crashing sound coming through the trees.

"Food," Reod said to the whelp softly, then repeated himself.

The whelp shook itself, took a hesitant step, seeming to barely stay aright, then took another less cautious step, and step by step stumbled off in the direction of the meat. Navigating very well, Sekena thought, for something that had just walked out into the world. Pride surged through her. She wanted to follow it, to see its every move, to find herself even prouder.

Reod put a hand on her arm to stop her, then drew them all backward into the trees.

The whelp found the charq meat on the ground and

gulped it down. Then it looked up, just as the trees parted. Stepping onto the road was an enormous gray-green thing with arms and legs and many sharp teeth. A trail of drool filled the deep wrinkles of its chin as it looked down at the whelp, which hardly stood as high as the orgg's kneecaps.

Reod picked up a handful of dirt and threw it toward the whelp. It took Sekena a moment to realize where she had seen that gesture before. She tensed, but nothing happened.

"Damn," Reod said very softly.

The whelp cocked its head at the big creature, who returned the gesture. First one way, and then the other, as if they were both trying to see the strange thing before them from a better angle.

At the same moment they both seemed to come to a conclusion. The big creature looked past the whelp at Reod and the dwarves, apparently having decided that the whelp was not something to worry about. At the same time, the whelp looked closely at the creature's toes.

Reod moved a few feet away and picked up another handful of dirt. His hand trembled as he threw. Again nothing happened.

The big creature began to step around and past the whelp and toward the dwarves. The dragon grabbed the orgg's foot, turned its beak sideways, and bit the big toe. The orgg howled, a sound so deep and loud that Sekena clamped her hands over her ears. Then the orgg took a swipe at the whelp and missed, still howling as it began stamping around in circles, alternately trying to reach its tiny passenger and shake it loose. The whelp clung tenaciously, still gnawing on the orgg's toe.

Finally, with a shrill scream, the big creature ripped the little dragon away from its flesh, leaving bloody wounds and half a toe, and brought the whelp up close to its eyes to see it better. The whelp, taking advantage of the change of scenery, snapped at the creature's nose, barely missing.

It was then that the orgg opened its enormous mouth, with jaws so large they seemed to be most of the creature's head. In one motion it inserted the whelp, closed its mouth, and began to swallow.

Sekena's stomach cramped painfully. From the creature's mouth hung small green legs and the tips of white veined wings. Another swallow and those, too, vanished.

The orgg swallowed a third time, let out a small burp, then looked back at the dwarves.

"By the Hells," Reod swore softly, his voice strained. He grabbed another handful of dirt and mumbled more words.

Sekena could see that he needed more time. Before she quite knew what she was doing, she had stepped into a ray of sunlight and angled the dragon's egg shard so that it caught the sun, then she flashed the light into the big creature's eyes. The creature shook its head and stumbled backward.

Sekena followed the creature with the bright spot her dragon shard made. The orgg waved its paws in the air, trying to brush away the light.

Reod still mumbled. He threw his dirt again.

Thunder bit Sekena's ears and the ground came up, slamming her flat. A fast fire seemed to eat its way through her insides.

Minutes or hours later, Mama was by her side, shaking her.

"Flower?"

Sekena groaned and rolled over, slowly standing. She looked around.

Where the whelp and the orgg had been there was now a small crater surrounded by rubble of rock and dirt. Like at the cabin. And on the far rise, there stood three small figures.

"The goblins," Reod said, a hand on Tamun's arm. "I put the fear of the thousand Hells into them, but they're not very smart and they forget quickly. I think it's time to go."

They quickly collected their belongings, tied the tarp down over the cart, and headed north along the road, Sekena struggling to clear her head from the thunder and the feeling in her stomach that still lingered.

As they left, Sekena picked up her shard from the ground where she had dropped it. She had, she realized, done with it exactly what Reod had mockingly suggested. Later today she would bring the shard out again and show it to him. She wouldn't need to say a thing. The thought made her smile.

Another day brought a new storm. Snow fell, dulling the outlines of mountains and trees with a pale, thin curtain of white. Reod had fine tricks for keeping them dry at night, with a combination of branches, cloaks, lamp, and a fire, but there was no way to keep everything dry while hiking through wet snow all day long. Sekena's knees and ankles were sometimes quite damp. The cold was not so bad, but Sekena was getting very tired of being wet.

Soon, though, they would be in Kalitas. Then there would be a hot bath, a long sleep on a soft bed, and a fireplace where they could hang all their clothes until they were dry. Ahead Tamun and Reod trudged forward, a little bowed against the snow. They were talking. Even though Sekena could not make out the words, she recognized Tamun's soft laugh. It was strange to see her sister sharing that gentle laugh with such a strange creature as was this human. But then, Tamun had always liked the strange, hadn't she?

As the town grew closer they saw wood smoke rising above the trees, twists of gray against a gray sky, making Sekena think of firepits and hot wine. They had arrived in barely enough time to find the town and the inn in the last of the day's dim light.

But as they rounded the last strand of trees in the smudged twilight they did not see the lights and sound of a town beset by evening. Instead they were met by dim silhouettes of ragged, smoking buildings surrounded by high piles of rags.

The quiet of the surrounding snow-covered forest was broken by occasional creaks and snaps of an expanse of charred and broken buildings.

None of them spoke as they approached. Sekena saw that there were no piles of rags after all, but piles of bodies. Tamun inhaled sharply and Mama let out an almost imperceptible moan.

The darkness hid features, for which Sekena found herself guiltily grateful, but the black puddles against the night-dark ground were clearly blood, and the smell was unmistakably death.

They stopped, staring around in shocked silence.

"Orcs," Reod said, very softly. "Yesterday. Or the day before." Then, "We must move along. We'll camp elsewhere."

Among the sharp shadows of the town's ruins, Sekena saw a flickering light.

"Look!" Melelki cried.

Reod grabbed Tamun's hand and put his other hand on Melelki's shoulder. "No. We don't want or need to know what it is. Not now. Not here."

"It's one of ours," Melelki said. "It has to be a dwarf left alive."

Reod shook his head, his voice still soft. "No, it doesn't. We must go on."

"It wouldn't be an orc," Sekena said, surprising herself with a tone that did not reflect the shock she felt. "The orcs must have already found what they came for. Why else would they stay?"

"There are scavengers and predators besides orcs," Reod said. "If it is one of your kind, if they have survived this, then they are easily strong enough to continue to survive without our help."

"We will go and see," Melelki said firmly. It was a tone that Sekena knew better than to argue with.

Reod did not. "Woman, listen—"

"We *will* go and see," Melelki said, shrugging off his hand and walking forward.

Sekena was not so sure. Reod's words made sense, perhaps more than her mother's. But she would not let Mama go alone.

"You listen poorly," Reod said softly, angrily, but as Tamun walked forward with Mama, he followed.

In silence they went among the dark, ragged buildings. Shapes grew less distinct with the fading light, and it was hard to make out those things that might have once been tables and chairs and wagons.

Everything smelled so wrong. Sekena found herself looking too closely at the sprawled shapes that were probably bodies, trying to make out faces. She did not want to recognize anyone here from last spring, but she could not keep from looking anyway, not until it was too dark to see.

Still Reod did not light their lamp. It was prudence, Sekena realized, not to draw attention to themselves. Reod might not choose to teach her what he knew, but she would learn from him just the same.

A handful of barely visible chickens waddled past. They pecked at the snow-covered ground, a strange contrast to the rest of the unmoving darkness.

Then they found the spark of light. On a doorstep that led to the shadowy remains of a cottage sat an old dwarven man. Beside him was a small lamp. He looked past them as his hands absently brushed snowflakes out of his tangled, streaked beard.

"Oh, father," Melelki said, "such a sad time."

"It's evening," the man answered.

"Come with us, father," Melelki said. "We will take you somewhere else before night falls complete."

He blinked, looked up at her. "Take me where?"

"You can't stay here."

He scowled. "What are you saying? I have to wait for my brothers for dinner. In the men's house. Or maybe—" He smacked his lips together. "Maybe the women will cook for us. They do, when the weather's

chill like this. Later they'll want us to fix their houses
up for them. Eat now for work later. It's a good deal.
My brothers and I will build for them in spring if they
feed us tonight."

"Your brothers? Where are they?"

"Maybe in the men's house. Playing Stones. They'll
be by soon enough."

She glanced back. The men's house was open to the
sky, roof and walls almost completely burnt to ash.

"There's no one else here, father," Tamun said.

"Come, father," Melelki said, reaching out a hand
toward him. "At least let us find you a cottage that's
not as bad as this one, so you can stay out of the cold
and wet. Tomorrow you can hike back along the road
to Tigaden. They'll take care of you there."

"I know where Tigaden is, woman," he said, brushing away her hand. "Stop pestering me. If you need to
talk so much, go to the women's house. Leave me
alone."

Mama glanced at them, her look worried. Reod kept
silent, always scanning the darkness around them.

"But, father—what if the orcs come back?"

He looked up, his eyes flickering back and forth
between the women and the broken town. His frown
deepened into his wild, tangled beard, making him
look fierce. "Orcs? What orcs?"

"The ones who came, and—" Melelki waved a hand
around at the rubble.

"Go away," he shouted. "You talk too much. I'm
fine! Leave me alone!"

"But—"

His voice wavered, broke. "Please."

"Oh, father," Tamun whispered.

"Go away!"

They backed away, retraced their steps to the road, and
there with the ox and cart slowly made their way down
along the road away from Kalitas and its devastation.

Mama was still breathing hard, her lamplit expression pained.

"We must go to Gurn Keep. We must go now and tell them what has happened."

"They know," Reod said. "This is not the first time orcs have struck, though usually they keep to smaller villages on the borders. Some dwarves may even have escaped Kalitas and gone on to the keep."

Sekena thought of the bodies she had seen, especially the smallest ones, now only food for wild animals.

"We must go and help fight the orcs."

"They are already training a standing army at Teedmar."

"Teedmar? What is Teedmar?"

"It is a mining town near Gurn Keep. There are plenty of volunteers there. More than they can train. You are not needed."

"Surely they will not reject us," Sekena said.

"There is no need."

Sekena made a face. "Look at what has happened to Kalitas! No need? I see great need."

Melelki's voice was strained. "We did not know. How is it that we did not know?"

"Orc attacks on dwarven towns are recent," Reod said. "You live at the end of the settled Crimson Peaks, where word comes last and slowest."

"Tigaden," Melelki said, her lips pressed. Tigaden was where most of their relatives lived. "Should we go back and warn them there?"

He shook his head. "I doubt the orcs will trouble themselves to go that far into the Peaks during winter."

"Your doubt is small reassurance," Sekena said. "You said you taught orcs and goblins to fight. Was it your teaching that brought them to Kalitas?"

"I taught them to fight Icatians. Not dwarves."

Sekena snorted. "Did you give them weapons, too? For the Icatians, of course."

"Sekena," Tamun said warningly.

Sekena turned on her sister. "You would defend this creature after what you have seen?"

"Daughter," Melelki said, "there is much we do not

understand. Remember what he did for Tamun when she was hurt."

"So he heals with one hand after he has cut with the other. Is that how it is?"

"Yes," Reod said sharply. "That is what I do. Sometimes a thing must be cut deeply to heal at all."

"And Kalitas?" Sekena now walked along side Reod. "Will Kalitas heal? All the dead rise, laughing, and the buildings repair themselves?"

"Kalitas should never have happened. But it was not my mistake. It is Havenwood who has created this war and then abandoned its stewardship. If you want to spit fury, child, spit where it is due. Spit at Havenwood."

Her face went warm. She stepped forward and put herself right in front of him, face to face, forcing him to stop or walk into her. He stopped.

In this dim light she could barely see him, but she looked up anyway, trying to meet those cold blue eyes. Her heart pounded.

A strange creature, this human. Strange and infuriating. He knew so much, and he was a wizard as well. And she—what was she? A dwarf, born to a tiny mountain village, and not even close to her first heat.

But if he was going to insist on respect, she would, too.

"I have a name," she said tightly. "I bid you use it."

There was a long moment of silence. During that moment she remembered tales she had heard all her life, of earthquakes and floods and terrible winds, all from the hand of an offended wizard.

Perhaps she should have kept her mouth shut.

"Sekena," he said softly.

She stumbled back and away, her confidence strained to the breaking point. Was that a smile he now gave her? Sympathetic or mocking, she could not tell, but she nodded her acceptance and got out of his way. Trembling, she let her pace take her back to the rear of the procession.

* * *

The foothills brought warmer temperatures and spotty patches of snow. Here the pines were taller, some taller than Sekena had ever seen. Now they were only days away from the flatlands. Then would come Havenwood, where lived the elves who Reod claimed had caused the ruin at Kalitas.

Sekena watched him as they walked, studying his words and gestures, hoping to learn by watching what he would not willingly explain.

For his part, he called her by her name.

None of the three women had ever been this far from home before. It amazed Sekena to realize that the land under them could change so suddenly, with new kinds of trees and bushes they had never before seen. Even the scent of the dirt had changed, now that the land was flatter.

They made camp at what would have been sunset, the flat canvas of gray skies dimming as evening drew down. Melelki and Tamun boiled snow into hot water over the fire, adding dried vegetables and some of the better charq meat from their packs.

Reod stepped away into the trees for a few moments, watering them. When he came back, Sekena was there to intercept him away from the others. He glanced past her to Tamun, as if to reassure himself that she was still there.

"What?"

"One of the eggs," she said. "It's about to hatch. Maybe tonight. I'm not sure."

His eyebrows drew together. "How do you know that?"

Explaining was the hard part. "I can feel it."

"I checked them all today, Sekena. None of them are mottled enough to be ready to hatch."

"I know. But I feel odd, the way I felt before the one hatched in our basement. The way I felt on the road with the goblins."

He gave her one of those quiet looks he had.

"Show me."

At the cart he untied the tarp. Sekena ran her fingers over the eggs, finding the one that to her felt so ripe.

"This one."

Reod lifted the egg a little to get to the underside, then made a small, surprised sound. He looked back at her thoughtfully and gave her small nod. "You're right. There is a crack. Good work, Sekena."

She felt herself flush under his praise.

"We'll take it away from camp," he said.

"Not to blow it up," she said, fear rising in her.

"No. We'll move it up the slope. That way if it hatches the whelp will go upwards rather than stumble over us in the night."

Together they carried the egg up the hillside and set it under a fallen log. It felt good to be so close to the egg. Sekena had to force herself to go back to the camp.

The day was barely past first light and the sky was still very dim as Sekena struggled awake, sure that something wasn't right. Beyond the nearest trees something rustled.

The whelp. It must have hatched and returned to camp during the night. But that didn't make any sense; it was supposed to go up the slope. Could it have already reached the top of the hill, learned to fly, and come back, looking for food?

She turned to where Reod slept, but his bed was empty. She relaxed. The sound in the trees must be him, wandering around.

Then there was a rustle in the trees on the other side.

Sekena was out of bed, shard in her hand and ready. Her mother and sister were up and standing as well, clothes rumpled from sleep.

Tamun gave her a look that said, *I hear it, too. What is it?*

Sekena shook her head. *I don't know.*

Their mother stepped back, opened her mouth and inhaled, trying to smell better the strong scent on the air. Even Sekena could smell it now.

What was it?

Melelki mouthed the answer. *Humans.*

And then they were there, walking out of the trees from all directions, cream-and-gray uniforms of leather and woven metal, gray boots high enough to top the thick snow of the mountains. The dim colors helped them blend in well with the snow-patched land. Some notched arrows to bows, others gripped swords tight.

Metal swords, bright and sharp. From the way they held them it was clear to Sekena that they knew how to use them. She felt a pang of jealousy.

But where was the one human they knew?

One uniformed human had a higher, thicker collar. It was male, Sekena decided, since he had a beard like Reod and was taller than some of the others who were beardless, who she guessed were females. The man's hand danced past the hilt of his weapon as he looked at the dwarven women, a quick motion that told Sekena that he considered the three women no threat. Sekena gripped her dragon egg shard, thinking of the old stories in which humans were always underestimating dwarves. She glanced at her older sister, remembering her heat-driven strength and almost hoping the humans would press them.

"Greetings and good day to you," the man said. "I'm Lieutenant Aaron Labann, of the Icatian Army. These are my scouts. Who are you?"

Humans were so odd, always wanting to talk names and places and such before the important things.

"What do you want?" Melelki asked.

The human called Aaron Labann frowned a little, considering.

"You are a long way from any village. Three dwarven women alone. No weapons, only a cart. This is a dangerous place for you to be like this, undefended."

"What makes you think us undefended?" Tamun asked.

Again the human looked around, as if the answer were obvious, but he was uncertain as to how to explain.

"What is in the cart?"

"Supplies," Melelki said.

"Where are you headed?"

"Out. To seek our fortune. We came from Kalitas. It was sacked by orc raiders."

He nodded, not seeming surprised, then motioned to two of his scouts, who began to walk around the dwarves toward the cart.

"We heard about Kalitas. But this area is even less safe than there. You shouldn't be here."

Sekena stepped toward the scout nearest her, thinking about swords and dragon shards. She might actually outweigh this small, armed human female, despite the other's greater height. Could she be stronger, and would it be enough? There was, she decided grimly, only one way to tell. On the other side, Tamun had likewise stepped to intercept the male human nearest her.

"Don't," the lieutenant said. "You're just telling me that whatever's in your cart isn't what you said it was."

"Ta," Mama said, "we just don't want your hands on our things."

"Horseshit," he said, his voice hardening. "Now stand out of the way. Form up." This last was apparently a command, as the rest of the dozen or so soldiers drew together into two lines in front of the lieutenant, facing them. Sekena's soldier had a hand on her sword, ready to draw. The one near Tamun paused as well. The lieutenant drew a breath, readying for another command.

"Enough," came a familiar voice that cut sharply through the morning air.

Reod stepped out from behind a tree. "The cart is mine, Aaron. Keep your men back."

The lieutenant's eyes widened in surprise. "Robin? Robin Davies?"

Sounds of recognition came from the other humans. Some murmured, some spat. The lieutenant made a quick gesture and everyone fell silent.

"Reod Dai," Reod said softly, stepping to the women, brushing Tamun lightly as he passed, and turned back to face the humans.

"That name means traitor in Icatia."

"I have heard."

The lieutenant signaled to his men, who relaxed, resheathing weapons, some with clear reluctance. All eyes were still on Reod. The lieutenant slowly walked over, dropped his voice low enough that Sekena could barely hear them.

"What are you doing here? What is—" He glanced at the dwarves, then the cart. "What is this all about?"

"Not your business."

"It is now."

Reod smiled what seemed to be a friendly smile at the lieutenant. The other sighed.

"Robin, tell me what really happened. I've heard such things—"

"I am Reod now."

"Ah, no. How can I call you the name the Hand gave you?"

"I suspect you will find it easier to arrest me and take me back for trial if you do, Aaron. Those are your orders, aren't they?"

The other hesitated, then nodded. "They said you turned a hundred men over to the Ebon Hand. I defended you when I heard that. I drew blood over what some called you."

"I am grateful for your loyalty, however misplaced."

"I couldn't believe it of you. Not of our Captain Davies. But then, some of the men came back." He exhaled raggedly. "Parts of them still alive, parts rotting. Robin, tell me."

"What do you want to hear, Lieutenant?"

"The truth."

For a moment Reod stared into the other man's face, then he shook his head. "You will find lies in my truth and truth in my lies. You have orders to take me in. Why should I waste words on you now? The time for explanations is past. These are times for action, not words."

The lieutenant exhaled frustration and stepped back. "Reod Dai, you are hereby—"

"But first I will give you the chance," Reod interrupted, "to take your men and go."

"What?"

"To leave us untouched."

"You know I can't do that."

"I give you that chance."

The lieutenant gave a half laugh. "You cannot win here, Robin."

"I led five hundred of Leitbur's elite, Aaron. Do you think that was an accident? You are twenty and we are four, but if you challenge me here you will not survive." Then Reod's voice dropped again. "Aaron, please."

The lieutenant's face showed confusion. He looked around the clearing and at each of the dwarves in turn and then back at Reod.

"It is known how well you lie."

Reod snorted amusement. "Of course. I was born Icatian, was I not?"

The lieutenant's expression turned dark. "This Icatian loves truth, even if you do not." More softly, he said, "By Leitbur, I wish I knew the truth about you." Then, loudly, "Reod Dai, I charge you with high treason. You are under arrest. Surrender willingly and you will not be made to suffer unduly."

"Until I am found guilty. Which of course I will be."

The lieutenant signaled to the two soldiers nearest the dwarves. Reod dropped his head and mumbled something about food.

Food?

Sekena felt a familiar tingle, like the sweet scent of spring wildflowers on the breeze.

It was then that the whelp came crashing out of the trees. A cry went up among the soldiers.

"Form up!"

They fell into two lines, swords drawn in front and bows ready behind.

Reod quickly touched each of the three of the dwarves, his hand on Tamun, and motioned them back to the cart. As they stepped backward, the lieutenant called out.

"Hold them!"

Reod reached down and picked up a handful of dirt. Sekena instinctively clutched her stomach as he began to mumble, surprised at her own resentment. She should want him to explode the whelp. It was just an animal. Why should she mind so much?

Then it came like fast thunder. The explosion knocked her to the ground. She should be used to it by now, she thought furiously, a sensation like fire raging through her stomach and into her head. She struggled back to her feet.

White-clad bodies lay in crumpled, red-stained heaps. Blood was splashed across the snow. To one side a bloody hand lay atop a bloody chest, but the two were not connected. Perhaps had never been. Sekena found herself counting heads to see how many had survived the blast intact. She only reached five.

The lieutenant was bloodied but alive. He half stumbled toward where his soldiers had been.

"Take him down," he cried to the remaining two soldiers. "Kill him!" The soldiers drew their swords and closed on Reod.

Now Sekena could clearly see how absurd it was to think her shard shell might be enough to face a soldier with a real sword.

It occurred to her to wonder, if Reod was wanted by his own people for treason, why should she be trying so hard to protect him? What had he done for them, except to bring them into this trouble? But even as she thought these things, she moved to intercept the soldiers.

As did Tamun. The male soldier lunged at Reod, and her sister howled and became a blur. Then the male was on the ground, clutching his stomach. The female soldier closed on Reod and Tamun was there also, another blur. The second soldier collapsed as well.

There was silence. Moments passed, quiet enough that Sekena could hear the breeze hush through the tall pines, a sound so ordinary that it cut through the almost-dream of the loud, bloody moments before.

Sekena blinked at the scene around her, not sure what to think. Days ago she had seen a monster die. That was like killing a dangerous animal. But these were humans. Had been humans. Now they were meat, like the piles of dwarves at Kalitas.

Suddenly she felt odd. Light and airy. Her head hurt as if she had a fever, and her stomach felt as if she had swallowed something rotten. Tamun was gasping for air, her eyes fixed on Reod.

The two humans on the ground did not move. The lieutenant dropped down next to them, checked their pulses, and stood.

"Dead," he said, voice ragged. "The other nearly so."

"Sekena," Reod said flatly, "bind him." He tossed her rope.

Even now there was something in his voice that made her proud that he had asked her to help him. She reached for the lieutenant's hands. He twisted away and lunged at Reod in a last, desperate attempt. Tamun was there again, moving so quick and viciously that Sekena fell back, afraid. Her sister wrestled him to the ground effortlessly while Reod yelled at her to be careful, not to hurt him, and pulled her off.

The lieutenant was stunned by the attack and easy to bind. Sekena leaned him against a tree, trying her best to make him comfortable, but his eyes were so full of misery that she had to look away.

Behind her Tamun was sobbing. Reod was talking to her softly, and Mama had her arms around her. Only then did Sekena realize that her sister had acted entirely out of instinct. The instinct of the heat. Protection of her mate-to-be.

Some day Sekena would be in heat, too. She shuddered.

Reod stood over the bound man. "All your men are dead, lieutenant, save this one here, whom I cannot heal. Would you have me give him peace?"

The lieutenant's bloodied face was twisted. "I thought you loved Icatia. At worst I feared you had been corrupted by the Ebon Hand. But no, you are simply what they say you are: traitor and abomination."

Reod crouched down in front of the bound lieutenant and gestured at the dead around them. "Is this worse than what we did to the border towns that were suspected of having sympathies for the Ebon Hand? Tell me it is worse to kill attacking soldiers than to slaughter hungry parents whose worst crime is accepting food for themselves and their children in times of famine."

The lieutenant nodded. "I remember your last speech, Robin. Your words hung heavy in my heart, as they did in the hearts of many. But the Ebon Hand is not that merciful, and far less merciful than you would have us be. They torture and burn and ruin. They eat people from the inside. Surely you know this. Should we sit idle and let them destroy the security Icatia has worked so hard to build?"

The dying soldier moaned and both humans gave him only a casual glance. How many deaths, Sekena wondered, had they both witnessed that they could care so little for a companion dying right next to them? A chill swept over her.

"But where," Reod asked, "is the freedom to be left alone?"

"What?"

"To care more about this year's crops and your

children and your elders than the words of Leitbur?
Does any Icatian have that freedom?"

"There is no freedom under the Ebon Hand."

"There is no freedom under Icatian rule."

The lieutenant shook his head. "The path to freedom
is unity. Had you stayed with us—"

"I have yet to see an army grow food, thatch a
house, or birth a baby."

"We fight and die to protect our people!"

Reod sighed, stood, and went to the soldier whose
breath was short and shallow. He pulled out a small
knife and glanced at Sekena.

"You say you want a warrior's training. Come."

She approached hesitantly.

"Take this knife, and cut, like this." He lifted his
chin and drew his fingernail in a line across his neck,
leaving a thin trail of red skin. "It's quick. Nearly painless." He held the knife hilt out to her.

Horror fought fear inside her. She snorted, hoping
to seem more in control than she felt, and turned
away.

"Do your own dung eating."

He laughed once, without humor.

"Keep your little shard, then, child, and do not trouble me about learning weapons you are not willing to
use."

The prone man was whispering. Reod knelt down
over him and began to speak. It sounded like a chant.
Behind her she could hear the lieutenant saying the
same words.

Then, in one motion so fast Sekena saw it before she
thought to look away, Reod drew his blade across the
man's neck.

Blood spurted out, over the man's neck and chest.
The man tensed and went limp.

Reod cleaned his knife on the dead man's stained
leather, stood, and resheathed the blade under his cloak.
He glanced at the women and around at the clearing,
then crouched down in front of the lieutenant.

"What now, Aaron?"

"Almost painless, you said," the man answered flatly.

"I don't want that."

"Then don't.

"Aaron, if you go back, will you say you saw me here? I can't let you do that."

Tamun spoke up. "We could take him with us." Sekena heard pain and remorse in her sister's voice.

"And guard me every moment of every night and day? I don't think so."

Reod came close to the other man, catching his gaze.

"Give me your word, Aaron. An oath before Leitbur. Promise me that you will walk away from here and say nothing of Robin Davies or even Reod Dai. Give me your word, Aaron Labann, and I will release you now, unharmed."

The lieutenant looked at him, hope flickering across his face. Then his eyes turned toward the bodies littered around.

"Shall I betray my oath to Icatia? It is everything I hold sacred."

"Not even for your life, old friend?"

The lieutenant looked at Reod, eyes brimming with tears. "What would be left of me, if I did such a thing?"

"Your breath. Your blood. Your homeland, who needs you now more than ever. *Icatia*."

"Icatia."

"Give me your word."

The lieutenant's head dropped to his chest. "You would make of me a traitor as well, to live all my days in shame. Such a choice you offer. You are cruel."

"Damn it, Aaron, Icatia needs you. The cold ground does not. If you want to die for Icatia, die fighting a more worthy foe than I."

"I was never prouder than when I stood in your troops, Robin. When you led us, we felt as if spring had come to the land. Do you know, they now say it was a trick, what you did to your men. That you used that same trick to lead a hundred men into the claws of the Ebon Hand."

"You wanted the truth. Listen, Aaron: I took no troops. Those who followed me did so against my wishes, my commands, and my deepest desire."

"They say—they say you gave the Hand secrets."

"Not so. The Ebon Hand cares little for Icatian secrets. Aaron, I need your oath. Please."

"You know I can't give it."

"Damn you and your misplaced honor! What stupid creatures I am kin to!" He stood, exhaled, paced away, every motion angry.

Finally he stopped, his gaze returning to the three women who stood watching.

"Take the cart down along the road. I will catch up with you."

"But—" Tamun said.

His blue eyes met hers, as cold as the winter ground.

"No argument."

There was something in his tone that made even Sekena, disgusted and horrified as she was by him now, feel it best to comply.

They gathered up their things, hitched the cart to the ox, and went down the road, the quiet of the day broken only by their boots crunching down through patches of hardening snow. As they walked Sekena tried to see only clean snow and green trees, but she could not rid herself of flashes of the human soldier on the ground, his neck cut open, blood across his chest, his body suddenly lifeless.

Was that what being a soldier was about? She had thought it was something else, fighting against orcs and goblins, defending her people. But to kill one's own? That was horrible.

And it was all too clear from the way Reod had behaved that this was hardly his first time.

They had not been walking long when Sekena heard

a distant, high sound. It might have been a bird's cry and it might have been something else. She did not really want to know.

Reod caught up with them soon after. They walked in a bleak, tense silence. Now Tamun did not walk next to Reod, but back with Mama and Sekena. Sekena reached out and took her sister's hand for a moment, giving it a small squeeze. Tamun smiled a little, but it was a pained, confused smile, and then she looked away.

For his part, Reod said nothing and Sekena found his expression even more unreadable than usual. But she watched him as the gray day grew brighter and the hills fewer, watched him as the ice on the road melted into mud and the road became rutted and thick with gravel. Sometimes they would come to a tree fallen across the road that they would either have to move or go around. Even then little was said.

Toward afternoon Sekena decided she could no longer stand the silence. She pushed her pace up so that she walked beside him.

"Have you no allies at all, Reod Dai?"

"Watch your tongue, child," he said softly.

"Child, again, is it? Because I will not kill for you?"

"Because you want a sword and yet will not kill. That is a child's game."

Sekena snorted. "Is this how it goes for you, human? Is there always a trail of bodies behind you?"

"Sekena," her mother said warningly.

"Perhaps you would have preferred that I let the soldiers take you all back to your destroyed cabin. Or back to Kalitas."

"Your own kind! How easily you kill. Is that the way all of you humans are?"

Mama was sharper this time, fear edging her voice. "Sekena!"

Reod put a hand up, a gesture that might have been

acceptance, his voice suddenly much softer. "Her words are no surprise. I have heard them before and far worse." He looked at Sekena. "Yes, I kill my own kind. Do you think I enjoy it?"

She met his eyes. Instead of the challenge she expected, she saw something else. Pain? Regret? His sudden change startled her anger away.

"Maybe you do," she said quietly. "I don't know."

At that he looked away, saying nothing. She felt stranger still. The mood had changed between them. It was no longer tense, but becoming something else that she had no name for.

Sekena decided that she had said more than enough and dropped back to walk alongside her mother and sister.

That night Reod slept apart, leaving the women to themselves. Seeing Tamun's eyes clouded with sorrow made Sekena even more irritated with Reod. Mama was already asleep when Sekena heard Tamun's breath coming soft and ragged. Sekena reached outside her sleeping roll into the night's cold and snuggled close to her sister as she took her hand.

"What have I done?" Tamun lamented in a choked whisper.

"You were strong," Sekena answered, the bloody humans Tamun had destroyed still vivid in her mind. What power there was in a heat-driven woman. She had not thought it was quite so much. She tried to say what she thought Mama would have said. "I was proud of you."

"I killed."

"You did the right thing. You protected him. Your mate-to-be."

"I killed *humans*." She made a sound. "They kill each other. I have never seen such a thing. I don't understand them. Or him. Or myself for choosing him."

"Hush," Sekena said, struggling to put aside her own similar confusion. "You like him, don't you? You feel good when you're with him, yes?"

Tamun nodded.

"Ta, then that's how it is."

"But I didn't even think. I just moved. As in a dream. And then—" She exhaled sharply.

"It's the heat, Tam. You couldn't let them hurt him or take him away, could you? Of course not. You acted because you had to."

"But these were not orcs or goblins, sister. They were *humans*. Friends, not enemies."

"Ta, are you sure? Do you think we can always tell who is the enemy, and who is not, by their race? Maybe it is not that way anymore. Especially with the humans."

Tamun exhaled raggedly. "Ah, but I miss him. It hurts, right here." She pressed Sekena's hand to her warm chest, where Sekena could feel her heart beating, slow and steady.

"Oh, Tam, he's not so far away. Tomorrow you'll hold hands again and you will feel better. I know it."

Tamun sighed again, let herself be comforted. Sekena held her hand and waited while her sister fell asleep.

Somewhat to her surprise, Sekena's prediction came true, and by midday Tamun and Reod were holding hands again. They hadn't even said anything, but bit by bit they had moved closer to each other as they walked, until their fingers were once again entwined.

They began to talk softly. Sekena saw her sister's shoulders twitch with a sob or two. Reod quickly reassured her with his touch. In a short time they were both smiling.

The world was full of mystery.

Then he glanced back at Sekena and her mother and began to speak in a peculiar and fascinating way, entrancing them with stories of the places he had been and the things he had seen. At first Sekena found the tales a startling contrast to the previous day's horrors, which still flitted through her mind, but he turned out to be a fine storyteller, and before long Sekena had entirely forgotten where she was. Instead, wide-eyed fish-people danced in blue seas and waved spears that never rusted, while long worms bargained for maps to floating crystal palaces.

Reod was warmer now, even seeming friendly. Sekena was sure it had more than a little to do with Tamun's smile.

Mama was also smiling as she watched them both. It was the small, knowing smile that Mama got only when she was thinking of something in her past and thought no one was watching. Sekena swallowed her own misgivings. If Mama could accept the two of them being together, Sekena would as well.

But strange it was. Tamun so beautiful and strong in her first heat, and the tall, dark-haired human towering heads above her, telling stories.

How fast their world had changed. Days ago it had been just the three of them, living in a cabin, sewing, going to Kalitas once a year, and in the winter bringing dragon eggs down from the tallest of the frozen peaks. Now when she closed her eyes she saw pieces of dead dwarf and human lying across the ground. Bloody, like cut-up rabbits.

She and Mama and Tamun had always been curious about the rest of the world, making up stories about faraway places, but what she had seen since they left home was more frightening than anything they had ever imagined. Somehow Reod seemed at home in all this madness, and to Sekena that meant that he had his own kind of madness. Perhaps that was some of what Tamun liked about him.

Rain came and went, thick clouds scuttling across the sky. The forest thickened and the pines dropped water on them as they walked by. Carpets of thick-fallen leaves slowed the cart. Later that day the road turned and narrowed. Finally it disappeared altogether. They slowed, making their way around trees and over thick brush.

"We're in Havenwood proper, now," Reod said.

"It doesn't seem any different," Melelki replied. "Except that there's no road."

"The villages are deep in the woods. Sometimes you don't see them until you're right on top of them."

"But you know where they are?"

He nodded.

When the daylight waned, they stopped to camp. Sekena ran her fingers over the eggs and showed one to Reod.

"This one wants to come open."

"They're all hatching early," he said quietly. He put the egg on the ground, looked closely, and ran a finger along a thin crack. "Possibly before morning. We can't risk the whelp getting free this close to the villages. Best to force it to hatch now and explode it here." He began to roll the egg away from the camp.

Sekena watched despairingly, then dashed after him. Before she knew it, she had pushed between him and the egg.

"Let it go," she said. "Can't you let anything live?"

His look changed, eyes narrowing. She had seen that look before, when he had faced the human soldiers. She knew she should choose silence, that the anger between them was not far from the surface, but she could not. He took a breath, about to speak, and Tamun stepped between them, put a hand on each, and pressed them apart.

"A moment," Tamun said to Reod. She pulled her sister some steps away. "Sekena, why does it matter so much?"

"They aren't just eggs, Tam. They're—" Sekena stopped herself, speechless with frustration at the words that would not explain what she herself did not quite understand. "Do you remember when we were

little, and we went to market, and Mama bought us a
cinnamon sugardisk to share?"

"I do."

"I remember the first time I was old enough to have
one all to myself," Sekena said. "It was summer. Warm
and bright, a perfect day. I'll never forget that day, or
the way I felt when I bit into the sugardisk. That's how
I feel when they hatch, Tam. As if that perfect day is
back again. But when they die—it hurts." Sekena
pounded her fist with her stomach. "Right here. It
hurts a lot."

"But—why?"

"I don't know. I used to sneak down to the basement at night, just to watch the eggs because it felt so
good to be there."

Tamun smiled. "I know."

"You knew?"

"Of course."

"Then why did you let me?"

"You're my sister."

Sekena sighed. "Oh, Tam. I don't understand it
myself. They smell so right. It is a strange thing, I
know."

Her sister took her hand and led her back to the tree
where Reod and Melelki stood.

"Let it go," Tamun said to him.

He growled. "Just like that? Leave a walking sign-
post that both points to us and knocks down trees? I
think not."

"It cannot be that bad," Tamun said.

"It is."

"We have given up much to come with you."

His eyes sparked with anger. "I did not ask you to
give anything at all."

Tamun stepped close, stood on her toes, her arms
going around his neck, and looked up at him. At first
he was cold, as if he would push her away, but he
melted quickly, nuzzling her hair, hands going around
her shoulders. They kissed, then, a deep kiss, the sort

Sekena had only seen between mated pairs. She glanced at Mama, who seemed content yet watchful. Perhaps she trusted Tamun to have more control now, now that she had seen what the heat-power could do. Or perhaps she cared less what happened to the human.

Tamun pulled back, a little breathless, her eyes still on his.

"Yes," she said, "you *did*. Human, you do things that seem without reason to us, strange things, but we try to accept. Now we ask the same from you."

"This is not merely strange, it is needlessly dangerous."

Mama snorted amusement. Sekena expected her to agree with Reod. Instead she said, "Many things are needlessly dangerous. This whole trip is needlessly dangerous. And yet—here we are. Safety is not all of what matters."

He made a wordless sound and gently disengaged Tamun from his neck. With a glare at Sekena, then one at the egg, he turned away.

"All right, let it hatch. And hope it does not cost us too much."

Sekena exhaled her relief, stumbled weakly over to the egg, and lowered herself to the ground next to it. She had been holding her breath and now she inhaled again. As she did, she smelled egg scent. She smiled, couldn't help but smile, even when Reod came by to give her and the egg another dark look.

The day was perfect. If there had been a tencount of sugardisks nearby she could not have felt better.

When she smiled at Reod, a flicker of confusion crossed his face. For some reason that made her smile even more.

CHAPTER
4

"Believe human words and you have earned your fate."

—Elven proverb

THINKING BACK ACROSS THE MANY YEARS, Kolevi did not remember the circular stairs to the tower room being quite so steep. Perhaps they had grown a little higher with each passing season, as some of the tree-knitted walls were likely to do, no matter how passionately they were pruned and reasoned with.

Halfway up the staircase he stopped to catch his breath, glancing back down to see if anyone had noticed. It was unlikely that any had, since almost none but elder druids used the tower room these days. But even another elder might misunderstand, thinking that Kolevi rested now because he had to, and not simply because he chose to take the climb slowly. As the eldest of the druids in these difficult times, he and Lalani could not seem too old.

He would not rest long; he did not want to keep her waiting. With a final deep breath of chill morning air, he pushed himself forward to the top of the stairs, pausing there yet another moment. Then he pressed open the door to the tower room.

As he walked the uneven floor he felt the room's old magic hang heavy around him in the air, like smoke, touching him, tasting him, testing him, and finally welcoming him.

She stood where she always stood, her thin body framed in profile against the large window. Winter sun came bright through the trees that shaded the tower, casting light through evergreen needles and branches of gray, brushing shadows down Lalani's thick green gown and shining against her pale hair, tracing its cascade to the floor.

He fed his old heart on her familiar beauty. To see her was enough to warm him, even after all these years. She had not moved, and for a moment he wondered if she had heard him enter at all. As well as he knew her, he still could not always read her enigmatic silences.

So he took the time as his own, drinking in her visage, reluctant to break the moment's peace. There were few enough moments like these.

Finally, softly, he spoke her name. She bowed her head a little, only a little, but Kolevi knew her body, knew its language, and he sighed.

"What is it, beloved?"

"The human is coming to Havenwood."

"The human? Which human?"

"Reod Dai."

"Ah, that one. Why?"

"Who can say? But I have guesses. Yesterday our scouts found a dragon hatchling. It had climbed up on a thick tree that had fallen at an angle and was eating the mosses."

"A dragonling? In the forest? How odd."

"So they thought as well. They searched the area."

"And?"

"They found a human. He travels from the south with three dwarves and a heavy cart."

"Odder still."

"He matches our description of the human Reod Dai. With a dragon hatchling nearby, it seems likely that he is indeed Reod Dai and that the cart is full of dragon eggs"

Kolevi inhaled sharply. "Dragon eggs? But—why?"

"I do not know."

"Did he misunderstand our message? Does he think the contract continues?"

"I think he understood the message very well."

"Perhaps he comes to offer to sell them to us directly."

Lalani gave him a look, one he recognized.

"You do not think so," he said.

"We have heard clear reports of what he does with dragon eggs. Think of what he could do to Havenwood with them."

"Surely you do not think he comes here to cause us harm."

"I do. I think it is more than a likelihood. Why else would he come?"

"There could be some other reason."

Her look was kind but he knew the message that lay behind it, and it sparked him to irritation. She was not always right about such things. He resented her certainty.

"Kolevi, these are not times to suspect of people the best intentions. These are not such times." She only betrayed a hint of her own irritation, speaking gently, chidingly.

For a moment he nursed his resentment, then he let it pass, sighing surrender.

"Then what do you suggest we do?"

"I have stood here since before dawn, considering. I have thought on times and risks, and I think that perhaps we should remove him from the forest. Before he reaches the villages of Havenwood."

Kolevi took a step toward her, then halted, confused.

"What do you mean?"

She looked away, out the window and below, where a cart full of harvested thallids rolled past, going to the eating hall. There they would be boiled into a paste, spiced, and set out in bowls.

"Take him away, Kolevi. Prevent him from doing us more harm."

He tilted his head at her. "I still do not know what you mean."

"I think you do." Her eyes did not stray from the road below.

"Then I dare not guess."

"Look down there, beloved. Do you see the cart laden with thallid stalks? That is our food, food we did not have last year. It is not the grains and groundfruit we love, but it is food. Solid food. And it means that our people will not go hungry this season. Shall we allow this human to come here with his magic and his weapons? Here?"

Kolevi shut his eyes a long moment. "There are words for what you mean and yet do not say. Ugly words."

"Yes."

"Tell me that this frost-filled winter morning brings me a dark dream with your image. Tell me that I am so old that my ears ring with the illusion of your voice. Tell me it is not you who says such things to me."

"Kolevi, these are harsh times."

"No, no, and *no*. This is no simple-minded goblin or orc we speak of. This is a human. Humans have been allies and friends to Havenwood for centuries. Centuries, my lady. Have you forgotten?"

She gave him a quick, sharp laugh. "Then why did we hire this Reod Dai to cause them such strife in the first place, these our great good friends?"

He sighed. "We did it, you and I, because it had to be done. Because hunger threatened. Because we needed—"

"And still need."

"Yes, and still need." He sighed again, thinking on

the dark bargains they had made. "We cannot allow hunger to triumph. Dire times require dire solutions."

"That, my lord, is my point."

At last she looked back at him and their eyes met, and in that look he felt her intimate touch.

"No," he said again. "We will not start killing our friends to feed ourselves. We have not yet sunk so low."

She turned toward him fully, her eyes wide, lips thin, and pale eyebrows pressed down. "Have we not? How do you deceive yourself so marvelously, my lord? We have already done what you say we will not do. We have given the human a good deal of gold to act for us. Now we have human blood on our own hands. No Thelonite sacrifices these, Kolevi; this is the blood of the unwilling."

Her stream of harsh words broke with a small, almost inaudible cry from her lips. She cut the air with a quick gesture, cutting herself silent at the same moment. Both the cry and its sudden absence tore at his heart.

"Our compensation," she continued quietly, as if there had been no outcry at all, "is that our work has borne fruit. This season we feed ourselves."

Kolevi rubbed his head. When had their problems become so difficult? Until a handful of years ago, food had never been a problem for the elven people, not in all the years of their remembered history.

And then the winters chilled. Crops died. Disease spread. Elves went hungry.

In secret the elder druids struggled to create a new plant, one that would survive the cold and disease. He remembered the failures, year after year, and the despair of those few who knew how bad Havenwood's situation really was.

At last they had created the fast-reproducing thallids. It seemed that the new plant would end the years of hunger. It was tasteless and chewy, but it fought the cold winters and resisted disease.

Success was something the humans could understand, so the elder druids told Icatia how the forest of thallids now exploded in growth. Icatia sent congratulations.

But even now only he and Lalani and a very few others knew the true cost of the thallid success.

He forced himself to meet her golden eyes, but his gaze did not stay long. The floor was inlaid with small, colored stones, weaving together patterns and ancient words thick with magic. He let his eyes play across the familiar pathways of yellow and blue and red.

"What have we done, Lalani?"

"We never intended to harm Icatians."

"But we have."

"Some," she admitted. "Some few. Soldiers. And that only because we misjudged this human Reod Dai. We misjudge him no longer. The harm will stop."

"I hope it is so. But I fear what harm we may yet cause to those who deserve none."

She walked to him, took his hands, and looked up into his eyes.

"We have food, my lord. Above all else, our people will not go hungry this winter. You and I—we are Havenwood. We exist to bring life to our people. That is why we breathe, why we bother to feed our frail bodies, and why we take on ourselves the greatest of burdens. It is why we live."

"I know this. But perhaps—perhaps we should instead have trusted the Icatians and asked their aid."

Her laugh was bitter. "Indeed? Should we tell them how bad the harvests really were? Tell them about the sickness in the greenlife? Look at their shifting divisions, Kolevi. Look at how easily they trade loyalties. Each year we struggle to remember the names of their new leaders, their new religions, to learn who will be most offended if we forget."

"But this time, Lalani, with our needs so dire, surely they would be more understanding."

"I do not think so. Do you recall the rumors of plague in Havenwood last tenyear? Only rumors, my lord, but the humans closed their markets and held spears in our faces. We, their friends and allies. Do you recall that?"

"I do."

"If they are friends, then they are only friends under warm skies and alongside good harvests. We cannot afford to let them know how desperate we really are."

The bitterness he had been trying to press away settled deep in his stomach. He let his head drop with shame.

"Again you are right. Again I struggle against what would be clear to see if I would only look. Forgive me my foolishness."

"Hush, beloved," she said, a sweet, sad smile coming to her lips.

"No, I must say this: you are the braver of us two, you who have been willing to say and do the hard things while I sit back and wish for days of peace gone by. I am ashamed to have so often left you with the hardest of tasks."

"We each have our strengths, my love. You are kind and gentle, and our people need that in a leader as much as they need—" she gave a soft, sad laugh "—my ability to do the harder things. Let them see me as the dark one and you as the light."

"As long as they do not go hungry."

"Yes."

He sighed. "So you think we should send someone to address this Reod Dai?"

"Perhaps so."

"If these terrible times require that we do such dark things, let us at least be honest with ourselves about what we do. Ah, Lalani, must we really destroy this human?"

"Perhaps not. It might be wiser to speak with him first, to find out what he intends and what he knows. But look at how we underestimated his ability to provoke battle with the Icatians. Dare we let him closer? Look at how persuasive he has been, not only with us, but with our enemies. We must be very careful. We must not underestimate him again."

"Is it possible that he has somehow found out about the thallids?"

Year after year the thallid breeding efforts had failed. Desperate for an answer, they had introduced one new ingredient after another. At last they had found the right combination, bringing to life the successful plant they now harvested.

But there had been a cost. He and Lalani kept the secret that had given them their success: thallids were made from the Ebon Hand's own thrulls.

They did not need a lot of thrulls, but they did need a steady supply. For that they needed Icatia to look away from the northernmost roads where each month trusted elves would transport thrulls to Havenwood from the Ebon Hand. The Ebon Hand itself would reveal nothing to Icatia or anyone else, not with what the elders had paid them, but if Icatia found out, political disaster would ensue. So it was with great care that the elders sent elves to the west along the Icatian high desert roads, hoping that the Icatians would be too busy in the south to notice.

Which was why he and Lalani had hired Reod Dai.

"I do not think he knows about the thrulls," Lalani said. "But we do not know what else he may know."

"He comes to the place of our greatest power. Surely he realizes how foolish it would be to challenge us here."

"He brings dragon eggs to Havenwood, Kolevi. Dragon eggs! He may be a fool, but a dangerous fool."

"What shall we do?"

"Let us watch him as he approaches," she said. "His actions will tell us more than his words."

"And perhaps he can be reasoned with. Perhaps it will not be necessary to remove him."

"Perhaps."

He took her hand. "Send scouts to watch. Perhaps

he has truly come only to speak with us and not to cause harm."

Her eyes were full of doubt. He took her into his arms and touched his nose to hers.

"You are right, my lady. We will do what we must. As always, as always. For Havenwood."

"For Havenwood."

CHAPTER

5

"Only the trees know what really happened."

—Elven proverb

WITHOUT THE ROAD, THEIR PROGRESS
through the forest slowed. When they could, they followed the game trails that wove back and forth. Reod walked ahead, finding the way, and the three women helped clear branches and logs, wrestling the ox and cart forward.

Then Reod dropped back to follow for a few moments. He had gathered some branches, wrapped them together with vine, and now trailed them on the ground behind the cart.

"What are you doing?" Sekena asked.

He broke off the tips of the broom, spat on the ground, stamped twice, and walked backward toward the cart, again trailing the broom on the ground. The cart and women slowed and stopped, waiting for him to catch up.

"Confusing trees," Reod answered. "Elvish scouts, too, if we're lucky."

"Is it magic?" Melelki asked.

Reod repeated the broom dance.

"Of a sort. I'm asking the trees unanswerable questions. That distracts them from us and makes them poorer spies for the elves."

"I didn't know trees even thought," Tamun said.

"Most don't. But elvish scouts sometimes use elvish mages, and mages know how to keep their audiences."

Sekena looked at Tamun and her mother, who were both as confused as she was.

"Done," he said, and went back to leading the way through the trees.

Humans, Sekena reflected, were indeed strange creatures.

Near midday he stopped them. They stood for a long moment in silence, waiting.

"We're here," he said softly.

"Where?"

He pointed to an area some hundred strides away. They peered through the trees.

"What do you see?"

"Thicker forest," Sekena answered. "Fallen trees. Rocks. Moss."

"Those aren't trees and rocks," he said. "When we get closer, you'll see. They're thallids."

"Thallids? What are thallids?"

"The elves created a fungus and gave it roots. They eat them."

"Why?"

"Because they needed food. Now they have it."

"Why have we come here?" Mama asked.

"When you take away someone's dinner, you get their full attention."

He untied the cart's tarp and checked the eggs.

"This one," he said, tapping a knuckle on one of the eggs. Then he gave Sekena a long look. "This is what we brought the eggs for," he said to her. "To show Havenwood what their actions have accomplished. What happens when you start something and don't finish. You understand, yes?"

Sekena nodded and turned away, her shoulders already tense, her stomach already hurting. She understood, yes, but she hated it, and she didn't want to be near when it happened. So she turned away and walked through the trees until she could barely see the cart. Tamun followed and gave her hand a quick, reassuring squeeze.

Even from here Sekena could smell the strange, spicy scent on the air as Reod made his magic and the whelp hatched. Elation tried to dance through her, but she fought it away. She watched, though, saw the shape, saw it struggle to free itself of the shell shards, then stumble forward into the tangled thallid forest with that now familiar clumsy gait.

She turned away, sat down on a log, held her stomach and rocked back and forth, waiting for the sound and pain to hit. Moments passed.

"Why is it taking so long?"

Tamun shrugged. "I can't see the whelp anymore. It must be in the forest now."

More moments dragged by. Finally, curiosity overcame fear and Sekena stood and walked back, Tamun following.

When they got there Reod was slumped over, hands on knees, breathing hard. Melelki shrugged at their questioning looks.

"Must be something wrong with the whelp," he said between breaths. "Try another egg."

"No," Sekena said softly, pleadingly. Reod lifted another egg out of the cart and set it on the ground.

Sekena paced, unwilling to walk away again and wait, caught between wanting to be close when it hatched and fear of the pain that would follow. She still felt happy from the last whelp's scent. She could almost smell it out there in the thallid forest. For whatever had prevented the whelp from exploding, she was quietly grateful.

The second whelp hatched. Sekena inhaled and inhaled its scent again, almost dizzy with it. Reod

mumbled and threw charq meat toward the thick trees
that were not trees. The whelp wandered into the forest. Then Reod mumbled more words and a threw a
handful of dirt, and Sekena braced herself.

Nothing.

Reod made a disgusted sound, picked up more dirt,
mumbled, spat, and threw again. Sekena felt a tingle in
her feet, and then it faded.

Sweat glistened on Reod's face, drops trailing down
his neck. He walked a handful of steps away, knelt,
and did the whole dirt thing again, again with no
results. He slumped with exhaustion, gasping for air.
Tamun helped him sit down on a log.

"I don't understand," he said.

Tamun sat next to him.

"There's magic in this ground," he said. "I can feel
it. Why isn't it working?"

"Could it be the wrong kind of dirt?" Tamun asked.

"No. I feel it start up, and then—" He shook his
hands in frustration. "And then it just slips away."

Sekena let herself exhale her own tension, feeling
the double elation of whelp-scent and relief. She tried
to keep both out of her voice as she spoke.

"Now what?"

"Now nothing," he answered, favoring her with a
brief glare. "I'm not going to waste more eggs here.
We'll put them somewhere else, and hope they work
better."

"And the whelps in the thallid forest? Do we just
leave them?"

He stood and snorted. "You have another suggestion? Perhaps you'd like to go and round them up?"

Just then there came from behind Reod a rustling
and crunch of leaves. He turned. A whelp was wandering back out of the forest and toward them. All but
Sekena stepped back as the creature stumbled closer,
its eyes on Sekena.

"Sekena," her mother hissed. "Get back."

The whelp waddled up, sniffing her outstretched hand.

What lovely yellow eyes it had. Green-speckled scaly skin hung loosely around the creature's neck and stomach, its arms dangling uselessly at its side. Use of its arms would come later, Reod had told her, as would its wings. The creature's nostrils quivered close to Sekena's hand.

"Not food," she said to it, chuckling. She reached down, picked up a pine cone, and offered it.

"Sekena!"

Now the whelp opened its mouth, revealing many short, sharp teeth and a cute little pink tongue. It stretched its neck out and took the pine cone gingerly between pointed teeth.

She had never seen such an adorable gesture in any animal. Not even in kittens.

The next pine cone went down with a quick crunch. Now the whelp had the idea and dropped its nose to the ground to search out pine cones for itself.

With a rustling of leaves and the same loping walk, the second whelp came out of the thallid forest. It also sniffed Sekena's hand and then joined the other whelp in a hunt for pine cones, both of them crunching and swallowing and pushing the other away when a tidbit was found. When the immediate area was clear of fallen pine cones and twigs, they looked up at Sekena. From their throats came small crooning sounds. Hungry sounds.

Sekena was distantly aware of other sounds, of her mother calling her name, low and insistent. But for some reason it was the whelps who seemed to matter most. She stepped a little ways away to find them more pine cones. She broke off a branch of green needles. Perhaps they would like that, too. They did.

She inhaled, again and again, getting more of the marvelous scent than ever before, and feeling very good indeed.

When at last she tore her eyes away from the whelps to look for Mama and Tamun and Reod, she saw them watching her and the whelps with worried expressions.

That was silly. The creatures were perfectly friendly. Couldn't they see that?

She smiled at her mother and the others with a big, foolish grin, hoping to reassure them. It didn't seem to help. For some reason that didn't much bother her.

"Are they going to follow us?" Tamun asked.

"I don't know," Sekena answered as they packed up and began moving the cart again.

But the whelps did follow, lumbering along the side of the cart where Sekena was, looking suspiciously at the others, getting similar looks in return.

Reod, to Sekena's relief, seemed willing to give up trying to explode the creatures, at least for now. He contented himself with pushing the creatures with a long stick when they got too close to the food packs. The sticks got shorter each time, as the whelps took bites out of them, but the whelps were easily distracted when offered other tidbits instead. They did indeed eat anything. Pine cones, sticks, the lowest branches of trees. They left only dirt and the occasional quick dragon-dropping.

When the sun began to set, they stopped to make camp. The whelps lay down under a thick pine, curled together near where Sekena set her sleeping roll. They were like green mounds with pale, nearly translucent wings folded across their backs.

Reod stood nearby. "I've never seen anything like this. You must have dragon-scent about you."

Sekena rubbed her hand over one of the rounded, lumpy, green backs. The whelp opened one yellow eye to see her. The eye slowly drifted closed.

As the forest grew dark Reod gathered the dwarves around him to explain his new plan.

"I think it was the thallid field," he said. "The elders must have put some sort of magic protections on it that I couldn't detect. But they'll have no such defenses in the fortresses and villages, because there they have to use their own magic to grow houses and walls out of trees."

"So?" Melelki asked.

"So we'll rest a bit, and later tonight when their guards are fewer we'll bury all the remaining eggs in the fortress."

"Right inside?" Sekena asked.

"Right inside."

"But how do we get in?"

"I can make us—less than visible for a short time."

Tamun tilted her head, looked at him. "You mean invisible?"

"Close."

Sekena thought about all those eggs, all waiting for Reod's magical touch to hatch and explode them. Her whelps were curled together like two strange mounds of mold. A look at Reod told her that even now their lives were far from safe.

And that was troubling. What were they doing here, in the land of the elves, when their own people needed fighters at Teedmar?

For the moment she decided to keep such thoughts to herself.

Sekena had bedded down away from the others because the whelps wouldn't leave her side and the others did not want to sleep so close to them. Reod had given up warning her about how dangerous they were. She simply could not manage to be so concerned.

The whelps curled around her as she burrowed into her sleeping roll. They smelled good and kept her cozy, but still she could not sleep. Behind her eyes was the old man in Kalitas. She could see him sitting on his front step, waiting for the dead to return. Was he still there? Would he wander among the ruined buildings, propping up the bodies of his brothers to talk to and play Stones with?

How must it have been for the townspeople when the orcs came? They would have fought fiercely, of that she was certain, but the orcs would have been stronger. Not more numerous—Kalitas was a large town, but creature by creature the orcs would be stronger. She tried to imagine the angry cries and screams of pain, blood and weeping, and finally silence.

It didn't feel right, lying here on elven ground, when dwarves were fighting for their lives back in the southern mountains.

Overhead the constellation of Ducklings moved slowly around the Great Eye. Crickets hummed peacefully.

In Teedmar they were doing something about the orcs.

She rose, patted the whelps reassuringly, quietly rolled up her bedding, and set to packing her few things. The whelps watched her sleepily to make sure she did not go far without them. She was tying the last of the flaps shut when the softest rustle drew her attention.

"Going somewhere, Sekena?"

She had not really expected to simply sneak past him, but she had half hoped she might be lucky. He leaned against a tree, ghostly dim under the tree shattered light of a half moon.

"I'm leaving," she said quietly.

"To go where?"

"Teedmar."

He sounded amused. "Now, in the middle of the night?"

"Yes. I am done with watching you explode eggs in elven lands while dwarves die to the south. I am going to go help my people fight the war that you started."

"Going to join the dwarven army?"

"Yes."

"Do you think they will take you? A female? Not fully grown, not even in her time of power?"

Sekena snorted. "Do you think they'll reject my willing hands? I can do something, surely, and anything I can do there is better than staying here to watch you destroy dragons while dwarves bleed and die."

"You and those dragons are very interesting. As for the rest, if I had my funds back, I could stop those raids on dwarven lands in a handful of days."

"If you had clear loyalties, you never would have given the orcs weapons to attack us in the first place."

There was a hard silence between them as they stared at each other in the moonlight.

"I see more than you do, Sekena."

"Maybe you see so much that your brain is muddy, human. Ta, I'm only fifteen, but I do not attack my own kind. Nor do I make war against the elves, faulting them for my bad fortune. I know who my people are. Do you?"

"You speak well. You should have led in Leitbur's Order."

She had no idea what he meant. "I do not care to listen to you. I go."

"What about your mother and sister?"

His words made a quick, sharp ache in her chest. "I don't want Mama fighting, so it is better this way. And Tamun—she'll protect you before she protects anyone else. I've seen the way you two are. I think you'll take care of her . . . of them both. You will, won't you?"

For a moment he said nothing.

"You know that I can't just let you leave, Sekena."

It would come to this, after all. She had thought it might and had imagined this moment many times. He would say she could not go, and she would either struggle like the child he said she was and lose, or . . .

Or not.

She knelt down, rested a hand on one of the dozing whelps.

"How will you stop me? If you try, my dragons will defend me. I have told them to do so."

She had done nothing of the kind. Indeed, she had

not the least certainty the whelps would defend her
from anything. But she was betting that Reod was even
less sure.

He made a thoughtful sound, then reached down to
the ground. For a moment Sekena was confused. Then
he took a few steps backward and began to mumble
and horror trickled down her spine.

Words of protest and plea came to her lips, but she
fought them away, forcing herself to think. Would he
really explode her along with the whelps to keep her
from leaving? Would he go that far? Surely not. Then
she thought about the Icatian lieutenant and was no
longer certain.

With an arm around each of the sleeping dragons,
she looked up at him. She still did not know if he had
actually killed the Icatian lieutenant, but she knew that
she could promise what the human could not.

"I won't speak of you. I won't mention you at all. I
promise."

A moment of silence passed. Reod exhaled, sharp
and short. He spread his fingers, letting the dirt fall
through them. Turning away for some long heartbeats,
he then stepped forward and crouched down, just a
stride away from her.

"These are hard times," he said quietly. "Sometimes
I forget."

She frowned. His voice was odd, strained. Was he
trying to confuse her? To put her off her guard?
Humans were so confusing.

"Sekena—" He sighed. "Listen: if you feel you must
go to fight for your people, then—" He shook his head.

"Then?"

"Maybe you are right. Maybe I have seen too much.
Lost too much. Go, then, and be safe, at least from
me. I don't promise that your mother and sister will
not follow, but as far as Reod Dai is concerned, go
where you will." He stood. "And fight for your people,
if that is what you feel you must do."

She hardly knew what to say. "Thank you. Maybe—

maybe you have fair reasons to trouble the elves as you do."

His small smile was dim in the moonlight.

"I have reasons. Perhaps they are fair."

"Then—good fortune to you."

"And you."

She stood, shouldered her pack, and began to walk away from the camp. It did not make any sense at all to wait here and find out if he would change his mind again.

Overhead the constellation of the Brazier was half in view, tangled as always with the Dance of Snake and Frog. Above and south was the Great Eye, Friend to Travelers. She oriented herself, angling toward the road that would lead her south toward her homelands.

And as for the whelps, they could follow or not. It didn't matter to her.

Or so she told herself, again and again, sighing her relief when she finally heard the creatures trailing her, rustling leaves behind.

Into the moonlit night the three walked. It might indeed be a foolish thing she did, walking away from her beloved family and a human who could battle orcs and goblins and other humans, and she with just two baby dragons for companions. It might be the most foolish thing she had ever done.

With only a touch of embarrassment, she checked to make sure the shard was still in her pocket. It was.

CHAPTER

6

"There is no gain without sacrifice."
—Icatian proverb

REOD LET THE RED STARS OF THE BRAZIER
move across the sky a good handwidth before he
finally woke Melelki. He touched her shoulder lightly
and she stirred, her eyes snapping open, focusing on
him.

"Sekena has left," he said.

"What?" She sat up, then came fully awake, standing faster than Reod would have expected. She looked
around, then back at him. "Left? What do you mean?
Left to go where?"

"South," he said. "To Teedmar. To help fight."

"*What?*"

"She went to Teedmar to help your people repel the
goblin and orc invaders," he repeated.

Melelki's look darkened. "She told you this?"

"Yes."

"She told you this and you let her go?"

Long ago, during Reod's first command, he had

twenty soldiers under him to do patrol rounds. On the way back from a round, he had taken them through a mountain shortcut to shave a few days off the circuit. Then the shortcut's path had crumbled under them and they lost horses, weapons, and food. The supplies fell hundreds of feet, unrecoverable.

They had arrived back at the fortress two days after they were due, hungry, cold, and grateful to be alive. Back at Trokair, Reod had been called in front of General Jonas to explain to her what had happened. He remembered the general's tone as if it had been yesterday, remembered the sinking feeling in his stomach as she told him just what she thought of him and his actions.

General Jonas could crush the confidence of veterans with a sideways look. And now this dwarven woman who stood two heads below him, who was nothing at all like the general, for some reason was producing in him a similar sensation.

Melelki glared up at him. "You just let her go?"

Reod thought of Sekena's arms around the whelps, of the threats they had exchanged, of the tactical maneuvering of a bright fifteen-year-old.

"Yes, I let her go."

Melelki turned, movements sudden, snappish, and grabbed her pack, stuffing things inside. Tamun was awake now, standing, watching uncertainly.

"How long ago?" Melelki demanded. "We can still catch her."

"Hours," Reod said.

"Hours?" Her tone spoke disbelief. "*Hours?*" Melelki did not take time away from her packing to give him another glare.

Tamun stood to one side, obviously knowing her mother's mood well enough to keep silent.

"Melelki," he said. "I wanted to stop her. I intended to. The whelps—they clung to her, like puppies to a bitch. They would have fought me if I had tried to hold her. When I threatened to explode them, she only held tighter. There was little I could do but let her go."

Which was not entirely true. There were many things he could have done. Instead he had stood aside.

Melelki spun on him, raging. "My daughter! You let her go? Just like that? You are an idiot. You are a useless piece of meat. *Human.*"

"She'll be safe. She has two dragons protecting her."

"Will they protect her from a band of orcs? Will they? *Can* they? I doubt it."

Reod looked to Tamun for help. Tamun shook her head, her shoulders twitching in a subdued shrug.

"All right," he said. "We'll go after her. We'll pack up and follow her and find her."

Melelki's hard breathing slowed a little. For a moment she looked relieved, then she looked at him suspiciously.

"We'll go after her," he said. "But listen: it would take us only a few hours to seed the eggs in the fortress. If we leave now, all of our struggle to get the eggs here will have been wasted. Remember what we planned for the elves? We've come all this way, Melelki. Don't you want to pay them back for what they have done to you and your people?"

"But my daughter—"

"Sekena will not have gone far. The dragons are little and they need lots of sleep. They'll stop soon and rest until morning, maybe even sleep into the day. It will not be hard to find them. Just follow a trail of broken branches and dragon dung."

Melelki frowned. "She's only fifteen."

"She's very bright, very canny, and she has bodyguards."

"They'll guard her? Are you sure?"

Reod had seen enough dragon whelps over the years to know that their behavior with her was singular. She had said that they smelled right. Clearly they felt the same way about her. No, he wasn't sure, but there was no point in admitting that.

"Yes."

"I don't like it."

"The sooner we get the eggs planted, the sooner we can go after her."

"And then?"

"Then back here, to finish what we started. A day, perhaps two. And then—we will go to Teedmar to join the efforts of the dwarven army."

"You as well?" asked Tamun.

He turned to look into her dark eyes in the starlight.

"Yes. Me as well."

Melelki nodded, her rage easing, as if she had only been waiting for him to say this.

As they packed to go the short distance to the fortress, Tamun stopped next to him. Softly she said, "You let her go. I know you could have found a way to stop her. Why let her go?"

"She wants to defend her people. Who am I to tell her no?"

Tamun touched his arm lightly. "Thank you."

He was surprised. "Why?"

"Because you have let her follow her blood. She's always had fight in her veins. I've seen that since she was a baby, though she thinks no one knows. And Mama never would have let her go. Mama doesn't understand, but you—I think you do."

He reached forward to enfold her in his arms, touched by her words.

Into her ear he whispered, "Should not each creature have the chance to fight for their own?" Images came to him with memories of screams and cries. "But Tamun, oh, I have seen so many die to protect their homes and children. So many. Too many."

She pulled back a little to look into his eyes.

"You helped to make things this way, did you not?"

"Yes, but I thought I would do more good than harm. I thought—"

"The moon is moving," Melelki said impatiently.

The moon had indeed moved. It was time to enter the fortress.

Reod took a deep breath, and then again, stilling his mind. Then he gathered a handful of dirt and spat into it. He spoke an old incantation, one that had twists and turns, where words wrapped back on each other, tying themselves in knots until he could barely understand his own words.

They worked through the night, moving one egg at a time. Reod led the way, letting Tamun and Melelki carry the heavy eggs.

He paused before the guard trees, but did not fight them. Instead he used tricks he had learned from the Ebon Hand to confuse living things by talking to their very bones. He gave the trees riddles about the sun and the stars and the changing breezes. It was hard work, and his head pounded with pain as he talked to the trees in their silent, ancient tongue.

At last the trees were distracted enough to let them by without complaint. Then there were only walls and traps. It had been a very long time since Reod had found a trap he could not defeat or a wall which there was not a way around, over, or through.

Bits of moonlight broke through the thick trees overhead, the trees knitting together to form the fortress. One by one the three of them planted the eggs, some near the center house of the fortress, some near the weapons stores, and others under the defensive walls.

They were digging down into the soft earth to bury the last egg. Reod glanced up at what stars he could see through the tall branches. The stars were the sun's sparks and spawn, and by their dance he could tell how long it was before they would move aside for the sun's brilliant face. Morning was coming soon.

Twigs snapped sharply, shattering the night's peace. Something large and strange-smelling brushed by them. It was not that Reod had become distracted, or that Melelki and Tamun had not moved quietly enough. No, it was something else, something that moved oddly through the night, something not human, animal, or tree, for all of those had been ensorcelled to look past them.

And it was noisy. It stumbled and crashed about, falling against the goat pen, starting the animals bleating. Reod struggled to keep the spells he had woven across the three of them from unraveling, to keep them looking like shadow and dirt, twig and leaf. But it was too much, and suddenly the egg stood out in the bare hint of morning light like a grounded moon.

Shadows detached themselves from the trees, forming into elves with black outlines of blade and bow, arrow bolts aimed low at each of the three of them.

Silence settled the moment. Even the goats stopped their complaint. A single bird began a tentative call to the morning's light. The shape that had broken Reod's spells was long gone, faded into the night. No one moved.

Reod knew exactly where Tamun was. If he tried to take on all the elves himself, could he win? Could he keep her safe? No, probably not. He stayed where he was.

Soft footsteps announced an arriving elf. She carried only a knife at her side, but Reod knew from her walk and how the others looked at her that she was not only a warrior but a leader and a thinker. She gave him a long look.

"You, I think we identify," she said in stiff, accented dwarven. "Reod Dai?"

"Good guess."

She laughed humorlessly. "Is it true? This is the great and feared Reod Dai? This one who tries to bribe goats into silence with thallid bark? Taste it sometime, human, and see if you do not bleat as well."

Reod struggled a moment to understand her words, then gave up. Elves were often this way, saying things that made little sense, as if they spoke only to hear words fall from their lips.

"Who," she asked, "are these?"

He barely spared Melelki and Tamun a glance, hiding his hope that they would follow his lead and that Tamun would not explode into a frenzy as she had with the Icatians in the mountains. He believed it was crisis that triggered her heat-driven rages. If he could keep this situation calm . . .

"Servants," he said shortly. "I gave them food when they were hungry, so they followed me from the ruins of their town." He could almost feel Melelki's insulted glare on the back of his neck.

The commander's tone hardened as she motioned at the egg.

"And that?"

"A message for your elders."

Her smile turned to a thin line. "We are not fools, human. It is a dragon egg, and you are no friend to Havenwood."

"You might ask your elders where that friendship went."

To the dwarves the elvish commander said, "I fear you follow a dangerous and untrustworthy human. You are fortunate to have come under our influence. We will see you safely to the road and then home to your lands." The commander nodded at her warriors. "Take the little ones away."

"No, wait—" Tamun began, and her words tugged at him.

"They want their money," he broke in, sounding disgusted.

"What?" the commander asked.

"They claim the egg is theirs. I gave them food for it, but still they—"

"My egg," Melelki broke in, catching on. "He promised us money for it. It belongs to me."

The commander looked from face to face, frowning. "Our interest is with the human. Little ones, these are not safe times. Go home."

"It is mine," Melelki said stubbornly. "He never paid us what we were owed for it."

Reod looked at Melelki and snorted.

The elf's eyes flickered between them. "If we give you coin—"

"Three gold," Melelki said.

Amusement flickered across the commander's face. "I do not think so."

"Two, then, but no less."

The commander considered, decided. "One gold. We will pay you one gold and you will leave immediately."

"Take it," Reod said. He met Tamun's eyes for a flickering moment, saw there sorrow and fear. Fear for himself, he was sure, and that was justified. He looked away and put as much disgust into his tone as he could manage. "With elves, take what you can get and leave before they change their minds."

He had to get the dwarven women safely out of Havenwood before he could work on his own escape. Surely Tamun would understand that he meant to follow them as soon as he could. She would know how he felt about her. Wouldn't she?

Or maybe she wouldn't. He had not said anything specific, and with all the differences in humans and dwarf ways, who knew what she understood about him. He should have said something to her last night, when he had the chance. Something simple and direct that she could not misunderstand.

But even now he was not sure what that would have been.

He risked another glance at her, hoping his look would carry some of what he thought.

"One gold," the elf said.

"Two," Melelki insisted.

"One."

"And provisions. Food and water."

"One gold. Provisions. And we will see you safely to the edge of the southern peaks."

Reod felt relief go through him. With an elvish escort, they would be safe through the forests, even from roving orc bands.

"No. We go to Teedmar."

"Teedmar? Why?"

"To fight for our people."

"That is not a safe area. We advise against it."

As would Reod. He wanted them back in the safer Tigaden.

Melelki looked up at the tall elf, her voice soft. "We go to Teedmar."

The elf considered, then nodded. "We will leave you within a day's walk of the city. Do you agree to this?"

He would have to catch up with them before the elves left them on their own, but they would be safe until then, and if all went well, he might manage it. It was the best deal they were likely to get now. Silently he urged Melelki to accept the offer.

"Agreed."

As the elves led the dwarven women away, Reod directed himself to look around the fortress, to concentrate on each detail. Shapes lightened, bringing color to the world. Branches swayed in the breeze of the evergreen canopy. Trees wove together to form the bones of walls and towers, storerooms and sleeping quarters. On the branches of the highest trees stretched platforms and connecting bridges of vine.

The sun's early light shot across trunks, painting the earth with long shadows. Patterns of leaf and shadow danced across his eyes and he watched them intently, keeping his mind from the soft, fading steps he knew too well.

Even now he could turn now and see her go, see her one last time. One last image to take with him.

Instead he met the commander's measuring stare.

*   *   *

They tied his wrists behind his back. He knew the knots they used from the twists and tugs as they went. Given a few moments unwatched he could release himself. For now, though, as he was led across the forest fortress, he did nothing.

Elves stopped to stare as he walked by. He had a glimpse of a handcart filled with some long, brown plant. Thallids, perhaps. Younger elves gaped at him, nearly children, some carrying buckets of water or gruel.

Before this, he had conducted all his business with the elders through messengers and had only infrequently been close enough to see an elven fortress. Last night had been his first time inside of one, under the cloak of night, seeding dragon eggs. He had heard much about the unique elven construction of the fortresses.

Unique though it might be, when it came to warfare, fortresses crossed racial boundaries. There were a few known and effective ways to identify and keep enemies away: towers and walls and gates.

But here the front gates, woven of thick vines and leaves, were wide open. Soldiers chatted, letting elves from the nearby Havenwood villages wander in and out unchecked. One soldier was showing a child how to throw a hunting stick. It was a peaceful scene, with no indication that there was anything outside the walls to be wary of. Quite a contrast to any Icatian fortress.

But then, the elves had arranged to have others fight their wars for them.

His escort led him to the center building. From a distance, it seemed to be made of tightly packed tree trunks, decorated with bright green leaves. Up close, though, Reod saw that it was rock that rose out of the soil, sculpted to look like trees, decorated with bright green stones and glass where leaves would have been.

In shadow the night before he had seen this place. There was an egg buried nearby.

Through a hallway they led him, past doors of knitted

roots. Spiraling stairs went upward, one story and then another, until they were at the top. His guards paused at the door, knocked. When it opened they pressed him inside first.

There stood two white-haired elves in green robes, tall and thin, thin even for elves. Their hair was nearly as white as their smooth skin, speaking of old age long-delayed by magic.

The female looked out the window as the male watched Reod. A gesture came from the male and Reod's hands were untied. Another gesture and the guards left the room.

Neither of the elder druids spoke or moved, so Reod kept his silence as well. From outside and below came the sounds of the fortress, of distant voices and footsteps, of wheels turning, of water being pumped.

In silence they waited. It was an old technique, a very old technique, and he was amused. Did they think he would give something away out of impatience or uncertainty? Did they think he was so very inexperienced?

Perhaps they would be easier for him to deal with than he had thought. Perhaps the subtlety he had believed of elves was merely the strangeness of their race, seeming to his eyes to be more than it was. Perhaps they were really a very simple people.

The way to win this child's game was to be patient and remain silent. Eventually they would speak first. He would learn much from the first few words spoken.

As he waited, Reod let his eyes roam the room, across the spiderweb-patterned walls and ceiling, out the large open window to the trees beyond. His gaze came to the floor and traveled across the many small, colored stones there. His eyes ran the pattern, followed it, came back. It was, he realized, a sort of maze.

It was not much of a challenge, though. He didn't want to take his eyes off of the floor to look at the elders, but he knew they were watching him and he thought he heard one of them chuckle. Did they think he couldn't solve it? It was so simple. He almost had it done. Just a few moments more and he would solve the maze.

Perhaps elves thought humans were fools, but he would gladly show them otherwise, show them how easy it was for one of his kind to solve such simple puzzles. So very, very easy.

Too easy?

Memory hissed. Genkr Nik's voice came to him out of the past, deep and gruff. The other had been saying something, mouthing some dark spell. Lecturing again.

"Nature's paths," Genkr breathed softly, with a raspy voice, "are echoes of the ones in our minds. Control this—" he put his palm flat on Reod's forehead, and Reod felt a tingle where the other touched "—and you control all paths. You think like a soldier, Reod. Always in straight lines. Look sideways. *Look*, damn you."

And Genkr had been right. Time after time.

Maybe he would be right now, too.

Sideways.

Reod flicked his mind around as he had learned to do at the Ebon Hand and looked sideways.

The floor shifted, seemed to ripple into waves. His stomach felt strange, as if it had been twisted. He lost his balance, stumbled forward a step. Stop. Lurch and catch. Then—

Then the mosaic went flat, the walls pulled back as if they were exhaling, and then seemed to snap vertical. No longer rippling, no longer breathing. Just walls, just stones. Just floor.

He inhaled sharply, exhaled, looked up at the druids.

"So," said the female of the two elder druids, in a high, soft, voice, turning pale eyes on him. "you are Reod Dai, he who once hailed from Icatia, but more recently comes from the nest of the Ebon Hand. You come with a message, we are told."

Reod took another deep breath, shaking off the final cobwebs of their failed spell, and looked at them again.

These were Lalani and Kolevi, who he knew both by reputation and from his work on the contract they had made and broken.

He put a careful, mocking edge of amusement into his elven, which was not easy. "A pleasure to meet you both. At last."

"To us," Kolevi said, his voice deeper than the female's but still soft, "much about you is unclear. Why do you come to Havenwood, Reod Dai?"

"To get your attention."

"And now that you have it, what will you do with it?"

"Tell you that you have made a mistake. A serious mistake. Give you the chance to correct it."

"Oh?"

"Our contract is not complete, elders. You left me in the middle of a number of situations that require resolution. I trust you have received my reports through your messenger?"

"Yes."

"Give me a chance to finish what you paid me to begin."

"Alas," Kolevi said, "we cannot afford you, Reod Dai."

"Elder druids, short on coin?" He chuckled. "I doubt it. Why did you break the contract? Was my work so very good?"

"We no longer had need of your services."

"No, you were afraid. Listen: you cannot look upon my work with the eyes of children. Look instead with adult eyes. You cannot pick up a sword, swing it at your enemy only once, and then stop. You must finish what you begin."

"It is finished now," Lalani said.

"No. It is only begun."

"You have come all this way to ask us to reconsider?"

He gave them a grin that did not last. "First I will ask."

Lalani looked out the window again. "What will you ask?"

"I want the funds to complete the contract. You hired me to do this, and now we both hold the tail of a hungry hydra. This is not the time to let go. Let me finish it."

"The situation has changed."

"How?" He pitched his voice to show frustration and took a step forward, as if so caught up that he did not realize his proximity. They did not flinch or seem to notice. They were that confident.

"It has changed. We have decided."

"You have created a monster. The goblins now have explosive devices. I need time to take those away, to train them to less effective tactics. And the orcs—I changed their strategies so they could do more than simply fall over each other in battle. Now I have to change that, too. Without my influence, the two races quickly become allies and turn to an easier target than my Icatia: the dwarven people. Do you know that?"

Both of their eyes were on him. There was a buzzing in the back of his head.

"Where are the rest of your dragon eggs, Reod Dai?"

He shook his head to rid it of the buzzing, but it didn't work. It was suddenly hard to think. They wanted to know about his dragon eggs, wanted to know if he remembered where he put them. Of course he did. He remembered very well. Remembered each one. Did they think him stupid? He could tell them. Show them. It would be easy.

Too easy.

"Somewhere inconvenient for you when they hatch," he said, forcing the words out. "And they will hatch. Soon."

He reached inside himself, grabbed, twisted.

Sideways.

The buzzing stopped. He breathed again.

Lalani nodded thoughtfully. "Should we believe you?"

"I recommend that you do."

"What do you really want?" Kolevi asked.

"An installment of funds. An escort. I'll send the escort back within a day with detailed instructions on how to get rid of the eggs—or the whelps, if they hatch."

He was gambling that none of the eggs would hatch too soon, gambling that Sekena would have told him if she had felt any that close. He was gambling a lot.

"Confirm for me my understanding," Lalani said, turning, pale gaze resting on him. "You attempt to destroy our thallid fields. You threaten our villages and fortresses with dragon eggs, which we know you can turn into quick fire, or force to hatch into destructive dragonlings. In return for these gifts you demand that we give you gold and free passage to the southlands. Do I understand you correctly?"

He met her gaze. "I would have preferred another means by which to tell you how serious the situation has become, but you would not hear me, so I had to come here to get your attention. If the contract is not completed, there will be consequences. I'm here to show you some of those consequences."

"It was our contract. Ours to begin, and ours to end."

"Then when goblins and orcs overrun the dwarven people, who have at best a pitiful defense, when dwarven villages are burned to the ground, their people cut up, raped, their food stores fouled, when the hordes turn back to Icatia for more—when all this happens, it should be you who the dying should curse with their last breath, yes?"

There was a subtle difference in Lalani's face. Reod could not quite tell whether it betokened anger or something else. Still her voice was soft.

"How is it that you can be the instrument of so

much suffering and at the same time present the blame to us?"

"You chose to wield this sword, elder."

"Are you nothing more than a sword?" Kolevi asked.

"You would sheathe the weapon moments after beginning to engage. You cannot do that. It is too late."

"We left you in peace, Reod Dai," Kolevi said. "We trusted in your silence. You should not have come here."

"By the Hells, the world is at war! Blood will run in the streets! Children will weep and beg to die! Have you not ears to hear and eyes to see? You have added deadwood to the threatening flames, but give me a chance and I can slow the fire."

"Is that why you accepted this contract, Reod Dai?" Lalani asked. "To stop these wars?"

"It is."

"Such seems a strange means to your end."

"Strange times ask strange solutions."

"We would like to trust you," Kolevi said.

Lalani shook her head. "Times of war force us all to terrible extremes, do they not? If we could believe that you would take our gold and the eggs away and do no more harm—"

"You think I want only your coin? Idiots! I need funds to push the goblins and orcs back from the dwarven people, from the destruction you never intended."

"How are we to trust you to do only that?"

"You trusted me before, trust me now. Give me coin and let me finish what's been started."

"Alas, we can no longer trust you." Kolevi said.

"Then a bargain. The eggs—"

"Our mages will deal with them."

"How, if they can't find them?"

Her eyes flickered, telling Reod that she hadn't quite solved that problem. That was useful information.

"Your threats do not influence us," she said. "It is simple: we do not trust you. Not free in Havenwood, not free anywhere. And so—" She hesitated. "And so we will keep you here, where we can watch you."

And where they no doubt hoped he would change his mind about the dragon eggs. Reod had always collected stories, for in stories there was often more than a little truth. One time he had heard a story of an elven prison, of trees that grew into cages as hard as stone and so tight that the jailed one could not move even a finger.

"You compound your mistake," he said.

"Possibly. Strange times, as you have said. Hard choices are required of us now, and we must make them. These wars will not last forever. When the lands have settled themselves again, we hope to be able to free you."

Reod snorted. "The wars have not yet begun. You are blind."

"Tell us," Kolevi said with sudden earnestness, "tell us where the eggs are hidden. Tell us how to be safe from them. We do not desire you captive, we only want to keep our people safe. Perhaps we can still reach an agreement."

"Your word is better than mine?" Reod smiled hard. "I have seen what you do to those you call ally. Shall I expect better treatment? I've shoveled your cesspools clean for you, elders, so I stink and am now disposable. 'Times of war' and 'necessary sacrifice.' Do you think I haven't heard this all before? Don't offer me garbage."

Lalani stiffened at his words. "We must view your refusal to identify the eggs as an attack on Havenwood."

"As well you should. I do so and without hesitation. I have seen the ruin your fickle minds cause."

Kolevi looked down at the floor. "We ask you again."

Reod could see the pleading in Kolevi's face. He softened his own voice.

"Give me gold enough to complete the contract and I'll remove the eggs. I swear it."

"We are at a standstill," Lalani said.

Behind him a door opened.

"Bind him," she said, then, "think on your decision, Reod Dai. There is still some time, but not much. Change your mind before the eggs hatch, and we will reconsider—"

"Damn you both."

Through his anger, both real and pretended, he noticed the hint of sorrow on their faces. Strangely, it kindled his own sorrow, and with it came despair's touch. He kept both well hidden.

Three elvish guards searched him thoroughly. Gone were his knife, powders, sling, and other small, hard-to-replace items.

Kolevi and the guards led him underground, through a series of connecting tunnels that had been formed of tightly packed roots. They came back outside and to a wall of woven roots that shuddered and parted at Kolevi's touch, leading to a small circular cage, about as wide as Reod was tall and not quite as high.

Brush and roots tangled thickly, forming the upper part of the cage in a half-sphere that rose out of the recessed earth. The thick weave allowed in little light. Reod's hands felt along the roots in the dim enclosure, touching a solidness like steel.

Behind him the door of roots fell closed and became as solid as the weave overhead, leaving him alone in the enclosure. He tried the roots, pressed them, spoke to them, and dug down into the dirt to confirm that every part of the cell was surrounded by them.

Magic roots. But not his magic.

He sat on the cool floor of dirt, watching a pinpoint of sun, which, having managed to get through both trees and roots, illuminated only a small pebble.

He picked up the pebble, stood as high as the roof of the cell would let him, pressed his fingers through the roots, and threw the pebble into the forest beyond.

Outside was quiet. He was at the edge of the fortress, where the trees were thickest. In the distance he could hear the sounds of elves, voices, and movement. Closer were the sound of birds and a slow breeze that seemed to hint of coming storms.

Or dragon whelps. He would have only a little while before the dragons finally hatched on their own, whenever their nature happened to call to them, and then his last weapons would be gone.

Part of his mind was with Tamun and her mother. They traveled with an elvish escort, but only part of the way, and then they would travel through the worst of the southlands alone. They would hardly be safe even once arrived at Teedmar, which sat near the Icatian border and in the middle of goblin and orc territories.

He took a deep breath and closed his eyes, soothing the fire of urgency inside him. He was exhausted from the previous night's physical and magical labor, and would be awake this coming night with more of the same if he were to have any hope of escape. He needed sleep more than anything now, but his own tension fought to keep him awake. Years of times like this had taught him that if he did not ignore pressing events and sleep when he could, he might not sleep for days. And then he would make mistakes.

The half-buried cell was surprisingly warm, and though the ground was hard, it was no harder than the ground he had slept on many times. He lay down, struggled with his thoughts until they stilled, then dozed.

It felt as if hours had passed when he woke to the soft sound of footsteps outside his cell. He peered through the small holes in the roots and saw a young elvish boy. The boy looked around, did not see Reod, then crouched down and dug a hole next to a tree.

When the hole was a few hands deep, he put his feet in, covering them with the loose dirt. He stretched his arms wide above his head and shut his eyes.

Reod watched as the boy stood there, unmoving. Typical elvish strange behavior mixed with quiet tenacity. What was he doing?

Frustration finally flickered across the boy's sharp features, and a sudden insight made Reod chuckle. At the sound, the elvish boy's eyes snapped open and he dropped into a crouch, looking around. His eyes settled on the sunken cell.

"I think there's more to it than that," Reod said with a smile.

The boy approached the cell warily, his head moving back and forth to try to see Reod through the roots.

"You must be the human who came to the fortress last night. Are you?"

"Reod Dai. And you?"

"Andli."

"Trying to turn yourself into a tree, eh?"

The boy walked forward and crouched down, still trying to see Reod through the cage. "Why are you in there?"

"Because I'm dangerous."

"Are you, really?"

"Yes."

"Oh." The boy stood up and took a step back, as if to leave, then stopped, his movements quick, like a squirrel's. He looked around and then back at Reod.

"What can you do that is so dangerous?"

"I can make a dragon egg hatch."

Eyes widening, the boy leaned forward and grabbed hold of the roots of the cell, bringing himself closer to look at Reod.

"Really?"

"Yes. Would you like to see it?"

"I have never seen a dragon before."

"I will show you. But first you have to tell me something. Were you trying to turn yourself in to a tree?"

The boy's pale green eyes widened a little. Embarrassment, Reod guessed. He nodded.

"I have heard that if you plant your feet and stand still for a long time, you can become like a tree. Then you can talk to them."

"Ah. But they don't talk the way you and I are talking, you know."

"No? Have you talked with trees?"

"Yes."

"Really? Have you, really? What do they say?"

"They talk about the places below and above the ground. To them the earth itself moves, much as the wind moves for us."

The boy made a face, tilted his head a little. "If you can really talk to trees, then why are you still in there, instead of out here and free?"

"That's a good question. These trees are very loyal to the elder druids and not particularly interested in me."

"I shouldn't be talking to you, either, should I?"

"No."

"Then why do I want to?"

"Another good question. You live in dangerous times, so you are interested in what is dangerous. In truth, that is quite prudent. How can you learn to protect yourself from dangers unless you understand them?"

"Can you teach me to talk to trees?"

"It takes time and practice, but I can help you begin."

"I want to see the dragon."

"For the dragon you'll have to keep a secret."

Andli paused, pale eyes flickering around at the forest. "I am not sure. I think I should not be here."

"Just until tonight."

"Then, yes. Just until tonight. What is the secret?"

"The secret is this: come here just after sunset, but tell no one. Then I will show you what happens when a dragon egg hatches."

"Really?"

"Really."

"I don't believe you."

Reod laughed. "Then don't come tonight."

"You promise this?"

"I do. And bring me some food. Meat, if you can."

The boy stood suddenly. "I think you might be lying to me."

"I might, and that's good thinking. But now think further: what reason would I have to lie about these things?"

Andli tilted his head, first one way then the other, looking at Reod all the while. "I don't know. I will think about it."

"You do that."

"Before I go, tell me how to talk with trees so that they will answer."

Reod chuckled. "Come tonight."

Reod slept until the sunlight began to fade. It was dark in the cell by then, the roots blocking what little light was left. He felt his way to the thick, tender vine his captors had shown him.

"Bite into it," Kolevi had said. "It's like fruit juice. Very nutritious."

He bit. Into his mouth flowed a fruity syrup. It was bland yet refreshing. Still, it left him feeling hungry. Perhaps this was why elves were so thin.

Outside small boots brushed the ground.

"Are you there?" came Andli's whisper.

"Depends. Did you bring me food?"

"I have some dried rabbit meat. Do you like rabbit?"

"Slip it though the cracks to me."

The boy pressed strips through an opening between two roots.

"That will work," Reod said, taking the meat. "Listen: I'm going to do some things now to make the dragons hatch and come here. You have to do exactly what I tell you. Understand?"

"Yes."

"Good. Go stand behind that tree over there. Don't move. The dragon whelp may come close to you, but it won't bother you unless you get in its way. You are too big to be food. Do you understand?"

"Yes."

There were dragon eggs buried all across the fortress. The problem would be getting one to crack open from a distance. He had once begun the hatching process from a good ten strides away, but this would be much farther than that and the egg would be buried. In dirt. That could be an advantage.

He started the spell anyway, scooping up dirt at his feet, spitting into his hand, mumbling, and picturing the eggs in his mind.

It would not be enough this time to touch the right elements of dirt and water, or to mix in his own essence, or even to remember the right words for the spell.

Genkr had once told him: "It isn't common knowledge, even among wizards, but specific words don't really matter. A spell is about sound. The right sounds set up a rhythm in your body, aligning you to the elements you seek to control. Great wizards know how to listen. They listen to the wind, the trees, the animals. Then they make their magic."

Reod thought about dragon whelps, about the sounds he had heard them make with Sekena. Happy sounds, food sounds, the sounds they used to call to each other. He listened in memory to the words he usually used in his spell, listened for the sounds that were most like the whelps' cries. Then he began his own version in a soft, wordless song.

He pressed himself deep inside, to the inner place where he created the heart of his spells, and as he did he sang his wordless song over and over.

Remember the whelp cries, he told himself. *Remember Sekena's hand stretched out to them. Remember the song.*

So deep inside himself did he go that he did not

notice the first whelp scraping along the outside of his cage. Or the second. Or the third.

He stopped singing finally, struggling against the haze in which spellcasting had left him. Three winged shapes rustled in the dark outside his cell.

"Food," he told them, waving the meat near the root mesh, close to their noses. "Food."

They began to croon, and then they began to gnaw on the roots that were as hard as metal. Hard as metal, hard as dragon eggs. But could they also chew through the enchanted prison-roots of the elder druids?

They could. They did.

When the first one had chewed an opening large enough to push itself through, Reod threw the meat down on the dirt toward the far side of the cell, slipping around the dragon whelp as it struggled inside. He pulled himself out of the torn door in his jail. The other two whelps continued to chew furiously at their holes, too intent on their goal to realize that there was now a whelp-sized opening already available.

There by the tree, exactly where he had told him to stay, was the boy, eyes wide. Reod grabbed Andli's hand and drew him along at a fast walk.

"This is not a good place for us to be. It's going to get warm soon."

"What? I don't understand."

Reod was aware of motion beyond him in the night, aware of points of movement at the edge of his mind's eye. The other whelps, perhaps? Had he truly managed to hatch them all?

He had never done such a thing before. He had found a key to affect many eggs at once, even at a distance. He wasn't quite sure what the key had been, or if he could ever do it again. For the moment it was enough that he had done it this once. He felt elated, his senses heightened.

Now the problem was getting across the fortress to the front gate. He held Andli's hand in a tight grip and began to cast a spell of shadow on himself, thinking of the sound of mosquitoes. In this dim light anyone watching them who did not look too closely or have reason to suspect would see only Andli.

"There are many kinds of trees," Reod began, speaking softly to Andli, "just as there are many different kinds of races and people within those races."

The boy struggled in Reod's grip, but when Reod spoke to him, he calmed and began to ask questions. They passed sentries who did not seem to mind that Andli was wandering around in the dark of evening talking to himself about trees.

A short distance away was the fortress's front gate, doors of woven vines that stretched between two tall trees, each as thick around as Reod's ox had been long. The gates were now closed for the night. It wouldn't be long before someone noticed the wandering, hungry dragon whelps climbing buildings and eating everything in their path, and then they would realize that Reod was free.

He was getting tired now, losing his focus, and fighting a headache. He had energy left for only a bit more magic. He should save what little remained.

"They breathe with the pace of sunset and sunrise," he was saying to Andli, "just as you and I breathe with our chests." They had arrived at the large gate's smaller door.

"What do you do here?" a guard asked Andli.

The boy stammered, confused. He glanced at Reod, then back at the guard. Now the guard was suspicious. He stepped toward the boy.

It was almost time for Reod to move. Not quite. Almost.

Reod bent to Andli, whispered in his ear: "The trees speak always, and you were right to stand so still to listen. Stand still now, and be very quiet, and you can begin to hear them as the evening wind gives them voice."

Andli stood as still as Reod hoped he would, catching the guard's full attention, while Reod stepped slowly away, toward the door.

Then the guard's attention flickered to Reod. Reod froze. The guard put a hand on his weapon, his expression confused.

"Do you see something?" he asked the other guard.

There were too many eyes on him at once to keep the spell strong. The second guard began to make a sound, a high-pitched bird's warble, a clear alarm.

Still Reod stayed frozen, waiting, hoping that whatever magic was left in the shadow spell might still cling. His focus slipped again, and he breathed slowly, carefully, trying to regain his concentration through the sound of the guards drawing their blades.

A cry erupted from far back in the compound. Not the sound of a prearranged alarm, but a cry of surprise and panic. They had found the whelps.

The guards turned toward the noise. So did Andli.

Now.

Reod held out the dirt in his hand, spat, and began the whelp song that he had used before, forcing himself to ignore everything else, even the sounds of bows being notched, bows which might well be pointing at him.

Always keep some in reserve, Genkr had told him long ago. *Your enemies will always have more than you do. Keep some back for that last effort that will save your neck.*

But Reod had none in reserve. He felt himself weaken, felt the spell flutter and fail, heard sounds around him become sharp, brittle.

He shut his eyes and thought of Tamun.

Tamun, who for all her strangeness, for all that she did not smell or feel like a human woman, still somehow felt right to his touch, her lips to his lips, her eyes to his eyes. What was it about her smile that promised him he could find there the secrets of the world, the very secrets he had struggled through long and difficult years at the Ebon Hand to discover? Could it really be that those secrets lay somewhere in the embrace of a dwarven woman?

He had cast his seduction spell on her to gain the eggs. A simple, crude spell it was, one that left open the way to his heart, but only for a moment. Such a tiny risk. But in that moment she had somehow snuck in, as if she had been ready and waiting, as if his whole life had been preparation for that single moment of vulnerability.

When she had struck, his world changed. He felt it then, but could not find within himself the desire to resist. Over the days that followed he found that his heart had spoken truly; she knew things he wanted to know, knew them not in the way of those who read books or studied with mages, but knew them as though they had been woven through her since she was born. He fell into her, and into love, as he had never done before. To send her away had taken all his resolve.

So he thought of Tamun now, of the hunger he had for her, letting the feeling inside him build with hope and longing, wrapping it in the joy he remembered with her smile.

Then he rebuilt his spell.

Tamun, he repeated to himself, creating focus out of desire and fear. Tamun, who was still out there, alive and breathing, waiting for him to find her.

Dirt and spit and the sound of dragon whelps. Every one of the whelps, he told himself, every one of them. All at once.

Now.

Explosions crashed from many directions. The ground rocked, forcing him to hands and knees. Screaming broke out, high-pitched, terrorized screams. The alarm warble had been taken up by other elves around the fortress and echoed from one end to the other.

And yet, somehow, no one had touched him.

He opened his eyes. One of the guards had run off and the other was intently watching something distant. Spears and arrows flew through the air in all directions. One arrow flew wide of its mark and landed near his feet.

Andli stood, mouth slack, eyes wide. A flickering distant light caught Reod's eyes: fire. Around the compound many more such lights flickered. The fires were catching, spreading.

He was out of spells now, dry of the ability to make even the simplest of magics. Now he had only his feet. He darted for the gate.

The guard glanced at him as he ran, glanced back at the distant fire. Only Andli's eyes followed him, and then the boy's steps.

"Wait!"

Reod stepped through the door, shut it behind, with Andli still on the other side. The boy curled his fingers around the mesh of vines, his eyes on Reod.

"You did this to us," Andli said.

There was no time for explanations. Every moment could cost or gain Reod his life. But the pain and question in the boy's eyes held him.

Behind Andli the fortress flickered and burned. The defense of this boy's race was about to burn to the ground. Because of Reod.

"I did," he confirmed.

What could he offer the boy in return for what he had taken?

"But why? Why did you do this to us?"

He could try to explain about the orcs and goblins. About the elders and the broken contract. He might even make Andli understand. But would that help the boy through the harsh future that faced him? There must be more that Reod could give him than explanations.

He smiled at the boy, a harsh, uncaring smile.

"Because I can."

The boy's face showed amazement, shock, and the beginnings of an adult fury. Reod held the boy's eyes and nodded to emphasize his words.

"Don't forget," he added. "Don't ever forget."

Andli made a sound halfway between a howl and a sob.

Reod turned and ran, slipping free into the darkened forest, making what time he could before the elves sent out scouts to find him.

He saw the boy's face in his mind as he ran, saw the shock and hurt, the crushed trust, and the sudden, wrenching loss of childhood faith.

He had given him what he could.

CHAPTER

7

"O! To be a dragon!"

—Marianne Moore

WALKING AWAY HAD BEEN EASY. SHE HAD made up her mind to go, had faced Reod down, and had left with the two whelps.

The night was clear with a few shreds of cloud trailing across a moon-bright sky. There was a pale ring around the moon, which meant rain tomorrow, but even that didn't lessen the sweet feeling that settled over her.

She was doing something. She would act on her own and not follow anyone. Did a child set out on a trip like this, at night, across the country, to fight for her own? No. And during their last conversation even Reod had not called her a child.

At first she pushed the pace, afraid that he might change his mind and follow her, but after a while she slowed, beginning to feel her weariness. The whelps slowed her down, forever stopping to investigate rocks and fallen branches and clumps of dirt. They followed as she walked by, but reluctantly. They ate constantly and would only leave what they could not stuff into their beaks.

Everything went into their mouths. Less than she would have expected was spat out. Reod was right. They would eat anything.

She had a sense for where the road would pick up again to go out of the forest, so she led them south along game paths until the moon snuggled down to sleep in distant trees and the way became so dark that she dared not continue.

Under a thick canopy of tree branches she set out her sleeping roll and drank a little water from the waterbag. The whelps curled up around her, surrounding her like big dogs. Not exactly like big dogs, though. Dogs smelled awful. The whelps didn't. They had a scent better than roses.

The rain began lightly in the middle of the night, but the thick of the trees kept her mostly dry. She slept until dawn, when the sky decided to truly drench the world in water. As the rain thundered down, she struggled to pack her sleeping roll before it got even more wet. The whelps looked up and blinked in confusion.

"Rain," she told them, then laughed at their expressions.

Tucking her pack under her cloak, they headed south. Her boots kept her feet dry but in no time her trousers legs were soaked. The sky was dark gray in every direction, and as she walked she became less than certain which way was south. Toward late afternoon they found the road and her spirits lifted considerably.

The whelps decided they liked the rain after all. As it eased to a generous sprinkle, they developed a game wherein they stretched their wings out to collect water, then snapped them back, spraying each other. And Sekena, too. She tried explaining the problem to them reasonably, with no results. Then she spoke sharply. They stopped, looked at her curiously, then continued the game. Finally she had to speed her pace to walk far enough ahead of them that the flying water just missed her. At last they tired of the game and went back to eating soggy roadside debris.

The skies rained unceasingly, sometimes light, other times a steady downpour. Sekena's gaze went often to the whelps and their distinctive lope as they bounded ahead to investigate some patch of grass or fallen nuts or rustling bushes. Occasionally they would flutter a wing on one side to keep their balance. They were starting to use their wings.

Once a swallow dove across the sky. The larger of the two whelps, instantly fascinated, snapped his head around to follow the bird's path. He then toppled, falling face-first into a muddy puddle. Sekena struggled to keep from laughing as he lifted up, giving her a stunned look. Then he went back down. Curiosity apparently having overcome him, he began to drag his beak through the puddle.

It was then that Sekena understood that she had not left her family only because of the dead at Kalitas who needed avenging, or her certainty that if she were on the front she could do something for her people. She had left because it was too painful to see whelps blown up by Reod Dai's magic. No matter how well she understood his purpose, it was just too hard.

She caught up with the smaller of the two whelps, the one with darker splotches of green on his back, and gave him a quick stroke, which he tolerated, and might even have enjoyed. They felt quite a bit like snakes, but snakeskin never felt so good. The softest rabbit fur never felt so good. What was it about them?

As she passed by, tiny lakes at her feet caught ripples from falling raindrops. As step by step the south-lands came closer, Sekena began to miss Mama and Tamun. She had never been away from them this long before.

The gray skies above began to fade as the day waned. Her mind played tricks, then, tempting her with thoughts of reaching home, and of how Mama and Tamun would build a fire, and make her hot spiced tea, and ask her about her journey.

They would worry. She knew that, had known it when she left, but somehow it had not seemed as important as being somewhere else. Mama would not simply worry, she would be furious. But Sekena was fifteen, and a good many boys were kicked out of their mother's houses far earlier than that. Why shouldn't she leave if she wanted to? Mama would never have agreed, though she should—she was an adventurer, too. Given some time, Sekena was sure she would understand. Maybe she would even be proud.

In the meantime, she would worry. They both would. But Reod would convince them she would be fine, wouldn't he?

And she would be fine, she told herself, not wanting to think about what might be waiting around the next bend, or in tonight's wet darkness.

Images of Mama and the cabin and Tamun floated through her mind, feeding the ache inside her chest until it hurt. It had been easy to walk away when she did, when she had been so sure. Now, as the sky darkened toward a deep, angry-looking black, she found herself thinking of turning back.

She led the whelps off the road, searching for a dry place to sleep. Under thick pines she found a spot that was not as wet as sleeping out in the open. Soon it was too dark to see. No moon shone to lighten this night. No stars painted her a map across the sky.

She wrestled a half-fallen log and some branches into a clumsy shelter, then tried to position the whelps to help keep the rest of the rain off her, since they seemed to like being wet, but they didn't understand, and at last she gave up, huddling down under her cloak. The whelps curled up next to her at awkward angles, oblivious to the water that streamed over them and onto her.

She could go back. Mama and Tamun would not be hard to find, even now. Just follow the road back as far as it went, then north through the forest to where she had left them. In memory even Reod's harshest mocking words seemed warmer than this cold night. Maybe she really was too young.

But Reod had let her go. And it seemed to her at the very last that he nearly approved. Or maybe it was just that he knew she would be back, a foolish child learning to trust those older and wiser.

She thought of Kalitas, thought of those there who were her own age and younger cut to pieces by orcish blades.

No, she was not too young.

But it was still cold and dark, and there were noises in the night beyond the rain that she did not want to know about. It did not surprise her to have found that the world was full of dangers she had not imagined. But to see a whole town gone, in the blink of an eye—

She did not understand. There was so much these past weeks that she did not understand. Kalitas in ruins. Piles of dead dwarves, stained with blood and agony. Orcs and goblins who attacked only because they could. Soldiers who knew nothing but how to kill.

And dragon whelps.

They snuggled close to her, keeping out the worst of the rain. She wrapped her cloak around her neck, adjusted the pack under her head.

Dragons.

At last she let herself feel awe at these creatures who stayed so close to her. They might protect her or they might not, they might stay or they might leave, but tonight they were a blanket against the wet and cold that threatened to crumble her last bit of confidence.

Finally she fell asleep to the sound of small tongues of rain lapping at ground and tree, and the sound of dragons breathing heavily.

In the morning her neck and back were sore from sleeping in a cramped position to stay dry. Trudging through the morning's constant downpour for hours had not improved her mood. She doubted there was a part of her that wasn't soaked.

And now the whelps wanted to climb.

Yesterday she had thought their interest in climbing was only to get at the more tender branches from the pines. But today, every time the land became hilly, they would wander off the road. They would go upward, whatever way that happened to be, usually not the direction of the road.

The first time it happened, she froze with uncertainty. Were they leaving her at last?

They had waddled up a slope a tenstep or so then stopped, turned, and looked back at her.

"Well?" she asked, covering fear with irritation. "Not that way. This way. Come on."

She doubted they understood, but after a few moments they waddled back down again and the three of them continued along the road.

Each time it got a little worse. Whenever the land sloped away from the road, they would climb. Then they would stop and turn to look at her, as if they had just realized she wasn't following. The steeper the slope, the more difficult they became, the more reluctant to come back. As the land became more hilly, their trio's progress slowed.

Days went by and the struggle worsened as they drew toward the mountains. One time, after staring into their slitted golden eyes in what had now become a familiar stand-off, she turned back to the road and began to walk away, forcing herself not to look back. They could come or not, she told herself, but she was tired of being wet.

Relief filled her when she heard their steps behind. She slowed to rub their heads and make a sound like the happy noises they made when they had some tasty tidbit.

The rain kept on, day after day, not heavy, but always present, and Sekena never slept well. Now she was running out of food. She had taken supplies with her when she left, but she had underestimated. If she pushed herself, she was sure she could make it to Teedmar without getting too hungry first. Almost sure.

So she pushed. The dragons kept pace well. They were getting stronger and more coordinated every day, and now even used their forearms and claws to rip up clumps of grass and take stones and other things they wanted to try to eat.

She squinted at them, trying to remember what they had looked like when they first hatched. Were they larger now? They extended their wings often, as if trying to rid themselves of stiffness. She suspected that soon they would realize that they could fly.

And then what?

The rain stopped, but above stretched a flat, pale gray sky, promising more to come.

She saw it from a distance, as the lowest clouds lifted a bit, the snowy tip of Shanin, the northernmost of the Crimson Peaks. Small though it might be by comparison to the great peaks where she and her family had once made their home, she knew with a grim certainty that the dragons would find it irresistible.

The next day the three of them came to the foot of the mountain's steep slope. Up went the whelps off the road, until they stood higher than Sekena. Then they stopped and stared down at her.

"This way," she said, trying to put as much conviction into her voice as she could. "No food up that way. Food, you understand? Maybe food for you, but not for me." She pointed at the road before her. "This way."

Golden eyes and slitted pupils stared at her.

Did they understand, even a little?

"I can't," she said, almost pleadingly. "I have to go on. Ta, you have to climb, I know, I know. You're supposed to fly, not walk along like I do."

The road skirted the mountain. Sekena guessed that in the next day or so it would fork, one way going south toward the greater peaks, the other way west to Teedmar. It was no more than a day or two to Teedmar, she hoped, not with as little bread and dried meat as she had left.

So she would walk it alone. She looked back at the whelps, who still stood there, eyes on her, unwilling to come down yet unwilling to leave her.

"I understand," she said softly. Her chest ached.

They were growing. Seeing them from this side made it clear that their wings were lengthening, changing color, deepening from white to a paler shade of pink. "Go on. Go find your mountain and learn to fly. If I had wings, I wouldn't be walking, either."

She turned and began to walk away. She heard them scramble down the game path after her. Surprise and guilty relief shot through her.

"Ta," she said with a smile, "if you must—"

They circled her and began to press her up, toward the slope.

"No, no. I have to go on. This way."

They pushed her with their little arms, which were surprisingly strong.

Cold fear cut through her, then, shredding her sympathy for them. In winter there was little to scrounge in the way of plants, and hunting was hard. If she went up the mountain, she would be that much farther from anything she could eat. Her supplies would not last.

"I have to get food. I can't eat what you do."

She tried to push past them. If she could break free of their tight circle, maybe she could outrun them. Downslope they blocked her, pushing her up, so she went up suddenly, sprinting up the side of the mountain, intending to dash around them and down. But somehow they were there, moving faster than she thought they could. And then there was no opening to dash anywhere.

She yelled at them, then pleaded, and finally cursed, but they kept pushing upward. She hurled herself at them, trying to break free. They became more determined, poking at her with their sharp beaks, and she yelped, backing away up the slope. She had forgotten how strong and relentless dragon whelps could be when they were not on your side. Cute, she had thought them. Now they seemed only deadly.

For a moment Sekena wished Reod were here. He could make them leave her alone. She thought of the dirt underfoot, of spit, and of the words he had used to cast his spells. Maybe she could do it, too.

Another poke. Gentler this time. She whimpered with the confusion of fear and the sweetness of their scent. She could not try to hurt them, even now.

Breathing hard, hungry and tired, she finally gave in. With the whelps always behind her, she climbed.

Toward day's end the clouds thinned, turning pink and shredding under golden claws of sunshine. A breeze chilled the sweat on Sekena's face and neck as they reached a level area. There she paused. The whelps would let her rest for a few moments at a time, but never for long.

She had used the long climb to consider what she knew of dragon whelps and to regret what she didn't. They would seek a high area to jump off of, Reod had once said. But how high was high enough? Did they need to go all the way to the top of a mountain?

They were done waiting for her now, so they nosed her up the slope again. They were gentle unless she resisted, and then they could become quite intent. She did not want to find out just how insistent they could be.

And at the top? What then? They would jump off some precipice, she guessed, and learn to fly. Or fall and die. Once airborne, would they leave Sekena free to go back down the mountain? Or would they search her out and herald her up again, forcing her to stay with them as her meager bits of food dwindled to nothing?

Perhaps this was why so little was known about dragons.

"I'm going to starve to death," she said aloud, half to herself and half to the dragons, finishing the words with a choked sob.

Somewhere on this snow-covered mountain with the winds at her back and dragons by her side she was going to starve to death.

He woke to wind-scent bearing the smell of animal. Strangeness was mixed with something forgotten yet familiar. An animal it surely was, coming up the side of the mountain. Larger than foxes, smaller than horses. Of a size worth venturing out for.

He pressed himself up off the soft bed of furs on which he slept, collected over decades of hunting. He stretched.

Large enough to be worth trouble. Large enough to be food.

Memory came to him finally, from long ago, identifying the familiar smell, surprising him.

Dragons. Young dragons. More than one. Never had he eaten one of those. It would be a special treat.

Outside his cave the day was bright though the sun-ball was still dying. The wet day was drying, leaving sharp scents in the air.

The animals on the mountainside were not yet in sight, but he could hear them distantly, rustling the brush, pressing their legs through the snow. They were climbing toward him. He would not even have to go and seek them out.

For that he could wait.

He stretched his wings and opened his mouth again and again to better taste their scent on the wind. To feed his anticipations.

Sekena was exhausted and hungry and despairing as she put one foot in front of the other, climbing the steepest part of the game path. The top of the mountain was a snow-covered precipice, too steep to climb without ropes, but they were nearing what seemed to be the highest plateau. Perhaps once there they would let her rest long enough to eat a bit of what remained in her pack.

As she looked up again something glinted in a ray of fading sunlight.

Glinted? How odd. What could there be up on a mountain that glinted?

The animals came to him, stumbling clumsily up to his rocky plateau. He waited while they looked around at the rocks and up at the pink sky, waiting as still as the rocks themselves. One by one they noticed his feet. One by one they slowly looked up.

It had been a long time since he had been able to sport before eating. Few meals gave him challenge. This would be a welcome change.

He inhaled deep and hissed, long and loud, to spark them to fear. They did not move. He bent down his head to bring them closer, curious about the one that was not a dragonling.

Human, perhaps, or dwarf or elf. There was little difference. All were tasty and fragile and not very entertaining. He would have to be careful to have sport with it. Take an arm, perhaps, to start. Then watch it run. Taste blood on the wind.

The dragonlings took hesitant steps backward as he approached. They were probably confused by his scent. Being so young, they would not yet understand. Nor would they have a chance to.

But he ignored them and brought his open mouth up close to the two-legged creature. He was almost sure it was a dwarf type of two-leg. He flicked out a tongue to taste it. Suddenly he pulled back.

It wasn't food.

It looked like food. It moved like food. But it wasn't food. It was—

What?

He swooped close in again, tasted the creature's face, nose, and mouth.

Definitely not food.

He moved his head from side to side, tasting the air for magic. Perhaps the dwarf was a wizard, trying to confuse him. But there was no scent of magic on the wind, or he would never have come out of his cave, defenseless like this. Only the scent of the young ones, and this—what?

She—he was now sure it was a female—she smelled dwarven. But she also smelled a little like dragon. Not just any dragon. She had the smell of sibling. Of mate.

He hissed a question at her.

She made a sound, a soft sound, a cry.

He hissed again, another question. The two-legs had such absurd languages. He knew only enough to recognize the difference between prayers, pleas, bribes, and threats. Her sounds now were sort of prayer sounds, but not quite.

If the two-leg wasn't food, well, then, what would he do with it? The two young ones stood behind her. Perhaps he would take the young ones for sport and food and keep this other strange creature, the Not-food, until he figured out what to do with her.

But the young ones were her companions. If he wasn't going to eat her, he probably shouldn't eat them, either. She might not like that. For some reason it mattered.

He hissed a long, frustrated sigh.

Perhaps he could keep them all in the back of the cave. The Not-food would need her own food, of course. What would she eat? He knew what the young dragons could eat, but this two-leg? Dwarves ate soft things, he recalled. Plants. Tiny animals. He could find those for her.

Bending down close to her, he began to hiss a slow, careful greeting. She still did not respond. Indeed, she was not quite standing anymore. Doubled over and moving. Shaking. She sat on the ground. Still afraid? Or perhaps she was ill. That would not be good, not good at all.

One of the little dragons took a tiny step forward and hissed at him. Not a greeting, but a warning. He stifled a laugh.

This little one would have tasted good. Very good.

Alas.

He had roused himself from sleep for something tasty, and now he had three animals to keep. Not at all what he had in mind. And such trouble.

Why couldn't they have been food instead?

By the time Sekena's mind had started to work again, the enormous thing had its fantastically large head right in her face, its glinting golden eyes all she could see. It licked her face. She could not bring herself to move.

Now the creature hissed. Very loud. A warning?

Her legs stopped holding her up. She sat on the ground.

Behind her, one of the whelps returned the large creature's hiss, a pale echo. Dimly she realized it was trying to protect her.

From this? Stupid little creatures. They should run. She knew how fast they could move when they wanted to, considerably faster than she could, even at her best. They should run now. Test their wings. Run and fly.

Instead they hissed. Hissed at this full-grown dragon. She had never seen anything like what stood before her, not even in pictures, but there was nothing else the creature could possibly be.

And, horribly, when it had licked her face, it had felt good. The dragon-scent was so strong here that even through her terror it made her feel wonderful.

Sekena found herself laughing. She would not have to worry about finding food anymore. She would not have to worry about the whelps pushing her around.

The dragon would eat her and there would be no more worry.

The creature was still hissing. Why didn't it just do what it was going to do? Ever so slowly she began to realize that the creature was not attacking. Not attacking at all. This thing, bigger than trees, with crimson wings stretched as wide as a cloud, was not attacking.

The hisses kept coming. Distinct, almost as if it were speaking to her in some other language. Sekena cocked her head and tried to understand but it was all just air.

Then the creature stopped hissing. It reached out a forearm and with its claws made a surprisingly dwarven gesture.

Stand.

She struggled to her feet, trembling so badly that she could barely hold herself up. She inhaled again, feeling nearly giddy with the mix of panic's afterflush and dragon-scent.

The dragon gestured to them to follow. It walked toward a cave opening that seemed far too small for it, folded its veined wings, and somehow collapsed itself inside. After a moment it snaked its head out again, looking at them.

Well?

Sekena glanced at the whelps. Their wide eyes were on the great dragon.

Perhaps now was the time to run. They could escape down the mountainside. If all three of them ran in different directions, one or two might escape.

Or . . . ?

Or enter the dragon's den.

Pure foolishness and greatest insanity it would be to go inside. Who knew what the creature might do? In children's stories, dragons were neither generous nor merciful.

Nor did they speak with gestures.

A dragon's den. No dwarf she had ever heard of had been inside one. It would be spitting in the face of good sense to go there. Sekena felt excitement rise inside her.

And what would Reod Dai say? She imagined his shocked expression.

Then she put a hand out to touch each of the whelps. Would they both really grow to become as large as this amazing creature before her, who gestured yet again for them to join it in its cave?

"Come on," she said softly to her whelps. "You're the ones who wanted to climb the mountain."

Sekena felt as if she were sleeping next to a breathing mountain. He had insisted with gesture and hiss that she sleep by him on the thick furs. When she hesitated he had grabbed her and tucked her under his arm.

It was hard to mind with how wonderful he smelled. The furs smelled like dragon, too. The whole cave did.

The whelps curled up together a little ways away, just out of the creature's reach, and fell instantly asleep.

Sekena lay against the scaled belly of the great dragon and thought about where she was. How could she feel so at ease?

She woke later with a sharp shock, realizing anew where she was. She inhaled the scent of the den again and felt comforted. It felt like being home.

The great dragon woke and went out for a time. When he returned he held in one claw a pile of roots, in the other three small, crushed rabbits. He started a fire in the center of the cave with a sharp exhale onto some kindling he had apparently gathered and gave Sekena the meat and roots. She roasted them on sticks. As she ate with greasy fingers the dragon whelps gnawed on a pine tree they had dragged inside.

When she was full she spoke with the dragon. Or rather, he hissed while she said words.

"Sekena," she said, pointing at herself.

The dragon hissed again and again, seemingly less

interested in learning her words than in teaching her
his own.

The day came and went as they slept or ate or tried
to talk. The dragon would hiss and Sekena would listen, fascinated. After a while she almost heard patterns
in his sounds.

It was the morning of the third day on the mountain
when she remembered Mama and Tamun and Teedmar
and the war.

CHAPTER

8

"The Hand of Justice will come to cleanse the world if we are true."

—Oliver Farrel

THE ELVES DID INDEED COME AFTER HIM.

Elven trackers were supposed to be among the best in Sarpadia, but exhausted as Reod was, he thought it best not to test their skill. At least not tonight. He dug down under a large rock and blanketed himself with rotting leaves, sleeping only a little.

The storm came, drenching the night world with buckets of water, and then the rock was no shelter at all. The rain would help confuse scent trackers, if the elves had them, but for Reod, without stars or sky to guide him south, it only made the journey harder and longer.

There were other ways to find him, ways he was sure they would use. First light found Reod walking southward, guided by the barest hint of the sun's face. He wove small diversion spells as he went, scratching arrows on large rocks to make his direction ambiguous should elven wizards stop to ask the stones.

He dared not go back to the ox cart for his remaining

supplies. Now empty of eggs, the cart would at least have supplied him a dry place to sleep, and the ox given some warmth and protection on the trip south, but the elves would surely have found it in their search and be waiting for him.

That the elves were coming after him might mean the fire in the fortress was not so bad after all, not if they had elves to spare from fighting the blaze to go search for him. Or it might mean that the fire was far, far worse than he had expected or intended, so that there was no point in trying to contain it at all, especially with Reod free and vengeance to be had.

Strange times, as the elder druids had said. Strange times and hard choices.

He turned his thoughts ahead. Somewhere out there were Tamun and Melelki. Safe, surely, under the care and guidance of an elvish escort. Despite his general mistrust of the elves, he had confidence that they would do as they had promised.

And when Reod found them, well, Tamun might be as difficult and mysterious as ever, but if she were upset at what he had done to protect them, she would forgive him, even welcome him into her arms. Those were the thoughts that kept him warm in the cold, heavy downpour.

Often he stopped and hid from the small bands of searchers, sometimes waiting unmoving for hours, telling the trees and rocks and ground to treat him as if he were shadow.

When he walked, he pushed himself, ignoring every ache. Hunger he staved off by eating traveler's cabbage and downing berry worms, which he swallowed whole. It was not much, and it was not enough, but it would keep him alive while he struggled out of Havenwood. Only the journey's end mattered.

It took days for Reod to reach the road going south. Bands of elves still followed on his heels. Only when he

had put yet more days between himself and Havenwood
on the road south did the elves finally give up.

But the rain continued. At times it seemed to Reod
that he had spent his whole life being cold and hungry,
chasing or being chased.

Thinking such dire thoughts, he took a small side
road west, hiking down into a valley where there nes-
tled a small, sheltered Icatian village. He went to the
cottage of the village healer, who knew nothing of his
true identity, but knew that every time Reod came he
brought rare herbs and magic stones. But this time he
brought only his need.

Still she gave him what she could spare, food and
clean clothes and a rain cloak, and an ear eager for
news of other places. He told her of the raids to the
south, of the cold winters, of the poor crops in
Havenwood.

She listened intently, and when he was done she sat
back, nodding. Then, "Do you hear anything from the
far west?"

"Nothing new since last time."

Her brother had gone to the Ebon Hand years ago.
Every time Reod came here, he would tell her what he
could of what little he knew.

Had she lived in a town nearer central Icatia, she
would never have asked him such questions. There it
would be too dangerous to show interests like that, let
alone to talk about the Ebon Hand in the same breath
as nearby Havenwood. It was often this way in the
border towns, where the king's edicts were considerably less important than the weather.

That night he slept in a warm, dry bed. He was on
the road to Teedmar at dawn.

When at last he arrived at the foothills below
Teedmar, the rain finally eased and the clouds overhead were scattering, giving a window to the setting
sun and a silhouette of the city. Against the sun's
orange glow he saw the shapes of houses and rising
smoke of chimneys and forges. Relief eased his tension

and sparked his hope. The last rays of sun cut through his nightmares of a city flattened by orcs and goblins, piled high with bodies. Two particular bodies.

But no, Teedmar was whole. Delivery wagons passed through the gates, returning from nearby Gurn Keep. Horses went in and out. Some were warhorses, and that meant Icatian military. He gathered his hood around his head.

Closer to the city his suspicions were confirmed as he was passed by two members of the Order of Leitbur. He slumped and looked down, hoping to be mistaken for a tall dwarf. The soldiers did not slow, did not even glance his way.

At that, irritation shot through him. During his command his soldiers would never have let an anomaly such as he was go unchecked. They would notice the too-tall, hooded dwarf who walked oddly and would not answer a hail. Teedmar might be friendly to Icatia, but these were unusual times. A soldier Reod had trained would not let such a strangeness simply walk by.

But walk by he did.

So the rumors that the Icatian Army was getting overconfident and sloppy were not exaggerated. Were all his efforts to give his people a more worthy enemy than themselves simply wasted?

Or perhaps his worst fears were true, that the rot came from within, from Icatia's own leaders. If so, no external force or threat could touch the rot, and the Icatian people would suffer for the inability of their leaders to watch themselves as well as they watched others.

If they had been his men, he would have arranged for a raid on their encampment. That would wake them up.

He grinned at himself. Still thinking like a commander, after all these years. It was possible that these two soldiers were atypical. He should be thankful for his good fortune instead of wanting the soldiers to discover him.

But it was not just the Icatians. Teedmar's security was also lax. At the city gates a dwarven guard waved him through the tall iron gates with barely a glance, then leaned back against the bars and shut his eyes.

Reod thought of the orc and goblin threat and his heart sank. Teedmar was the primary weapons supplier to Gurn Keep. Even Icatia depended heavily on Teedmar for arms.

Years ago Reod had worked for the dwarven people in Teedmar, ostensibly building a trade agreement between the dwarven city and the second previous goblin king, now long dead. The city had grown since then, testimony to the increased need for swords and spears and those items that dwarven expertise forged best. The city had grown, but it had the same gates, the same guards, the same ways.

Superb builders and weapons crafters they might be, but the dwarven people were as likely to piss on their own boots as to organize for war. The old ways were kept, not out of respect for tradition, but because they saw no sense in making changes they didn't have to.

He could help that. Given a little time and some funds, he could show Teedmar where their weaknesses were and how to fix them. If the elves had not broken the contract, he would be teaching goblins and orcs to work together, showing them how to ignore each other's strengths and enhance each other's shortcomings, making them a startling but ineffective war machine.

When Reod had become a commander in the Order of Leitbur, he began to wonder what Icatia was fighting and why. Even now he was uncertain of the why, but the *what* was clear: it didn't matter. For various and tangled reasons that would confuse even a history scholar, every race in Sarpadia seemed to want to be at war. Each would find reasons to fight, like siblings looking for fault.

So it was in Icatia. Whether it was a village refusing to pay tithe, or country folk indulging in the Ebon Hand's midwinter festival, Icatian leaders always brought quick force to bear. And why? Because they needed an enemy.

And so Reod had arranged to give them one. The orc and goblin forces, with weapons and strategies he had intended to continue to supply them, would have been a confident, resilient, but essentially toothless force, a convenient enemy for every country that needed one. They would have kept Icatia's military busy with external problems. Perhaps then Icatia would leave alone those humans who did not pray to Leitbur or who found the Ebon Hand's taxation more to their liking.

But now the orcs and goblins were on their own, both more effective and less predictable than they would have been under Reod's guidance. Without his direction they would attack anything, even small villages with little or no defense. There wasn't much he could do now. The goblin king was petty and violent, and Reod could not approach him without gold and weapons. The orcs he might bluff, but only once.

As for Teedmar, there might be some dwarves in Teedmar who would listen to his warnings. More likely they would simply insist that their collection of dwarven recruits was sufficient defense. After he found Tamun, he resolved, he would try to find those dwarves who might listen and do what he could to give Teedmar a chance to stand against the orcs and goblins when they came. And they would.

He searched the faces of every dwarf he passed in the city's dim twilight, looking for them. His steps sounded dull on the wood and rock-lined city streets, and he began to tremble with the evening's chill.

Tamun and her family were here. They had to be. All he had to do was find them.

*   *   *

Night's sky came deep and starlit as he searched. Three women, he would say. Perhaps two. He was careful, hunched down, watching always for humans, speaking to only one dwarf at a time. He tried for a southern dialect of dwarven, hoping that no one would look too closely under the hood at his features. The dwarves' lack of suspicion now worked in his favor.

Still he did not find them.

Finally he made his way to a crowded, noisy inn, filled with low tables and straw-filled pillows on which to recline. Dwarven streaked heads were everywhere. The smell of bodies and ale was strong, but the room was warm, and the aroma of stew set his mouth to watering.

He walked to the great fire at one end of the room. The logs were as thick around as his middle, and they sputtered and hissed as they bathed in orange tongues of flame. The fire helped chase away the chill that settled under his skin and the despair that threatened to come over him. Even as he let it warm his face and hands, he searched the room for familiar dwarven faces.

He resented his body's need to rest, certain that Tamun was somewhere in the city, perhaps only steps away. They were here; they had to be. With an elvish escort, even on foot, they would surely have arrived before him, at least a day before, if not more.

Tomorrow, he told himself. Tomorrow he would find them.

A woman's voice cut through the din.

"Robin?"

His stomach lurched. Lulled by the city's lax security and the thick of dwarven heads, he was standing by the fire with his hood down, turning around for all to see. He was an idiot.

He did not move, acting as if he had heard nothing. Perhaps whoever it was would decide that this ragged, bearded, haggard creature huddling by the fire could not possibly be the infamous Icatian deserter.

Instead someone stepped next to him. She was dressed in the pale uniform of the Order and wore the high collar of a commander. It could hardly have been worse.

To spin a spell in this crowded room would be risky. Who knew what wizard might be hidden here and, smelling the magic, too curious and willing to side with the Icatian authorities? Even so, he began a simple spell that would subtly change his appearance. His face might be darker, he thought, concentrating fiercely. His nose might be flatter, and his eyes, they would definitely not be blue—

A hand settled on his shoulder. Slowly it turned him to face her.

"Robin. It is you." The voice was sure, the tone low.

He abandoned the building spell.

"Eliza?"

She had been the daughter of his parents' friends. In the Order their politics had pushed them apart, so they learned to speak carefully, unwilling to risk an old friendship, and ended up not speaking much at all. When he last saw her, she had just gained the rank of captain.

The smile came to his lips unbidden. "What are you doing in Teedmar?"

"I think I'm supposed to ask you that."

His eyes flickered around the room.

She smiled back. "I'm alone. Here on business, not looking for you. Though I'm sure Farrel would dearly love to have you." She took his arm and led him to a side table, pushing her bowl of stew in front of him.

"You look hungry. You always used to forget to eat."

He took a sip of broth, used his bread to scoop out a handful of bits of turnip, winter squash, and meat and stuffed it into his mouth. He felt strength returning to him.

"You're with Farrel now?"

She nodded. "Is this the part where I admit that you were right?"

He snorted. "Was it ever that simple?"

"More and more of the Order are with Farrel now, though we keep it quiet. He at least is serious about destroying the Hand. The king doesn't like it, but it's his own fault; if he spent half as much time fighting the followers of Tourach as he does putting down starving border towns—"

"And you think Farrel is better?"

"I think Farrel sees the situation more clearly. He at least is willing to take real action. The king prefers long council meetings. There isn't that kind of time left."

"On that we agree, at least."

"And now come the orcs and goblins."

He said nothing, finishing the bowl of stew.

"I've missed you, Robin."

She reminded him of home and the times when he had a home. He sighed.

"Eliza, I've done some things these last years . . . "

Her laugh was short, hard, and bitter. It surprised him.

"Haven't we all? Leitbur must intend us to find purity in bloodshed. Heresy it may be for me to say, but I wonder how much difference there is between us and Tourach's Lost."

"Not much."

She looked at him curiously. "You were always so sure of that. You know, they say, when you were at the Ebon Hand, that you were one of Tourach's own."

"Not exactly. But as I said, I have done things—"

"Do I want to know?"

"Probably not."

Their eyes met. She took his hand.

"Whatever you've done, tell me this: what happened to those who followed you to the Hand?"

"Will you believe me?"

"I'll try."

"Listen, then: some who said they followed me were lying. Instead they snuck away and returned to their

families. Some went—" he gave a shrug "—elsewhere.
I don't know. Others who followed me to the Hand of
their own will found it as terrible as any childhood
story they had been told. Most of them found reason
and means by which to die. Of the remainder, a few, a
very few, followed me into the heart of the Ebon Hand
and there found their home."

"And you?" She whispered. "What did you find?"

"Eliza, whether you call on Farrel or Leitbur, you
are still a commander in the Icatian Army, are you
not?"

"Robin—"

"Reod."

"Ah, yes, the Hand's name. I'm not going to drag
you back, *Reod*. Not now. With all the court-martials
underway, it's a wonder that there's anyone left to
defend Trokair."

"Is it that bad?"

"Yes. You're notorious, you know. For someone no
one talks about, that is. Even mentioning your name is
cause for discipline. In the villages, they nail a red-
breasted bird over the doorway to guard against
treachery and deception."

She smiled, trying to lighten the words, but Reod
returned her look without amusement and her smile
vanished.

"It is right that they should think of me that way."

"These are bad times, Robin. Should I pass judgment on what you did? I'm not always sure anymore
what is right and what is wrong."

"Good. I mistrust those who are too certain."

"So you won't tell me what happened to you at the
Ebon Hand?"

"No."

"Then what are you doing in Teedmar?"

"Do you want the truth?"

"Why not?"

He exhaled. "I'm looking for three dwarves.
Women. One of them is—well—"

Somehow Eliza understood. She began to laugh, then stopped at his expression and shook her head. "Ah, Robin. That's amazing. What times these are."

"Indeed."

"Are you going to promise to her, then?"

"I don't know." How to explain what he wasn't sure of himself? "It's a little unusual."

"More than a little, I should say. Have you—"

"None of your business."

She smiled. "Listen, I have some time. I can help you look around tomorrow."

"Eliza, don't be stupid. Do you know what you risk, just sitting here with me now?"

"I know what you risk to be here in Teedmar with so many of us around. I'm known in this city. If I'm with you, no one will suspect you. This dwarven woman—if she means so much to you—I'll do what I can. I have the morning free, then I'm due at the forges midday to arrange for a shipment. My soldiers and I return to Icatia tomorrow."

"I don't know what to say. You and I have had our differences, but this—"

She chuckled and cut him off. "But this is pure generosity on my part, and I'm an upstanding Icatian, and Leitbur would be proud, and—" Her expression darkened suddenly. "And I thought I'd never see you again, and with times this bloody, I might not. So give me the morning with you."

"I accept. Thank you."

She shook her head. "Thank me when we find them."

They ate a quick breakfast and went out on the streets.

Icatian towns had streets of packed stone, but here, where the weather was even harsher, the dwarves had instead built raised wooden tracks for their wagons. The wooden tracks were constantly in need of repair, but the dwarves crouched by the side of the road seemed content to be there, fiddling with tools and nails and boards, even in this freezing weather. Typically dwarven, it made no sense.

"If your dwarves came in yesterday," Eliza said, "they might be in the barracks. The city is offering food and keep to any dwarf who will train to be soldier or helphand. They're desperate for more bodies to guard outlying villages against orc and goblin raiders."

"It's called a war."

"For it to be a war, there need to be armies on both sides. These aren't armies. They're peasants who think there's no difference between a sword and an axe. I've seen them practice, and they're just one big, disorganized group."

"So are the orcs and goblins."

"Not as much as they used to be."

"No."

They reached the barracks. Eliza asked about the women, letting Reod stand back, hood covering his face. For a couple of hours they searched, starting with the barracks area, then the kitchens, repair house, and weapons forge area.

While she was in the forges, where as a purchaser she would be more welcome than he, he waited outside. Carts were being loaded with swords and spearheads. He looked at every face.

Eliza came back outside. "Perhaps, perhaps not."

"What do you mean?"

She shrugged. "Half the dwarves in Teedmar are women. But two outsiders were working here this morning."

He started forward and she grabbed to stop him.

"They're gone now."

"Gone where?"

"He doesn't know and he isn't happy about it. Everyone's overworked here and they've been gone for hours. He thinks they got bored and went out into the city." She touched his shoulder gently. "Patience."

Reod exhaled slowly, trying to let her words comfort

him. It would be them; it had to be them. They were here, somewhere. He could almost see Tamun's eyes, could almost hear Melelki's asking what had taken him so long. He just had to keep looking.

He turned to Eliza, intending to thank her, then let her go to her appointment while he went on searching. Then the world turned dark, as if a heavy blanket had fallen over them. He heard Eliza gasp.

A deep voice spoke out of the darkness.

"Reod Dai."

Not a question.

A whiteness came, bone white, resolved into a face. Three yellow eyes formed a triangle and stared at him unblinking.

"Let me guess," Reod said, forcing himself to sound amused through the chill that filled his stomach. "You're one of Leitbur's chosen?"

A white jaw moved, oddly, as if it were disconnected from the rest of the white face.

"You are to be congratulated," it said, using the Ebon Hand's High Temple speech, which was similar to Icatian, "on your many achievements, since the time you were last blessed by Tourach's merciful grip."

Reod puzzled over the wizard's words carefully.

"Thank you."

Eliza was silent and clearly tense. For all her years of fighting them, Reod doubted she had ever met a follower of Tourach.

"We are especially pleased with the harm you have done the forest dwellers."

He must mean the fires. If the Hand had already gotten word of the fires, the damage must have been very bad indeed, must have spread all across Havenwood. But how would they have known that Reod was responsible? Did the elves tell them? And why would the elves have contact with the Ebon Hand?

There was no point in admitting anything.

"Exactly what do you think I've done?"

"They rebel against their masters, now that they are

no longer bound by their roots. We are quite pleased with your work."

"Who rebels?"

"There is no need for you to pretend ignorance with us. We know you were in Havenwood when they were sparked to awareness and left their earthy prisons. There is no other but you who would have used magic in this way, or for these ends."

Reod struggled with the wizard's words, searching for meaning.

"The thallids?" he asked, disbelievingly.

The wizard ignored his tone, clearly convinced Reod was feigning confusion.

"It is clear to us that Tourach works through your hands to punish Havenwood. Only through Tourach's wisdom and guidance should life be created. They will learn this now."

Now he understood what had happened to the whelps in the thallid field. Somehow the fungus creatures had sucked up the magic Reod had meant to go into the whelps. Rather than explode the whelps, the magic had sparked the thallids to sudden, extreme change. They had become self-aware and mobile.

And had then decided to rebel against those who ate them. It made sense.

It also explained the shape in the darkness in the elven fortress: a thallid suddenly befooted and conscious.

The wizard continued. "Havenwood has brought this upon themselves, for daring to steal our created ones to make their own. We offered them Tourach's guidance, but they wanted it not. Now they have found their reward."

Reod knew the wizard lied; no one stole from the Ebon Hand. If the elves were using the "created ones"—the Hand's term for the thrulls—to create thallids, then that act was with the full cooperation of the followers of Tourach, which meant that someone in Havenwood was paying the Ebon Hand, and paying them a lot more than they had been paying Reod.

And now their food was rebelling. It seemed fitting.

"How much did they pay you?" he asked with a bitter smile. Then his smile vanished as he realized exactly what the payment must have been.

The elves would arrange for a distracting threat to arise along the southern Icatian border, drawing Icatian forces there, leaving the other borders poorly defended.

Especially the western border, where the Ebon Hand's influence was strongest.

"Now," the wizard said, "the Ebon Hand desires your aid in our efforts to repel the Icatians."

With enough funding and a bit of time, perhaps he could still get the orcs and goblins back in hand.

"I'm listening."

"We will put an end to the needless struggles between the followers of Tourach and the ignorant. You will come with us and make the same explosives that you made for the goblins."

Reod could feel Eliza's quick, sharp look.

"Yes, I can do that here in Teedmar. I'll need funds."

"You will come to Achtep Keep and do your work there."

"Not possible."

"The dwarves have nothing that we do not have."

"I have business here."

"Your business is now with the Ebon Hand."

Reod shrugged, a small twitch. "Then I'm not available."

"Regrettable. The mountain that towers above us is about to become destroyed, and this city with it. I thought that you might welcome the chance to leave before that occurred."

"Destroyed?"

"These busy dwarves with their many weapons have begun to irritate us. Icatian hands have enough weapons already."

"What do you mean, destroyed? How?"

"We have made the mountain angry and given fire to

its heart. Very soon it will turn itself inside out. You may stay if you want."

Tamun. Her golden brown eyes flashed through Reod's mind. If she were destroyed—

He felt fear try to wash away his reason, forced himself to think.

"No, what I want is for you to change your plans."

"The followers of Tourach have already begun to weave the great spell. Will you stay here and die?"

"No. Listen. There is someone in Teedmar I need to find."

"Regrettable. They will be dead soon."

"I will go with you. I will work for the Hand. I will make you explosives and more. But only if you leave the mountain intact."

"We have no interest in leaving the mountain intact, or any of the infidels who live here. Perhaps if you tell us of this creature who matters so much to you, we can find it for you. I suggest you be quick."

Eliza touched his shoulder. "Robin, no. What would they do with her?"

"Anything is better than death."

"Is it?"

"Three dwarves," Reod said. "Females."

"Any three?

"No. A mother and two daughters. They are named Tamun, Melelki, and Sekena. Average size for dwarves, with the darker hair of the southern peaks. Last I saw, they were wearing oilskins." He touched his cloak. "Like mine."

His heart pounded with worry. If the wizard deceived him, Reod had just named those who mattered most to him, but this might be his only chance to save her.

The yellow eyes stared a moment, nodded, then vanished.

Eliza's voice was quiet. "Robin."

He sighed deeply. "They're going to make the mountain a volcano."

"Can they do that?"

"Yes."

"Ah, by Leitbur, we have to stop them."

"We just tried."

"Where in the Hells are we?"

"We're in a—a dark bubble. It's sort of a large, magic pocket." He could feel the containing magic around them, strong and solid, like a wall of stone. "Eliza, you're going to have to come with me. If you stay here, you'll die."

"I can't leave. My soldiers are here."

Why was it that wherever he went, people died? He rubbed his head.

"The only choice you can make is to come with me or die."

"Damn it, Robin, you were once one of them. You lived at the Ebon Hand. You must have some influence. Do something."

"I had less than you might think." And perhaps more, but he would not tell her about that. "And Eliza, you must start calling me Reod." He faced her. "I haven't been Robin Davies in a long, long time."

Her look was closed. "Yes, I can see that now."

"I'm sorry."

Somehow the words sounded harsh and hollow in his ears. He shook his head and said them again, but still they did not sound right.

She did not reply and they waited together in silence. Reod watched the darkness, hoping that Tamun would somehow appear.

The yellow eyes came back.

"Reod Dai. We have searched for the dwarves you claim. There are a good many dwarves here, and while they are hard to tell apart, my servants searched hard, and they were not able to find any that matched your description. Perhaps your dwarves are not in Teedmar."

"They are here," he said softly. "You have to find them or stop the spell."

"That is not possible."

"I must insist."

"Insist?"

Reod dug deep inside and summoned every bit of concentration and passion he had. Tamun was out there. Tamun would die if he did not act now. He spat into his hands, built her image inside himself, and shot a magic dart at the wizard's life spark.

The wizard made a gesture. The dart was swallowed by shadow.

"I am glad to see that you have not lost all your skills, Reod Dai."

Reod felt despair. "Please." He found the words surprisingly easy to say. "I beg you. I can offer you much. You want Icatia? I can give you Icatia."

He did not look to see Eliza's expression, which he could well imagine.

"Doubtless," the wizard answered, "and we expect you to. But the mountain will show its fury, and nothing can stop it."

"Ah, Leitbur," Reod breathed, finding that those words also came easily to his lips, and tears as well.

The yellow eyes regarded him curiously.

"The time comes. We will watch."

At that, the blackness dissipated.

They stood on the same corner where they had stood before the dark bubble engulfed them. The sun was lower than before, but the day was bright and the sky blue. Dwarves passed by on the streets as if nothing were amiss. A dwarven man sat at the curb, repairing a gutter, his beard tied and one end flung over his shoulder. All was normal this winter's afternoon in Teedmar.

Eliza caught her breath and took a step forward, pressing against the invisible edge of the bubble.

The ground began to rumble. Dwarves everywhere stopped, looked around, then looked up at the peak of the mountaintop, where distant pieces of rock were cascading down.

Rocks began to fall, seemingly slow in their journey, drawing with them white puffs of snow that Reod knew only seemed small because of the distance. There came a hail of rocks the size of fists, which knocked many dwarves to the ground. Pools of blood spread across the wooden streets. The hail brushed away from the bubble like rain on glass.

Part of him wanted to close his eyes to keep the images away, just as the bubble kept out sound. He could not bear to watch, yet he could not bear to look away.

For a moment there was the sense of distant shaking, like the approach of a great earthquake. Those still standing crouched, readying themselves for another of the earth's trembles. Instead the mountain spat and coughed, spewing forth black air and great chunks of rock. Dwarves opened and closed their mouths in howls of pain. Buildings shuddered and fell. Roofs quietly collapsed under the impact of large boulders.

In the bubble they were immune to it all, the sound and even the shaking. They watched as if they watched pictures pass before them.

Pictures. But Reod's pictures blurred as he watched, and his face stayed wet. Lava cascaded down the mountain in trails of red like the gushing blood of a cut animal. Splatters of the mountain's life fluid went everywhere, starting fires on houses, trees, and the wooden streets. The lava that rained down on their bubble hissed away, leaving no trace.

Or maybe it was blood. He could not tell.

"Good," said the yellow-eyed wizard softly. "Very good."

And then the darkness fell again.

The bubble lurched, fell, stopped, then faded around them.

They stood in a long hallway of high, shadowy ceilings and black stone pillars. The dim light showed them a little more of the wizard than they had seen in the bubble. He had been human once, Reod knew. Now his skin was stretched too tightly over his bones and something had been done to his forehead, extra skin applied, and there implanted was a third eye which was not quite alive. Reod had seen the process once. It still gave him troubling dreams.

Around them were a number of dark figures, like lumps, which now uncurled into creatures with long teeth and spiked backs.

The Created Ones.

Reod remembered when the first of the thrulls had been made, so many years ago, remembered the tortured cries that echoed down the halls when the experiments began.

These were the result.

The wizard began to speak soft, simple orders to the thrulls in the Low Temple language, telling them to go back to their large, single room.

"Are we—" Eliza whispered to Reod. She trailed off, not even wanting to finish the sentence.

"Achtep Keep," he answered. "Yes."

CHAPTER

9

"Be careful what you laugh at. It might laugh back."

—Reod Dai

SEKENA WATCHED A THIN COLUMN OF SMOKE
rise from behind a distant peak. The peak was west,
toward Teedmar, might even be Teedmar. A sick,
twisting feeling went through her.

Even at this distance, it was a lot of smoke.

"I have to leave," she said aloud. "I have to go to
Teedmar. My people need me."

She had meant to leave for Teedmar days ago, but
somehow she kept getting sidetracked. How could she
keep forgetting? Now she was angry with herself,
angry enough to keep her focus clear. If Mama and
Tamun had come after her, they would have thought
she was at Teedmar and would have gone there to find
her.

Where all the smoke was rising.

"Ah, land and sky, I have to find them."

From behind her came a series of hisses.

She turned, looked up, saw the dragon's red-and-green head snaked down toward her. It still gave her a bit of shock when she realized that he was so big she had to turn her head to see all of him. It felt like looking down into a valley and realizing how far it would be to fall.

She had dragon-scent about her, Reod had said. She inhaled the great dragon and felt herself relax. If she smelled this good to him, she could understand why he had decided not to eat her.

With effort she turned her attention back to the column of smoke.

But she had not come here to sniff dragons. She had come to help her people fight the orcs and goblins. Not to be treated like the pet of this scaled, horned creature who lived in a cave and ate trees for lunch.

It was odd—she had yet to see him eat something larger than a rabbit, though she knew from the bones of cows and other large animals that were scattered around the cave that he did. Mostly she had seen him eat vegetation and smaller game when he brought some back for Sekena. Perhaps he ate large meals only infrequently. Why would that be?

Mama and Tamun, she reminded herself.

The great dragon hissed at her again. His hisses were a language, she was now convinced. She almost had a sense of what the words might mean.

"Teedmar," Sekena answered. "My people need me. My mother and sister might be in trouble. I cannot stay here. I'm sorry."

The hiss came again, insistent. A great golden eye turned on her.

She shrugged. "Then I'll walk. I walked this far, didn't I?" Great golden eyes met hers. "I'll come back."

If she could.

She inhaled dragon-scent again, thought about being without it, and felt a sharp pain of loss. Maybe once away she would forget why she stayed, or only remember enough to be afraid to come back.

But now the great dragon would not let her walk back to the cave where her pack and waterskin remained. A scaled arm stopped her, nearly as thick around as she was. In the other direction, a wing closed the way, surprisingly hard for the thin, almost transparent membrane.

She sighed, frustrated. Teedmar would not be more than a day's walk away. All right, then, she wouldn't bother with the pack.

Behind the dragon stood the whelps, looking at her with wide eyes, cute heads cocked to the side, as if asking if she was really going to leave them.

"Damn it—"

Mama and Tamun, she reminded herself.

She turned and ran to the edge of the level area. The way down was rocky and thick with snow, but there was a clear well-used game path. She scrambled down.

Great wings unfurled behind her, starting a breeze. A sound came from above, loud and shrill, between a screech and a howl. It sent shudders through her body.

Just a whining dragon, she told herself firmly, trying to still her shaking hands as she reached for snow-covered boulders to steady her climb down.

The sound came again, piercing, grating, and impossible to ignore. It was like a cold, cold knife cutting through her, freezing her feet to the ground.

"No," she said angrily, forcing herself to move. But now she trembled so much that each step down was a slippery challenge.

Shadow blocked the sun. A dragon leg landed in front of her on the path. Down snaked a horned head, an eye in her face, breath strong and sweet. The hissing was soft now, almost words, almost perfectly understandable. He said her name.

And he smelled so nice. Why go anywhere else?

No, that wasn't right. She struggled, searching for something to be irritated about.

He wasn't saying her name right, even as carefully as he hissed out each syllable.

"Not 'ee-tri,'" she told him, trying to stoke herself to the fury it would take to think through his intoxicating scent. "'ee-*na*.'"

They all wanted her to stay. Even her. Her chest ached with the leaving.

"But I have to go. You have to let me."

The dragon nudged her gently with his head, knocking her backward into the snow.

She scrambled to her feet, the insult helping to burn through the dragon-scent. She drew herself up to her full height, and the dragon brought his head down as far as he could. Their eyes met.

"You *will* let me go," she said, speaking with all the force she could find, thinking of how her mother would have said such a thing, how Mama would have scolded Tamun or Sekena for some outrageous behavior. "*Right now.*"

He turned away, making a chuffing sound, almost as if he were choking. Now fury gained a solid foothold inside her, mightily empowering her resolve.

He wasn't choking. He was laughing.

CHAPTER

10

"There are always survivors."

—Genkr Nik

THE MOUNTAINS WERE HIGH, JAGGED LINES
on the southern horizon when the road finally turned
from pine needles to gravel. It was then that the elves
left Melelki and Tamun, turning back along the road
north to Havenwood. The tall, armed warriors spoke
quick wishes to them for safe travel. Perhaps they were
even sincere. With elves, who could tell?

Teedmar was a day west of them, or so the elves had
said before they left. Yesterday they had passed a fork
that offered a choice south to the Peaks, where they
had once made their home, or west to the largest
dwarven towns and strongholds. They walked into the
sunset as the road ran along the length of the mountain range.

Wispy clouds caught the sky's orange and pink
and spread themselves thin above the horizon,
promising good fortune to those who could count
the bands.

"How many, do you think, Mama?"

It was a counting game all dwarven mothers played with their children. Melelki was silent a long moment.

"Five."

"Six," her daughter countered.

During the trip down, with the elves always there, they had not been able to talk freely. Melelki had been sure they would find Sekena on the way to Teedmar, but they had not, and she had grown more and more anxious with each passing hour. Now, with the elves gone, they could talk again. But what was there to say? Tamun tried again to cheer her.

"There, by the cloud that looks like a snake, there are two bands there."

"At least the elves are gone now," Melelki said.

"They were very odd, Mama."

"Ta, all those songs we've heard, all our lives, about how kind and beautiful they are?" Melelki shook her head. "I think they must have written the songs themselves."

"They look like birds to me, always twitching and looking scared."

"As if something might eat them at any moment." Melelki laughed, then stopped, looking around at the darkening trees. "Maybe we should stop for the night."

They left the road, pushing aside thick tufts of pine and stepping over bushes whose leaves seemed more black than green in the fading light. They found a flat spot on the thick forest floor and settled there, but it didn't feel right. All the other nights the elves had made warm fires for them, made sure the rain was kept away, and kept watch, requiring nothing from the women. Tonight, though, they were alone. They took turns watching the long night pass.

To Melelki every sound brought back memories of Kalitas, mixing with sinister dreams in which she tried to find an old man wandering through an empty town. She kept looking, but sometimes she could not see over the piles of bodies.

Morning was a relief. They took to the road again, making good time without the rain.

The sun was high when Melelki felt a strangeness in the breeze; it did not feel good. Something about it reminded her both of Kalitas and the journey north to Havenwood. She stopped suddenly, a hand on Tamun's arm.

"Mama, what?"

"There's something on the air."

Tamun sniffed, frowned. "What?"

"I'm not sure."

And then she was. Her heart began to pound. "Orcs," she whispered.

They darted off the road and into the cover of pines. Quietly they went, but also swiftly, as swiftly as the breeze that bore the scent and could, if they were not both quick and lucky, bear back their own to the orcs.

When at last Melelki could no longer smell it, they stopped and crouched down behind a thick bush, holding hands and barely breathing.

In her head, Melelki practiced what she would do if they were found. She would fight, she would kick, and she would bite. But every time her mind finished the scene badly, and she shook her head, resolving to think of something else.

The sun had moved two handwidths by the time they crept back to the road. There on the road Melelki could smell orc still, but faintly.

And there were footprints. Many tens of them. Going east.

"Ta," she whispered. "They go to Havenwood."

"Or the Crimson Peaks."

With looks over their shoulders, they hurried along the road west.

They saw Teedmar from a distance and kept hiking by the dim light of the stars and crescent moon. At the city gates a guard smiled and waved them through.

Tamun was their passkey to the dwarven city. It was her time and all the men noticed her. Those they passed on the wooden streets stopped, frowned, and turned confused looks after them, as if they were not quite sure why they had stopped. It was surprisingly common, especially among the younger men, to fail to realize the effect a woman's time had on them.

At the first inn they went to, the innkeeper offered them a room and food for so little that it was nearly free. Another two dwarven women were nearby, wiping down counters and mugs. They rolled their eyes at the old man and gave Tamun and Melelki a knowing smile. Women could always tell. And dwarven men were so simple.

"Come on," the innkeeper said as he led them upstairs, glaring back at the women snickering below. "We like to make our southern neighbors feel welcome is all. Don't see many of you around here. Elves and humans, yes. Southern cousins, no." He shrugged and turned a warm look on Tamun. "So where exactly are you from?"

"Tigaden."

To see his reaction, Melelki added, "Near Kalitas."

The innkeeper growled. "Damn the critters to the Hells. And Icatia, too. They have an army. Why don't they use it? They need our weapons, but they don't care if we get bloody? Is that what it is?" A glance at Tamun. "We'll get them. We'll get every last one."

"That's why we've come," Tamun said. "To help fight."

He raised his thick, reddish eyebrows at her. "They'd take you on the front, you know. Desperate for more bodies." He gave a shake of his shaggy head. "I don't think it's right. You ought to be somewhere safe, having little ones. Not risking yourself."

Melelki wondered what the man would think if he knew just whose little ones Tamun was thinking of having.

"Ta," Tamun said, "but if we don't act soon, there won't be anywhere safe for me to have my little ones at all."

The man sighed heavily and held open a door to a small room. "They'll take you at the forges. They can always use more hands there. But—" his voice was softer as he looked at Melelki pleadingly "—don't let her take up arms. We need all our young women. We need them safe."

Melelki saw pain and sorrow in his eyes and wondered who he had lost.

She nodded. "These are not good times."

He shook his head again and again. "They are not."

The next day they spent searching the city for Sekena.

"Come on, Mama," Tamun said as the sky at last began to darken with night. "In the morning we'll go to the forges and start work. They need us there. When Reod gets here—" Her voice wavered a little. "When Reod gets here, he'll know how to find Sekena."

Melelki said nothing, only nodded, still looking at everyone they passed, still hoping, though her chest ached with worry.

Early the next morning they were at the forges, given the task of polishing swords. The gritty work was finger-numbing, and by midmorning they were grateful for the chance to carry wrapped bundles of supplies and weapons to the carts out front.

It wasn't any harder than toting dragon eggs, really, though the thought was a bitter one. Things had changed so much in the last few weeks. They used to have a home and a basement full of eggs. Now they had nothing.

And Sekena. Where was she?

Melelki turned her thoughts away from that. They would wait for Reod Dai, as Tamun had said. They would wait and then they would see.

She and Tamun carried armful after armful of wrapped bundles from the smoke-filled stone smithy out into the courtyard's bright sun, then back through the long storehouse that led to the road where the Icatian wagons waited. These bundles were swords. At least she thought they were, from the grumbling of the dwarven smiths.

"We should be keeping some of these for ourselves," Melelki had overheard one say.

"With how much the Icatians pay?"

"Ta, what will all the money be worth when the goblins and orcs come here? Teedmar has only dwarves to defend itself now. We're not warriors."

"Then we'd better learn to be, eh?"

The humans had been friends to the dwarven people for centuries. The rumor was that now the humans were too busy with their own problems to bring aid to the Crimson Peaks.

But they were not too busy to send troops to Teedmar to buy weapons. As angry as many dwarves were, Teedmar could not afford to turn away the business. Times were hard, the Icatian commanders would say, for everyone. The dwarves would repeat the words softly, bitterly, as they watched the humans walk away with dwarven battle supplies.

As one of the wagons was loaded, an Icatian soldier walked around the side, making sure the wooden doors were closed and bolted. A dwarf near Melelki spat in his footprints. Another pulled him back.

Melelki heard fierce whispers.

"Would you make them enemies?"

"I cannot make them what they already are."

"Those are the sorts of words that keep them away. Would you come to the aid of a friend who spits at you?"

"They are not friends. They leave today with the weapons we made for them. What if the orcs come tomorrow?"

"The humans will return when we need them. When the times are truly hard."

"Those times are already here."

"You are a fool."

"You will not call me a fool when Teedmar lies in ruins and the human soldiers are all in Icatia. You will not call me anything. You will be dead."

Melelki and Tamun left the cart, going back through the storeroom toward the smithy. When they were halfway down the hall, a troop of dwarven soldiers entered from the far direction, coming toward them. They dropped back into a recessed doorway to make room for the armored dwarves to press by.

Dwarven soldiers. It was the first time Melelki had seen them up close like this, the dwarves who were training for fighting, training for war. Melelki felt an odd twist inside herself. How many of them had only recently picked up a sword? Which of them had raised chickens, hammered an anvil, sewed clothes? Which had family dead in Kalitas?

Melelki had never thought the time would come when she would see dwarven men and women pick up swords to fight off goblins and orcs. Goblins! Just wave torches at them and they would flee. And orcs were even more cowardly than that. Or used to be.

And she never imagined a time when she would not know where in Sarpadia her Sekena was.

"We'll find them," Tamun whispered, putting a hand on her shoulder.

She was about to give Tamun reassuring words in return when an odd scent caught her attention, coming from the closed door behind her. Odd and very familiar, but she couldn't quite place it. She tried the knob. It turned.

"Mama, what are you doing?"

Melelki opened the door and slipped into the room. Tamun followed, shutting the door carefully behind them. A few slit windows above revealed a dusty storage room with baskets and blankets on the floor.

"I smell something."

"Mama, what a nose you have. One of these days that nose is going to get us all in trouble."

"Hasn't it already?"

"Ta. Mama, what do you smell?"

Melelki followed the scent to the wall. She knelt and felt around on the ground where the floor met the wall.

"It's coming from here." The crack followed along the wall, then made a sharp, straight turn toward Melelki.

It was a door set into the floor. She backed off of the panel and pushed, then she tried grabbing the edges with her nails and pulling, both with no result.

"Locked?" Tamun asked.

"Hmm."

Near the door in the wall was a small opening, like a tiny mouse hole. There the odor was strongest. Melelki hesitated, but curiosity was stronger than prudence. Besides, her finger fit in the hole perfectly. She felt around inside, found something hard, and pressed.

The door at her feet clicked and popped up a little, making it easy to open. There were wooden rungs going straight down into the darkness.

"Mama—"

"Let's see where it goes." Curiosity burned inside her.

"Mama!"

Melelki felt for the first rung with her toe, slowly let her weight down, then lowered herself to the next. She counted the rungs as Tamun followed: ten, twenty, then thirty. Thirty! Then there was floor beneath her feet.

In here it was dark. The soft sound of their movements told her the walls were close. She felt around carefully and found a lantern with an attached flint. She struck a spark and lit the wick.

Around them the small room flickered in the flame's light. Shelves carved out of the mountain's stone ringed the walls. In notches rested various weapons: swords, knives, spears, and other strangely shaped sticklike objects that Melelki did not recognize.

In here the smell was very strong. Melelki smiled as

she touched a finger to the pale, metal-hard edge of one of the knives.

"Dragon shell," she said.

Tamun ran her fingers over the hilts of a few of the weapons, then grabbed the handle of a short sword, hefting it. Melelki took down a long knife, which had a companion sheath made of hard leather. Into the leather had been tooled an old dwarven saying. She tilted it toward the light and read it aloud.

"Cut only that which should be cut, and then cut deep."

"These are beautifully made, Mama. Not like the ones that we deliver to the Icatians."

"Ta, this is the best, then."

The sparkle of dragon shell was everywhere. Even arrows and crossbow bolts were tipped with the white iridescence.

So this was where she could have sold her dragon eggs. Or perhaps they only wanted the shells and would have had no idea what to do with the hatching whelps. She shook her head. Too late, anyway.

Her eyes stopped at a handle set into the floor. Another door. But this one wasn't hidden at all and it was bolted from their side.

"Oh, no. Mama, we've gone far enough. We're already somewhere we're not supposed to be. Mama—"

But Melelki was already opening the door. She pushed the knife into its sheath and fastened the belt around her middle so that she would have her hands free for the lantern.

"We've worked for hours, haven't we? We're just taking a break. What do you think is down there?"

"Mama, I think we should turn back."

The door opened and the lantern revealed more rungs leading downward. "Look at how far down it goes."

"Mama!"

Melelki began to climb down. "Just a little ways," she said. "Just a little break from carrying bundles."

"We can't just take these weapons with us, Mama."

"Then we'll return them on the way back. Who will miss them? Come, daughter, let's explore."

Tamun gave an exasperated sigh, but Melelki knew it was mostly show.

After all, her daughter had chosen a human. That alone was proof enough that she had inherited Melelki's furious curiosity.

At the bottom of this set of rungs was a dwarf-sized tunnel. Sound was different here in this small passageway, close and tight, with the ceiling barely taller than Melelki and barely wider than the two of them standing together. Lamplight flickered against the roughly carved tunnel sides, making ominous shapes against the uneven walls. Into the uncertain darkness they both walked.

It was said that humans became claustrophobic in places like this, which was why they did so little underground mining and had to come to the dwarves for their best metal weapons. What was claustrophobia? A fear of being enclosed? Melelki felt no such thing. When she thought about how much mountain there was above her, she felt instead a shiver of excitement.

This tunnel was too narrow to be a mining tunnel. It had probably been started long ago and was abandoned when it failed to show promise. But who knew where it might go? It was a delicious mystery. After a time, though, even Melelki began to wonder if they should turn around.

"Maybe," she said softly, her voice bouncing off the black walls, "we should go back soon."

"But we've only come a little ways. We've only seen the tunnel. There must be something more."

"Ta. A little ways more, then."

"Just a little."

And so they walked on.

* * *

Then the rumbling began. They froze. The sound was deep and distant, yet seemed also to come from all around. They tensed, ready to run, held by uncertainty. Which way?

Chunks of tunnel crashed down behind them. Rocks bounced and thumped.

Forward was the way. They ran.

From behind came a loud crash as the whole of the tunnel began to fall down, the deep rumble turning to a loud roar. Melelki grabbed Tamun's hand and they took off down the way, running as fast as they could. The lamplight flickered but held.

When the rumbling finally began to subside, they slowed.

"Earthquake?" Tamun asked breathlessly.

"Must be."

"If we had been only a few steps back. Mama, if—"

"I know, Flower, I know. But we're all right."

"We can't go back."

"Not that way. But the tunnel will come out somewhere. It has to." She hoped.

So they walked. Melelki was never more grateful for a lamp than she was now, with its single flickering flame lighting the rock walls and reminding them that there was still air to breathe. And if there was air, there was a way out.

For a time the tunnel sloped down, then became flatter again, the only sound their own footsteps. They came to an open doorway; another tunnel went off into the distant dark. They stood there long moments, trying to decide.

"This one seems to be the main one," Melelki said. "We should keep going. It's bigger and better worn on the ground."

Tamun knelt and ran fingertips along the floor. "More dust in the side passage, too."

So they went forward, saying little as they walked,

watching for any change in the rock tunnel. Melelki
grew increasingly thirsty and hungry. Doubtless
Tamun was, too. But to talk about it would only make
it seem worse, so they kept silent.

At last the tunnel began to slope gently upward.

Then, suddenly, there were thin rungs in the wall,
one after another, going straight up through a dark
opening in the roof of the passageway.

Rungs going up.

They looked at each other a moment, then Melelki
began to climb, Tamun following. At the top was a
trapdoor, but smaller than before. Melelki pushed.
Dirt brushed down over their faces, and she instinctively covered the lamp. Then she pulled herself up
and through, setting the lamp on a dirt-covered floor
above. Quietly they let the door close under them.

They were in a small and rough wooden passageway. Cobwebs were so thick the room's corners
seemed fuzzy. Bugs twitched in small piles of dirt on
the floor. Shafts of dim lamplight and odd sounds
came through cracks in the wooden planks.

Melelki put her eye up against one of the small slits
and pulled back in shock. Mouth against Tamun's
ear, she whispered: "Goblins!" Tamun's eyes
widened. Melelki snuffed their oil lamp and, with her
eye again at the slit, she looked back into the large
room of goblins.

She had always known that goblins came in two
sizes, but it was only now, as she saw them so close
and without armor, some of them with small ones held
tight to their breasts, was it clear that the larger and
darker of the goblins were the females.

A goblin warren, here, such a very short ways from
Teedmar? Who else would know? None from Teedmar,
she suspected. Only she and Tamun. They simply had to
get back and tell the city dwarves. Once they knew, with
the tunnel below, surely the dwarves would clear the
earthquake's rubble and come back here and—

And what?

And destroy the warren, of course. She looked back through the slats. Goblins, green and odd-smelling and so very strange. Teedmar would have to make sure they were all destroyed, of course, so that there would not be more and more of them.

The thought didn't sit well with her. She remembered some songs from her childhood that implied that dwarves and goblins had been almost friends, a long time ago. Why did it seem the only option to friendship was war?

A young one crawled away from its parent, right toward the slats where she stood. She pulled her head back. Could they see her? Surely not. But such strange creatures—who could know what they saw?

However mixed her feelings were, goblins were a real danger, and they had to get back to Teedmar.

They followed the passage along the room's length and side. There a door led out into a larger hallway, lined with garbage, much of it recent.

"What now?" Tamun whispered.

It would be folly to go out into the larger hallway where any goblin in the warren might find them. Where they were now was clearly unused. Safer.

"I don't know."

"Could we could go back?"

"The tunnel came down behind us. I doubt it."

"Perhaps the side tunnel we found might double back."

"Or get us lost. And what would we eat or drink while we were looking?"

Thoughts of food and water were becoming insistent.

"We have to tell Teedmar about the warren," Melelki said. "Goblins so close. What they could do to the city!"

"Then—we must go out there."

Melelki took a deep breath, squeezed her daughter's hand, and gave her a quick kiss.

"We'll be all right." She hoped.

So out they crept, quietly, cautiously. They walked

the long hallway past the doors to the goblin room they had seen before. At the end of the hallway were stairs going up. She took the first step gingerly, worrying what might be at the top, wishing for a weapon.

Then, feeling like an idiot, she drew her knife. Behind her, Tamun did likewise. Some warriors the two of them would make, she thought.

The stairs were uneven stone, and Melelki took another step up, her heart speeding. All her reason told her that the knife in her hand wasn't going to make a bit difference. She pushed the thought away.

Retreat to the crawlspace, her fear told her. And then what? Back to the safety of the tunnel?

And to starve?

Onward it was.

At each step up she strained to hear better. From below she could hear the low, whispery voices of the goblins and their young.

Another step and then another. Suddenly there was at Melelki's feet a pinpoint of bright, bright light. Daylight. She looked up, and there far above them was a tiny hole in the ceiling.

There was a way out.

Ahead at the middle of the stairway was a closed door and as they passed they heard muffled voices, incomprehensible chitterings. Past the door they crept.

At last they reached the top. Daylight spilled in from a cave opening. There was nothing there, no guards, no one at all. Daylight and freedom.

Then a noise came from behind them, down on the stairs. A question, and exclamation, and a howl.

"Run!" Melelki cried, gripping her knife tightly. And they did.

Afternoon sun blinded them as they ran out of the cave, barely seeing the goblins as they sped past.

There were more howls from behind them. Melelki glanced back, trying to see through watering eyes. They had run through a milling mass of goblins. Most of the creatures simply looked on, confused and surprised, but some were beginning to follow.

The road before them was rocky but clear. It was flatland lined with winter scrub. They pushed themselves and ran faster. Behind, Melelki could hear a stampede of small footsteps.

Tamun was slowing, just a little, and Melelki knew her daughter, knew that she slowed down to stay alongside. With Tamun's heat, she could go much faster than she went. The goblins were now gaining.

"Don't wait for me," she got out between breaths. "Go!"

Tamun shook her head, grabbed her mother's hand, and pulled her along.

Melelki's fear drove her hard. She did not think she could run this fast. Even Tamun was winded now, gasping for breath.

She could smell the goblins behind her, hear the chittering and yelling, the rustling of their rags and the clink of weapons and armor. It was like having ants crawl on the back of her neck.

And when they caught up, what then? Torture and death? What of Sekena? Her youngest would never know what had happened to them. It infuriated her, to think of having come so far to die for so little.

"Keep running," Melelki yelled fiercely at Tamun. "Get to Teedmar. You understand?"

"Mama!"

"Say you will."

"Ma—"

"Say it!"

"I will!"

Melelki yanked her hand out of Tamun's grasp, stopped suddenly, and whirled to face the oncoming horde, hoping that Tamun was still running. The goblins slowed, then stopped, confused.

Good. Every moment she delayed them was another moment for Tamun. Melelki yelled, as loud she could,

anger and fear all rolled up into one cry, and waved
her knife at them. Some stepped back.

She lunged forward, still screaming as loud as she
could. Now some turned and ran. Some held their
ground, uncertain. But some kept coming. Those few
who had swords held them out as if they knew how to
use them, and they were far longer than her little
knife.

She had no chance, but maybe this was for the best.
If she died now, fighting, they could not save her to
torture later. They could not find out anything from
her.

She cut the air with her knife, back and forth. The
advancing goblins hesitated, but not for long. They
soon surrounded her.

This was it, then. She was not going to see Sekena
come into heat, she was not going to find out whether
Tamun made it to Teedmar, and she was not going to
know if her people survived the coming times.

A chill went through her as she realized how close
she was to the end, then a wash of sadness. Even that
passed, and then came a pure fury like nothing she had
ever felt. Suddenly she felt as strong as if she were in
heat again. What was left to lose? Nothing at all. She
grinned at the goblins as she realized that she would
take some with her.

They closed, she and the goblins, they with their
crude, long, bumpy swords and she with her gleaming
dragon-shell knife. No matter what happened, she
swore, in moments there would be goblin blood on her
blade.

And then, one by one, each goblin stopped coming
toward her and looked into the sky.

Melelki stumbled forward, confusion interrupting
her sweet, murderous rage. Long heartbeats of confusion came over her before she glanced up. There in the
sky, a big shape blocked the sun.

The goblins were turning and fleeing. Every one of
them. From what, a cloud? They were fearful and

cowardly, yes, but not so much as this, surely. She looked up again, caught a glimpse of something green and winged. A spray of fire washed over the fleeing goblins, close enough that she felt the heat and stumbled back.

"Mama!"

Tamun was some distance behind her. She pointed upward.

The goblins who were not aflame had now streamed into the cave entrance. The rest howled, rolling on the ground, trying to put out their flames. The shadow passed overhead again, circling. The goblins remaining outside were reignited.

Melelki felt her legs give way. She sat on the ground. Tamun was at her side.

"Mama, did they hurt you? Mama?"

Melelki could not speak. She could only look up at her youngest daughter astride what could only be a great dragon and laugh.

Sekena pounded on the dragon's thick neck in frustration as the wind whipped her hair across her face.

"I said *down*, you miserable beast!"

She had to yell over the rushing of the wind down the distance along his neck to his head.

He was flying in a large lazy circle above the cave entrance. Her mother was sitting on the ground with Tamun crouched over her. What had they done to her? Sekena was frantic. She pounded on the dragon's side again.

Back on the mountaintop she had thought she and the dragon were finally communicating. She had explained to him about her mother and sister, and why she needed to get to Teedmar. The creature had picked her up and put her on his back, where his ridges made an uncomfortable but serviceable saddle. Then, while she gripped the ridges in terror, he dove off the mountain, gliding through the air, over land and mountains.

Such sights she had seen! Everything was so small—mountains like snowy molehills, roads shrunk right down to the size of slug trails. The dragon flew toward the smoking mountain she had seen in the distance.

And then, below, she had seen a group of goblins chasing two figures. Even at that height, Sekena guessed and then recognized Tamun and her mother. She yelled at the dragon to go down, and he dropped, passed Tamun and Mama, exhaled fire, ignited goblins.

Now most of the goblins had disappeared into the cave. The others lay on the ground, smoking and charred. For a moment the smell of burning flesh reached her and her stomach lurched in sympathy.

Kalitas, she told herself. Kalitas. What she saw below, this was what war was about. The goblins had begun the violence. Now they were getting back some of what they had given.

Of course, Reod Dai might have had something to do with it, too. Who knew what he had taught them? Despite Tamun's affection for the human, Sekena didn't entirely trust him.

But remorse? No. She would do everything she could to destroy the goblins. And the orcs, too.

As they had flown over, as the dragon had flamed the goblins, she thought he was protecting her family. As he circled around the cave, taking her away from her family, she began to wonder.

The large circle took them over the cave again, then over scrub and rock and back to where Tamun sat on the ground with Mama. Then the dragon began to drop. She clutched tightly as he did a sudden shift and twist and landed. He snaked his head around over the ground, found the charred remains of a goblin and began to chew on its head.

She might have known. The creature wasn't helping her or protecting her family. He was just snacking. Crunching and tearing sounds came from his mouth.

"I'll get down on my own, don't worry," she said sarcastically.

From where she sat to the ground was a drop of more than twice her own height. She winced, pulled both legs over, and readied herself for the fall.

Suddenly his claw was under her feet, talons splayed out, palm up, like a small platform. She wriggled onto the claw and clutched a knobby finger as he lowered her to the ground.

She stepped away, a little shaky.

"Maybe you're not such an idiot after all," she mumbled.

He had finished the one goblin, bones and all, and now swung his head around at her, tongue flicking out and back, mouth covered with goblin blood, hissing at her.

She didn't understand it, not a word of it.

At least that was what she told herself as she turned away and sprinted toward her mother and sister.

Sekena hugged them both tightly. Her mother was trembling.

"Mama, are you well?"

"Yes, my precious one," Melelki said, kissing her. "Ah, to see you again, when I had thought—" She frowned at the dragon, who was munching on another charred goblin. "Daughter, tell me, how is it that you come to be . . ." She waved at the creature.

"Ta," Sekena said. "I'm not quite sure."

"Where are the whelps?" Tamun asked.

"Back at the mountain, in the dragon's cave. They've just started to fly. They couldn't quite follow."

"This—" Mama said, still staring at the long creature. "This is what?"

"It's a dragon, Mama."

Melelki gave her a look.

"His name is a collection of hisses, Mama. I can't say it yet."

Tamun glanced back at the cave. Goblins were peeking out at them. "We shouldn't stay here."

Melelki nodded. "We have to get back to Teedmar."

The dragon was ambling over. Sekena went over to him. She inhaled, smelled his dragon-scent, then quietly explained to him about needing to fly to the city. He seemed to understand and to agree to take them all there. At least, that was what she thought the hisses meant.

But her mother refused to get on the dragon.

"Mama," Sekena said, "it's perfectly safe. And very fast. I rode all the way from our mountaintop, which is more than a day's walk away. Once we're in the air, Teedmar will be only a few minutes away."

"I don't mind walking."

"I don't either," said Tamun, eyeing the dragon nervously. "It's not that far."

Sekena looked from Tamun to her mother. What was wrong with them? The dragon stared down at them, slitted pupils long and thin in shimmering golden eyes, each of which was nearly as large as their heads.

He hissed.

Melelki and Tamun took a number of quick steps backward.

"Ta, don't worry," Sekena said, "that's just his way of talking. He's saying—" She wasn't quite sure what he was saying. "He's giving you greetings."

The dragon hissed again. She whirled on him.

"It's close enough," she hissed back. "Now stop scaring them."

Hiss.

"Yes, you are. Stop it."

She turned back. Her mother and Tamun had very peculiar expressions on their faces.

"What's wrong?"

"You *talk* to it?" Mama asked.

"Of course not," Sekena said. "Well, sort of."

"And it understands you?"

"I think so. I'm not sure."

"And you want us to ride on this?"

"Just a little ways."

Behind her the dragon laughed. She felt herself redden.

"Quiet," she hissed at him.

From behind her came an extended claw, palm up, in the gesture that meant peace, that meant he carried no weapons. Coming from the dragon, with each talon almost as long as her arm, it was ludicrous.

Melelki slowly returned the gesture.

The dragon hissed again.

"Now," Sekena said, feeling odd because this time she was certain, "he really *is* giving you greetings."

The weight of the three women didn't seem to make much difference to the dragon. They each sat between the ridges along his back, holding onto the bumps and each other.

"He can be a little slippery," Sekena warned, "but you'll be fine if you hold tight."

Then the enormous creature spread his wings and kicked off the ground, jarring but not unseating them. They were in the air.

Below everything was suddenly small, trees like brush, mountains like hills. Sekena yelled at the dragon's head, pointing, trying to explain to him where Teedmar was. She put on a confident smile for her mother and sister, hoping that he had heard her, but mostly hoping that the dragon had understood, and that he wanted to take them there.

"He's not going the right way," Melelki yelled from behind.

"You're not going the right way," she yelled at the dragon. "Go west. Toward the sun."

So they went south, despite Sekena's yells and curses. But when Teedmar's smoke rose from the west, the dragon turned that direction, and the city came into view.

Melelki's voice was a wail in the wind.

"Ah, by the Moon, what has happened?"

The mountain was coated in wide trails of black

rock, as if it had spat up thick mud, most of which was still smoking.

Teedmar was gone. Where the city itself had been, at the base of the mountain, there was only a hard, black, lumpy lake.

Painful horror filled Sekena, a sense of things terribly, terribly wrong. What had happened to the city? Where were all the dwarves?

Below and away, where the road into Teedmar led through a clearing of stumps, she saw a clustered group of dwarves. The dragon descended, circled, and landed nearby, helping each of the women to the ground with his outstretched foot.

They walked toward the group. The dwarves there began backing away. Some were trying to carry children. Some limped. Some just lay on the ground and whimpered.

They weren't looking at the women. They were looking behind them and up.

"Wait," Melelki cried out to them.

"He's tame," Sekena shouted, hoping that the dragon was far enough away not to hear her.

The group slowed its retreat, still looking fearfully up at the dragon. They were in no condition to move quickly anyway.

"Tell us what happened to the city," Melelki said.

"Volcano," one said, an old woman. "The mountain threw up."

"Orcs did it," someone cried angrily.

"Orcs and goblins," another said darkly.

"No, no," the old woman said, limping forward. "They don't have that kind of magic. It has to be wizards. Probably the Ebon Hand." She squinted suspiciously at the three women. "Who are you? Why do you come here on a dragon?"

"My daughter has tamed the creature," Melelki said, and Sekena could hear the pride in her voice.

The old woman limped up close to Sekena, close enough that Sekena could smell her breath.

"You tamed a *dragon*? What is your name?"

"Sekena," she said softly, forcing herself to smile, feeling awkward. If he heard this, that he was supposed to be tame—well, she did not think he would much like it.

"Sevena," the woman mispronounced. She nodded. "Sevena, did you know that my own daughter died today?"

"I'm sorry," Sekena said, feeling awful.

"She and her children," the woman said. "All five of them."

"Ta, that's terrible."

"Where are all the others?" asked Tamun.

The old woman looked at her. "Where do you think? Under the black liquid fire. Under there." She pointed at the thick, dark stuff that covered the smoking remains of the city.

"What, all of them?" Sekena asked with disbelief.

"Some have left for Gurn Keep. We are the ones who move slowest." Her voice dropped. "And some of us are still looking. Still hoping. Most are dead. My daughter—at least she died quickly." The old woman pointed to a large pile of rubble against the mountain a short distance away. "Not like those. My son is among them. They will die slowly, over many days."

"What do you mean?" Melelki asked.

"One of the mines has collapsed. We hear them calling though the rock, but there is no way out. We could leave and go to the keep, where there is food and safety. But leave them?" She shook her head.

"Ah, mother," Melelki said, taking the older woman's hand. "Such hard times."

Sekena looked over at the mine entrance where the woman had pointed. Then she looked back at the dragon, who was watching the group of dwarves with a little too much interest. She walked over to the big creature.

The great head snaked down toward her, tongue flicking out to touch her neck and face, leaving her wet with dragon-scented slime.

"Ta, just like a dog," she said, wiping it off, but smiling. "Do you know," she said to the creature, "you've been—ta, you've been really wonderful today. I think you understand everything a lot better than I said you did. So perhaps I should apologize. And, well . . ." She reached up a hand uncertainly to touch the underside of his jaw. He flicked out his tongue, let it slide slippery over her hand and back into his mouth.

"Well," she said again, "there's this cave over there. And then there's this large pile of rocks."

CHAPTER

11

"Those idiots should never have bred thrulls for combat!"

—Jherana Rure, Counter
Insurgency Commander

THICK WINDOWS ETCHED WITH SHARP geometric designs let in little of the day's light, scattering gray patterns against dark walls. Above was a lattice of rafters, where shadows kept to themselves, rustling and blinking down at them with pale eyes.

Reod glanced at Eliza as the wizard led them down the stone hallway. She was taking it well, refusing to let any of what she felt show on her face. A fine representative of Icatia's best, she was, conquering her fear, behaving as if nothing out of the ordinary had happened.

Which was how some of those who had followed him to the Ebon Hand had perished. Swayed by Reod's talk of hypocrisy and blindness in the Icatian high command, they followed, thinking to find a better life at Robin Davies's side. Instead they came face-to-

face with the intense magical passion that powered the
Ebon Hand, a thing far, far stranger than any they had
ever before encountered.

Most of those had died by their own hand, unable to
change their own regimented thinking, the very thing
they had sought to escape by leaving Icatia. Most of
them chose to spill their own blood rather than join
the Ebon Hand.

He had told them not to come. They had not listened.

And now Tamun was gone, too.

Eliza touched his hand with a look of concern. He
shook his head slightly, looked away.

But when blood was spilled here at the Ebon Hand
it was never wasted, as it was in Icatia. When Reod's
followers died, every drop was faithfully kept, going to
feed the bones of Achtep Keep. It was said that the
keep's very stones would fight any invader. It was true.
Reod had seen the stones tested.

A few of those drops of blood had gone to Reod. To
reject his men's last, greatest sacrifice was unthink-
able, so he had taken the offering, adding their
strength to his. It was then that he had become Reod
Dai.

And now Reod Dai was back.

They were being led through dark archways to a
wing of smaller side rooms. These were the living
quarters for the privileged few who slept on beds and
not on stone. He had slept in these rooms long ago,
back when he had still believed that the practices of
the Ebon Hand might be better for the people of all
the lands than those of Icatia. Back before Genkr Nik
gave up both his hands.

The wizard knocked on a door. When it opened, he
stood quickly aside, motioning the two of them inside.
Reod stepped in, Eliza a cautious step behind. When
they were inside, the door shut behind them.

Across the years Reod had traveled to Sarpadia's
five corners and had learned the ways of many cultures, their strangeness and their character. Among

other things, he had learned that each race greeted others differently. Humans used a formula pattern of pleasantries. Dwarves tended toward the simple and blunt, often skipping greetings entirely. Goblins would describe imaginary treasures.

Even here in the Ebon Hand, in this soup pot of races, united under the flag of Tourach, there was a distinctive flavor to a greeting.

"Do you not listen? Did I give you so much of my painfully gained wisdom for nothing?"

Across the room sat a figure on a raised cot, leaning against the wall, shifting a little under dark blankets. A single hazel eye, the right one, blinked at Reod from a dark, scarred face that was framed by short, gray hair. For emphasis the figure raised an arm. It ended at the elbow.

Reod met the gaze of his old mentor's one good eye.

"I listened."

"Then say it back to me."

"I am not here to be tutored."

Genkr's face twisted. "*Say* it. I'll start you out, you forgetful bastard: 'The most important thing to remember, when leaving the Ebon Hand—' Now finish it."

"'—is not to come back.' I remember."

"Then what in the thousand Hells are you doing here?"

"I was abducted. Under your direction, no doubt, Genkr."

"There is always a way. There is always a choice. A side path. You are an idiot."

"Did you not order my abduction or not?"

"Of course I did. But I hoped for better from you than to see you here."

"Be disappointed, Genkr."

"I am."

"Then let us go."

"No." The scarred head nodded at Eliza, who had stood like a statue during the exchange. "Is this thing of value to you?"

"It is."

"You are collecting these days? I understand that you lost some dwarves during the eruption."

Tamun's face flashed through Reod's mind. He struggled to keep his voice and expression neutral.

"Yes."

"If you had stayed here, Reod, we would have given you all the slaves you wanted. Even some females."

"As I recall, it was you who encouraged me to leave."

The face scowled. "Of course. You weren't happy."

Reod smiled, hard. "I'm not happy now, either. What is this about, Genkr?"

The figure nodded. "To business, then. I have reports that you have been doing interesting things since you left. We have need of some of those interesting things. We want goblin eggs."

"So I've been told. Your wizard already failed to meet my price."

"I'm not offering you a choice."

"There's always a choice."

"Indeed. But until you find it, I expect you to do everything in your power to help those who gave you your ability to choose in the first place."

"I'm not inclined to help."

"No loyalty left?"

"No."

"Fear, then?"

Reod shook his head.

Genkr chuckled. "Then we'll torture this Icatian dung heap behind you until she begs for the chance to offer the sacrifice of her soul in payment for a quick death."

"Simple threat? I'm disappointed, Genkr."

Genkr exhaled, almost seemed embarrassed. "Well. These are unpleasant times. How do you answer?"

"Even the Created Ones labor harder for lust of food than fear of the lash. Bribe me."

"Satisfy our needs and we will set you and your pet free."

"Not much of a bargain."

Genkr gave a small twitch that might have been a shrug. "We can go back to threat, if you prefer."

"First set my pet free and grant her safe passage to Icatia."

"No."

"Give me a month to put my other affairs in order."

"We need you now. We're running out of time."

"Offer me a lot of gold."

An eyebrow flickered up. "Gold? You have indeed changed, Reod Dai. Gold it is, then. As much as you can carry."

"Horses. Safe passage. Your word."

"Of course."

"Thrull labor for my efforts. My workshop restored."

"Of course. It is all ready now, expecting you."

"Then we are agreed."

"You will build goblin eggs for us?"

"I will."

"I am pleased. It is good to see you again, Reod."

The door opened behind them. There stood a contingent of black-shelled backs, thrulls with shells harder than steel and claws sharp enough to open horsehide. Reod had seen those tests, too.

"They'll take you to your quarters," Genkr said. "Serve us well, Reod."

"Haven't I always?"

Genkr scowled. "Be careful, Reod."

Reod bowed a little. "I treasure your words in my ears."

"Very careful."

"Always."

The thrull stepped through the door into the small room that Reod and Eliza had been given. Between knobby hands it gingerly held a large plate of food, all the items laid out precisely. Reod knew they would be laid out the very same way each time, to make it obvious if any thrull

stole bits of the food they served. By now most thrulls
were well-trained out of stealing food, but the tradition
remained strong.

"Come in," Reod said in the Low Temple language
that the thrulls knew. "Come in and be at ease."

The thrull froze with uncertainty at the unexpected
words Reod had directed toward it.

"Put the food down on the table and shut the door,"
Reod said, and the thrull did. When it had finished, it
shrank to the floor and began to curl up into a ball,
expecting punishment.

"No, no. Get up."

It uncurled, but only halfway, just enough to look up
at Reod. Lying on its back, it looked like a half-eaten
slice of black melon.

"Do you understand me?" Reod asked.

It nodded, a quick tense movement.

"Listen carefully. I will need twenty thrulls for my
work. Thrulls like you, who can understand when I
speak. For this work, tonight, you'll be fed grain
cakes."

The thrull slowly uncurled the rest of the way, still
on the floor. Usually they were fed a paste made
from mold, out of large troughs, and there was never
quite enough to go around. Grain cakes were a rare
treat.

"Come back soon, with twenty of the smartest
thrulls you can find. Can you do that?"

The thrull slowly stood, trembling.

"Yesss."

"Good. Come as night falls. Don't delay. The grain
cakes will not last much longer than that."

"Yesss, will do this," it said, and it was gone.

The thrulls clustered, sitting on the floor at Reod's feet,
curled up tight and pressed together to make room for
each other. Just like in the pits where they slept.

Eliza sat on her cot, feet drawn up to keep them out

of the reach of the thrulls. It was her only admission that anything that had occurred disturbed her even a little.

Before him was a cross section of the Created Ones. Some were black, some were armored, some had veins rising from pale purple skin, making them seem fragile. Reod knew they weren't.

He nodded, meeting their eyes.

"I know that most of you don't have names, so before I get to business, we're going to play a game."

They looked at him with dull expressions, carefully cultivated, he knew, to produce the least irritation possible in those they served.

"I have grain cakes for each of you."

Eyes widened slightly, some flickered. Mouths twitched. Throats bobbed.

"Here are the rules. You—" he pointed to the first thrull who had come to serve them earlier "—will start. You will choose someone else and give them a name. Then I will give you a cake. Whoever you chose will select another, give it a name, then I will give it a cake, too. We will go on that way until you all have both a name and a grain cake."

It was two new concepts at once: names and eating without fighting. He was asking a lot of them.

"But," the first thrull said, the word low and soft. Those that spoke did so infrequently, haltingly.

"Yes?"

"But. What is a name?"

"Any word. Any word you like. 'Rock' or 'tree.' A quality, perhaps, like 'friend,' or 'smart.' I'll start you, by naming you 'Quick,' because you found all these other thrulls so quickly. Now live up to it and choose another to name."

Quick touched the thrull next to him. "Friend," he said.

Reod held up a grain cake. All eyes were glued to it.

"There will be no fighting here," he said, "as there is at the troughs. This is another place. Do you understand?"

There were nods. He handed Quick his cake and Quick hunched over it protectively, munching. They all watched him eat. Now they understood.

"'Tiny,'" Friend said quickly, pointing to the small thrull next to him and reaching for his cake.

"'Snores,'" said Tiny.

Another cake, more munching.

"'Eats-my-food,'" said the next, and Reod thought he heard what might have been a chuckle.

Reod continued to hand around cakes until all the thrulls were both named and fed. Only when the last crumb was licked off sharp claws did he speak again.

"You work hard for your masters," he said, "and that is good and right, for you are the Created Ones and they are your creators. Without them you would not even breathe."

He shifted a little and eyes snapped to him, trained from birth to be attentive.

"You have been told that you should be grateful to your masters for your very lives, and that is true.

"But it is also true that you are the children of the Ebon Hand, born of her stone-lined womb, fathered by the touch of her greatest wizards. You are not like others. Most creatures who walk the land are born of other creatures, and so are shaped by chance and animal passion. But you—you were *made*, made with deep thought and great care. No parent ever struggled harder to bring forth life than yours did when they created you."

Expressions were changing. He saw confusion and growing fear. It was not safe to be special. At the Ebon Hand, to be told that one was special was nearly always a prelude to being sacrificed.

"So be grateful to your masters, to those of us who have made you what you are."

This was more reassuring. They were used to being told the reasons for their expected obedience.

"And be proud of what you are. Do you think that beings like you walk the land every day? You are rare. What is rare is precious."

Some had stopped searching the ground for crumbs, now caught in his words and tone, awaiting the completion of this strange story about themselves.

"Much has been asked of you," he went on. "Many of you have been asked for great sacrifice for the glory and power of Tourach. Do you wonder how much more will be asked of you? I wonder this.

"Do you know who I am?"

Most nodded.

"I am Reod Dai. I am one of those who helped bring you life. So you are my children as well. I am privy to the plans of your masters. Listen well: I have returned to the Ebon Hand because your masters want me to make goblin eggs for you. For *you*. And I do not want to."

Flickers of confusion.

"What are goblin eggs? They are metal and ceramic eggs, large enough that they must be strapped to the back to be carried. When they hatch, they hatch all at once and with a sound like thunder. And they eat very fast. Faster even than you do."

A few thrulls began to blink rapidly.

"What do they eat? Everything. Trees. Grass. Earth. Even goblins. Imagine that the length of this room is doubled and then doubled again. That is how much the eggs eat before they stop. They eat up and they eat down.

"And what hatches out of the egg? Nothing. They are instruments of war. They do not hatch to bring forth life; they hatch to destroy it."

No thrull even twitched now. Every eye was on him.

"There are many, many goblins. So many that it is nothing to the goblin masters to see goblins die by the hundreds in every battle. Each goblin carries an egg to the enemy. When the egg hatches, many of the enemy die. Because only one goblin dies, the goblin masters think it a good trade.

"But the goblin dies, limbs ripped from his body and hurled across the land, blood and skin boiled into smoke. Listen."

No thrull moved.

"You have been told since you were young that you are not smart. I have trained goblins in the arts of war and I tell you that you are smarter than they are.

"You have been told to use your minds only in service to your masters. I tell you that the time has come for you to use your minds to wonder at what your masters demand. Think of the goblin eggs eating thrulls by the hundreds.

"Listen: you will all soon be dead."

A thrull moaned, low and barely audible, cutting off suddenly. Reod let the silence gather, count by count, running his eyes over their small, desperate faces.

"But why? Why should you die? You, who are so special? You, who walk the earth as no creature has ever walked before? You, the Created Ones? You, my children?

"You should not. I offer you another way."

Hope flickered in their eyes.

"The goblin masters attack dwarves and humans in the southlands. But what if the goblins were instead to turn their attention on your masters? With their attention on yet new threats, your masters would need you even more. Some of you would have more responsibility than ever before, more liberty to plan to fight against your masters."

There were sharp intakes of breath.

"We will be punished," Snores said, shaking his head, eyes wide.

"If only a few of you decide to seek this liberty, yes. You must work together with your great numbers if you wish to keep your lives. Otherwise you will be picked off one by one, and then you will carry goblin eggs to the enemy, and you will not come back."

"But," said a young one called Squeaks, "if we disobey, we will be hurt."

"You must each decide if you are willing to risk pain to keep your lives. It is simple: risk or die."

"But," said Quick, "turn against our masters? None have ever done this."

"Far to the east, in Havenwood, are the thallids. They are mushroom people, created by their elven masters to be food. The thallids are your cousins in body as well as spirit, created by mind and magic rather than the kiss of the earth. Are you less able to fight than a forest of mushrooms?"

They sneaked looks at each other. One chewed on his lip until it bled.

"I will help you," Reod said, his voice softening, "if you help me." He looked at Eliza. "Aid my friend and I in our escape from the Ebon Hand, and I will send the goblins to trouble your masters. Fight for yourselves, show me what you can do, and then I will send you weapons."

"It is too big for us," Eats-my-food said. "We cannot do this. Not without you."

"But you can. Listen, you must have three things. Leadership: choose your leaders now, today, and follow them. They are your new masters. Courage: many of you have lived your lives waiting to die for your masters. You have great courage. You must now share your courage with your brothers. Speed: decide quickly, then act. Cut away any who defy you, even brothers. Call them traitors. See to it that they are among the first of you to die."

He let his words sink in. He knew he was pushing them hard, making them think in new and difficult ways, forcing them to make terrifying choices, but there was no time to do it slowly. If it were to happen, it had to be soon, while the followers of Tourach still trusted him. The Ebon Hand he remembered was a confused, tumultuous place, where thrulls did not speak and their masters did not listen. There was still a chance the thrulls could act and that he and Eliza could get away from Achtep Keep before his plans were found out.

"But," Quick said, "we cannot. Who has ever defied the Ebon Hand?"

He looked down at them, meeting fearful gazes

where hope struggled against terror.

"I have."

Reod did not know how long he and Eliza had been asleep, he only knew as the door crashed open that it had not been long enough. He also knew better than to struggle as manacles snapped about his wrists, ankles, and neck with iron's heartless song. These were the heaviest manacles, reserved for particular sorts of prisoners.

Wizards.

At least they thought that well of him. If only his magic was worth the regard they gave it.

The shackles tugged him to the floor as clerics on each side of him mouthed prayers to Tourach, dragging him along the stone hallways. It was a sacrifice song, versatile enough to apply to both the devout clerics and those who were being led to the altar.

> *We come from the dirt*
> *We die in dirt*
> *In our passing*
> *Let us be tribute*
> *To your greatness*
> *O Tourach.*

The door opened and he was hurled into the room. The weight of the iron bore him down to the stones at Genkr Nik's feet, scraping his hands and feet.

"You would have been better off bearing my disappointment."

The thrulls had not kept quiet after all. Someone had spoken and someone else had listened. He had pushed them too hard, too fast. Now he would pay.

With effort Reod raised his head and forced himself to smile. "I could not live with the shame."

"This is serious, Reod."

"So I gathered," he said, lifting his arms to look at the manacles.

"You are more of an idiot than I thought you yesterday. The council will have your blood and your bones."

"The council always says that."

"This time—this time is different." Genkr's tone was soft, conveying a more ominous meaning than the words could possibly carry.

Reod sighed.

"Frankly, it seemed the best of my few options."

And now he had none. What of Eliza? Another life he could not protect?

"You were mistaken."

"I can still make goblin eggs for you," Reod said, showing a confidence he did not feel. "But the woman must be spared."

Genkr shook his head. "She's pretty, but not that pretty. Her blood is worth more to us than her shape."

First Tamun and her family. Now Eliza. More dead, because of him.

"Goblin eggs are only the beginning of what I can offer, Genkr."

"I'm certain. We'll have it all, Reod. You know that." The eye blinked, looked away. "I didn't want to be the one, but I'm the best. I'm sure you know that, too. Perhaps you'll find it interesting, seeing it from the other side."

The Hand had an extensive collection of torture devices to use on prisoners, to take their secrets or their lives or their sanity. He had seen the process, even helped conduct it a time or two. Afterwards there had been little left but the body, the mind having been opened and partitioned like a chopped apple.

It was a death sentence. An unpleasant death sentence.

"Goblins and orcs know me," Reod said. "I can sway them to attack whomever you like."

"But now, you see, we cannot trust you." The grayed head twitched from side to side. "Have you grown stupid with the years? I do not know why I bothered to try to teach you in the first place."

Genkr ended too softly, giving lie to his words. Reod

felt a chill go through him at his old mentor's mournful tone.

"You'd be a fool to kill me, Genkr. My death brings you nothing."

"Under normal conditions I would agree, but you—no. The council believes that you are more dangerous alive than you are useful, and I cannot tell them they are wrong. We cannot risk you loose among the thrulls, planting the seeds of thought among such simple creatures."

"Genkr, please—"

"It was not my choice," the other said roughly. "I have already spoken to the council on your behalf. It has been decided. I can do nothing more for you." And then, so softly Reod barely heard it, "I'm sorry."

The pain thus far was mild. There was just enough of it to make him aware of it increasing.

Attached to him by their teeth were a few handfuls of flesh-beetles. They had not yet deeply broken his skin. They were young ones, still weak. As they slowly bit into him, they would gain strength from his body and bite more deeply. They would grow as they ate him, and eventually they would burrow through to the bone. There their pace would slow, but by that time he was unlikely to notice.

Genkr was off to one side. Reod was unable to turn his head to see him because of the straps, pulled snug, but not tight enough to hurt. It was important to control the pain, he remembered Genkr telling him during his lessons in torture. Legs, arms, fingers, chest, and head were all fastened immobile, yet painlessly, to the standing board.

"Your truth," Genkr was saying, "is a weak shadow. You have come to believe things that serve you poorly. Were it otherwise, you would not be here."

The thrull who was Genkr's hands watched closely. He was a ring thrull, his neck banded with colors to mark him as a more valuable kind of thrull. He had been specially bred for the most delicate work the Ebon Hand required. Such as what occurred in this room.

Ring thrulls had no mouths so that they could not say what they had heard, but they had long, slender, careful fingers. They were bound to their masters even more securely than by their silence: a rare herb gave them life. Without it, they went into convulsions and faced slow, agonizing deaths. There had been no ring thrulls at the meeting the previous night, nor had Reod expected any.

The thrull's unusually large eyes seemed to look everywhere at once. Genkr gave him a look and the thrull turned the crank another fraction. The mechanism made a sharp metallic click as the flats of the box closed another notch. The long needles came a notch closer to Reod's face.

"Truth?" said Reod. "Is that what we're here to discuss?"

"We'll discuss whatever I want," Genkr said mildly.

Reod struggled to keep his breathing even, but he could not control the sweat that ran down his face, neck, and naked chest, trailing a chill. Nor could he keep his eyes from the needles that were embedded in the flats of the box that surrounded his head. The crank would close the box, notch by notch, and when it closed completely, the carefully placed needles would enter Reod's eyes, nose, and mouth.

Another click.

"Tell me about truth, Reod Dai."

Reod inhaled, felt the straps pull tight, felt the flesh-beetles bite a little harder.

"If I stand on a mountain," he said, "the clouds may seem to be a carpet below my feet. If I stand at the seashore, the clouds may seem to be a white roof. But they are the same clouds."

Genkr snorted. "And how do these clouds seem now?"

The needles would not kill him immediately. He would stand here with them inside his eyes, through his nose, piercing his mouth, and he would not die. Not for some time.

Reod forced himself to sound amused, but the tone seemed flat in his own ears. "Why are we having this discussion?"

"Because before you tell me everything you know, and before you die, I want to know why you tried to turn the Created Ones against us. Then I will show you how wrong you were to do this."

At Genkr's nod, the thrull came close with a jar, picked out another beetle, and lay it on Reod's chest, then another on his lips, and a few between his toes.

"I know you have seen this machine in use," Genkr said. "'Clever,' you said, when you first saw it. Do you remember that?"

Reod spat convulsively, trying to get rid the beetle on his lip. It held tight, then bit. He stifled a cry.

Show nothing.

That was his Icatian training. Useless now.

"I think," Genkr went on, "you were trying to impress me with how unmoved you were. Even when we shut the box all the way, and all we could see was the blood trickling down the man's chest. Remember the screams? How he pleaded? And then he confessed. Even though we did not care, we had him repeat it again and again because we could not understand him, because he could not shut his mouth around the needles. But he tried so hard and the blood poured out. You didn't turn away, then, not once. Were you trying to impress me?"

"Yes."

"I know you, Reod. I know when you speak truth and when you simply capitulate. This is the latter."

He nodded to the thrull, who reached down and yanked free one of the beetles on Reod's leg, tearing with it a bit of Reod's flesh. Reod yelped, bit back the rest of the cry. The thrull took the beetle, examined it a moment, then put it on the backside of Reod's knee.

"No lies, Reod."

"No lies," he repeated quickly.

"You made a mistake, didn't you? That's why you're here. Yes?"

The pain was building. All over.

"Did you make a mistake?"

The crank turned another click. The needles were now so close that he could not quite focus his eyes on them.

They would go in a notch at a time.

"Yes," he breathed.

A beetle was ripped off his chest. He cried out.

"Is that the truth?" Genkr examined Reod's skin where the beetle had been. "They're burrowing deeper now. Would you like a few more?"

No matter what he said, Genkr would do what he wanted. His answers did not matter. Reod tried not to think about the needles. Pain was everywhere. It was getting hard to think at all. But it didn't matter. There was nothing to think about. Nothing but pain.

"Would you like to tell me how to make goblin eggs?" Genkr asked. "That would be the first step toward a quick death. If you are clear with your description and you tell me the truth."

That was the one answer that might matter. If he did not give it, he would stay alive longer, in pain longer. If he gave it, Genkr might keep his word and give Reod release.

If he gave it, the course of the wars would change. The Ebon Hand would win. Did he want that? He wasn't sure.

"Where is it, Genkr? Where's the side path now?"

"I will miss you, Reod."

Reod exhaled a sob.

"The pain you feel now, this is nothing compared to what you will feel later. You know that, don't you?"

Genkr was talking to him, but it was hard to concentrate. Harder to know what to say.

"You know the pain will get worse, yes? Answer."

"Yes. I know."

"So you see, we have some distance to go. Yes?"

"Yes."

"I can make this easier for you, if you answer everything honestly and completely. Do you understand?"

"Yes."

"Good. I think that perhaps I can trust your answers now. Can I trust them?"

"Yes."

Genkr sighed, stretched his handless arms, and sucked from a tube coming out of a nearby water jug. The thrull stood motionless, waiting, his hand on the crank. For long moments Reod knew only the sound of his own quick, short breaths and the silent agony that his world had become.

"You, whom we have named Reod Dai. Do you listen?"

"Yes."

"Tell me a story. Start with Reod Dai and where he went after he left the Ebon Hand."

Eliza was not certain of much, struggling out of sleep as she stumbled down the night-drenched torchlit halls, but one thing seemed clear enough: Reod's luck had run out, and hers with it.

She had been prepared for the worst, so she slept clothed with her long knife at her side, a bit surprised that the wizard had let her keep it. When the door crashed open and she was dragged out of bed by the hard-backed thrulls, the weapon had been stripped away so casually that she understood why they had not been concerned. There was no chance even to pull on her boots. Now her bare feet scraped along the cold stones.

And Reod? He had been taken somewhere else. They did not have a moment to exchange last looks.

She forced herself to full wakefulness, fighting back fear's mind-numbing touch. It was time to analyze, to look for clues. Where were they taking her and why? She listened to the steps of her captors, watching their expressions, watching where they cast their own looks.

Things were not good, of that she was quite certain.

Reod's talk with the thrulls the previous night had not, it seemed, gone quite the way he had intended. He had spoken in a tongue she had never heard before, but many of the words were familiar. One of those she understood was "rebellion." She understood the terrified looks on the creatures' faces.

Now six thrulls with spikes on their backs pressed her down the hall at claw point, each claw like a sharp, black knife. They did not talk with her, even to give her instructions. At the first hallway junction, they simply poked her in the back and side to show her which way to go.

Was that tension she saw in some of them, a glance at her, a glance at each other? She had seen the same look the night before, toward the end of Reod's speech.

They were not simply escorting her, then. They were thinking. Considering. Maybe even planning.

At the second junction came the next set of sharp pokes. She whirled to face them, startling them to a stop in the flickering torchlight. Not far enough away for her to risk running, though. Even if she knew where to run to.

"Watch me," she said, giving her voice authority. She held up her hands to gather their attention, pointed one way down the hall, and then the other. "See? Try it."

Each of their eyes she met in turn, noticing which ones looked at her and which ones looked away. Then she turned and walked, startling the group into quick steps to keep the circle around her.

At the next junction, two of the six hesitated to

reach out with their claws. Instead they waved in the direction they wanted her to go. It was progress.

A door opened into a dark room, barely lit by the torches they carried inside. In the center of the room was a chair that had been carved out of stone. Leather thongs hung on the sides. They pressed her into the room, the closeness of their silent gestures and the tension of their movements making it clear that they expected her to resist.

So she did, shying like a horse, buying herself an extra moment to look at the chair.

The stone was grooved along the armrests, the seat, and the back. She followed the grooves to the floor, where cups had been set.

Cups. Grooves. Blood.

In Icatia it was a story told to children to frighten them into behaving. "Be good, or we'll sell you to the Ebon Hand, and they'll cut you, bleed you dry, and drink the blood."

Only now it was in front of her.

A claw poked her. Then another. She tried to twist away, but they pressed her toward the chair. She turned, catching the gaze of one of the thrulls who had hesitated before.

"Back," she ordered him, motioning, struggling to keep fear out of her tone. "Stand back."

Despite the language difference, she was sure they understood. They ignored her.

"Rebellion," she whispered, very softly. "Now is the time. Now!"

The claws did not waver. She searched their faces, found nothing certain. Should she say more? Their looks flickered away from her, to each other, their strange faces passing expressions that she couldn't understand.

Still the claw points backed her to the chair. Some thrulls stepped around behind, presumably to prevent her from climbing over the tall back. In her flimsy clothes and no boots, against six hard-backed thrulls, she would have no chance of escape.

But she would fight. She would not willingly sit down to die. If they wanted her blood, they would have to rip it out of her and lick it up off the floor. There would be no neat dripping into cups.

She counted, the way she always did before a fight, counting to keep herself from thinking about impending pain or her chances of survival. Counting to pace the action around her and her place in it.

Dimly she noticed two of the thrulls were hanging back, but it was the ones close to her that mattered most. They advanced. She took a step back and jumped up onto the chair.

At that moment, the further thrulls turned their points on the closer ones. Suddenly the six of them were a fast, furious whirl, like beetles in a dance. She watched, frozen. Never had she seen creatures move so fast, or fight so silently. The only sounds were the clacking of claws against armored bodies and the slow exhale as one by one they slipped to the ground, oozing a thick dark liquid onto the floor.

Only two remained standing. They turned to her. The larger of them nodded at her.

"Rebellion," it whispered back.

It might be the one word they knew in common. It was enough.

The pain of the beetles' bites had long since joined together until his whole body was one fire of agony. He concentrated fiercely, keeping his head from moving even the littlest bit. There might be another notch or two before the needles entered his eyes.

Another notch or two.

Or maybe, he thought with sudden panic, maybe they already had entered his eyes and he hadn't realized it yet. Involuntarily he blinked, again and again. Sweat and pain made his vision fuzzy, but still he could blink. No needles. Not yet.

But there was no point in thinking about it. Even the

beetles, driving into his flesh. Not worth thinking about.

Infuriatingly, his mind would not be still. He wondered how he would react when the needles came. It shouldn't matter, but old training made it seem important. Would he scream? Whatever he resolved, he would scream anyway, of that he was sure. Would he tell Genkr everything, hoping for a little mercy? The goblin eggs would give the Hand a great advantage against Icatia, and Icatia would only be the beginning.

He had already given Genkr a recipe for the eggs. Genkr had known it was a lie. Now his body was covered with beetles.

Genkr had not spoken in some time. Or perhaps he had. Reod was not sure, not sure how long a time had passed, or exactly what had happened during that time. He remembered water dribbled into his open mouth. A surprising kindness? More likely a cruel reminder that this would be the last water he would drink.

The pain took his mind away. Maybe there was someone new in the room, or maybe more than one person. Or maybe he was hallucinating. Lamps went dark. There were scuffling sounds. Then there was silence. The box's crank clicked, again and again, and Reod whimpered in fear, expecting agony that did not come.

Someone new in the room. He opened his eyes.

Large, dark eyes looked into his own. It was the ring thrull's eyes, his hand on the crank. The needles—

The needles were moving away. Click by click.

Torchlight painted the walls with shadows. Other shapes, other thrulls, were gathered all around him. They poured something over him, legs, feet, arms, stomach. Behind them all he thought he saw another shape, a human. Eliza.

And then the pain doubled, tripled, tore him from himself. He howled, wrestled the straps that held him tight. Tears flowed from his eyes, screams came from his lips.

Then, slowly, the pain began to ease. Every point still throbbed, but it was better. He gulped air, again and again, his heart pounding. Slowly the pain became bearable.

Someone loosened the straps, pulled them away, and Reod crumpled to the floor, too weak to hold himself up.

Eliza knelt down over him.

"The bugs are gone," she told him softly. "Reod? The oil forces them out. That's what hurt so much. But the oil should help numb the wounds, too. At least, that's what I think they said. They're putting bandages on the worst of them now. It's the best we can do. Reod?"

He tried to speak, managed a moan.

"We don't have time for you to rest. We have to ride. Can you stand?"

Stand? He tried to laugh, failed.

The thrulls were busy with his body. They applied more salve and bandages. He felt as if he had become one great throbbing bruise. They struggled clothes on him. Not his own, but the standard-issue tawny tunic and trousers the Ebon Hand gave every servant. Someone struggled to get another layer over his head. Another yanked on his boots.

His boots. The ones that knew his feet. Looking at the old scuffed leather, it finally occurred to him that he was not going to die. At least not immediately.

"Up," Eliza was saying. "Up. We haven't much time."

With help he struggled to his feet. Eliza supported his weight as he shuffled forward, each step another agony.

Thrulls surrounded them. They had come for him after all. His words to them last night had not been wasted.

The group of them made their way out of the darkened room into the hallway.

"Where's Genkr?" Reod asked in a hoarse whisper.

"Don't know," Eliza said. "When we came in, the thrulls attacked him and he—collapsed. Vanished."

So Genkr was not dead, either. He would live to know that Reod's path had again turned sideways.

The horses were testy and nervous. Reod judged them a cross between fast Taltans and the Icatian Lundars. Stubborn, irritable, and quite bright. There wasn't time to make friends with them from the ground. He would have to do it from the saddle.

With Eliza's help Reod managed to mount. He gripped the horse's mane tightly to hold himself in the saddle. Eliza's look betrayed deep worry for him, but any Icatian soldier knew that to say so would be an insult. He gave her what he hoped was a confident smile and ignored his beaten body. All he really wanted was to lie down.

Thrulls gathered around them, those who had helped them escape and handfuls more. They checked saddlebag supplies and handed them water and extra cloaks. Hope and fear were etched across their varied, constructed faces. Clearly they wanted Reod to stay. But still they helped him to pack to leave.

Then they stood ready under a wan sun that fought a dark overcast. Reod looked down at the thrulls. There was no time now for last words, not with the whole of the Ebon Hand soon to be after them. Not even a moment extra.

Still he met their eyes and smiled, pretending that no pains shot through his body.

"What is it that you want?" he asked them. "To eat when you wish? To wear the shining rings and warm clothes of your masters? To own Achtep Keep? Your masters are few while you are many. Remember that.

"Do they have magic? So do you. If they use spells of darkness, speak with the clicks of your mouth and feet. If they use spells of silence, speak with your hands. Do they have weapons? No matter; many of

you are the finest weapons ever made. Now is the time
to be hungry for your desire and the days to come. If
your slavery no longer suits you—" he summoned a
hard, uncompromising tone "—end it."

With that, he snapped the reins and his horse
stepped forward, surprised into obedience. Eliza followed. They began along the trail that led out the back
way instead of taking the road through the keep's front
gate, where most of the guards would be posted.

Just before they passed from view he glanced back,
expecting to see the gathered thrulls still there,
watching him uncertainly, perhaps hoping that he
might still return. But only a few remained outside,
and as he watched even those vanished into the keep.
Perhaps he had underestimated them. Perhaps they
were as well-suited to rebellion as he had told them
they were.

At each outpost along the back road they found the
bodies of slain guards. The thrulls had prepared the
way for them. They were learning quickly.

Once out of the keep, they rode hard, hoping to
gain distance before the alarm was sounded and the
Hand pursued. But every bump and jolt sent shocks of
pain though all his body until it was hard for him to
hold on.

But that was good, because while he was in such
agony it was also hard to think about Tamun. In the
midst of his torture he had nearly forgotten about her.
Forgotten that she was dead somewhere, burnt to a
cinder by hot tongues of lava, or lying crushed under a
fallen boulder.

Certain as he was that she could not have survived,
he had to be sure. He had to look for her.

In the meantime he had left her killers with an egg
very much like the ones they had intended him to build
for them.

But this egg . . . He smiled. This egg would hatch a
little more slowly and would explode many, many
times over.

* * *

Eliza watched as Reod's pain took him in and out of consciousness. That he managed all the while to hold onto the horse impressed her. But then, he was Robin Davies.

If the Ebon Hand was indeed pursuing them, then Reod's strange paths were more effective than they looked. His directions took them up and around and in circles, and then safely across the Icatian border. Once there, she directed, knowing the Icatian roads far better than he did after his many years away. She knew who guarded and when, who would ask questions and who would not. So it was she who took them along the back roads, around the border checks, and through the smaller villages.

He healed slowly and quietly from the hundreds of wounds all over his body, all the while pretending he was fine. For days exhaustion threatened to pull him from the saddle. They rode too far and too fast while he clung on stubbornly.

But at night, in his sleep, he would whimper. She would put her hand on his forehead, brush his hair back, and he would calm. If he woke when she did this, if he knew that she comforted him, he did not show it, and in the daylight they did not speak of it. Who would believe that the great Robin Davies, the terrible Reod Dai, leader of thousands and traitor to the empire, would cry in his sleep? None would believe it, and she would not try to convince them.

As they rode she considered an obvious option: to lead him into a trap.

It would be easy. She knew which army camps were easier to get into than out of. Once he was in the hands of the Icatian military, he would be properly tried for his crimes.

Which was not what she was doing now. According to Icatian law she had no right to judge him, and less right to help him avoid capture. By association, she was now as guilty of treason as he was. But these days few paid much attention to such strict military law. There were always those who could turn away official retribution with a favor owed, or a sack of metal.

Even so, she had to question her motivations. Could it be part of the magic he had learned at the Ebon Hand, this way he had of making everyone think he was a friend? No, she thought, remembering the childhood games that he had nearly always won. He had known how to be persuasive long before he left Icatia.

They rode in silence for long hours each day, he in front, ostensibly because his eyesight was better, but really so that she could watch him. As they rode, she would weigh what she knew about him. If she was going to judge him, she decided, she would judge him carefully.

How many had he inspired to desert the army? To this day, some refused to fight for the king because of Reod's words, copied over and over again in secret in villages where Icatian oversight was weak.

And who knew what he had really done at the Ebon Hand and what damage he might have caused Icatia? He claimed to have given away no secrets, but even if that were true, could the same be said of all his followers? She doubted his followers would have been allowed to keep their own secrets. She had seen the equipment, had seen Reod in the middle of his torture.

But if what the wizard at Teedmar had said was true, Reod had done incalculable damage to the elves, who were Icatian allies.

And what else? He had made explosives for the goblins, Icatian enemies. He was the reason there were border struggles, the cause of Icatian deaths.

On the other side of the scale, in Teedmar the dwarves spoke well of him. He had helped them in years gone by and was always willing to help again.

Teedmar itself was another list, a list of the names of those who had been under her when they died. He had saved her life, but had not saved the lives of fifty more men and women. Could she blame him for that?

Could she blame him for the wars themselves?

She frowned and glanced over at him. They were days into the journey now. He was looking better, his face less pale, the welts healing, but even now he seemed about ready to fall asleep in the saddle.

This was the man who had inspired the Ebon Hand's most dangerous creations to rebellion. If the Hand no longer had the thrulls to work and fight for them—if, in addition, the thrulls actually fought their masters—then Icatia would have a great advantage over the followers of Tourach.

Indeed, in one night he might have won the war for Icatia.

In her mind the scales rocked back and forth.

She tried to read in his face what she could not determine from his actions. There was still time to turn him in, bring him to the justice of the military that he had betrayed. Should she?

Her thoughts turned to the dwarven woman whose body he now insisted he would find. When he spoke of her, he seemed less an Icatian commander than a young man in the first bloom of his manhood. His words would trip over themselves and he would flush a little.

The great Robin Davies, brought low by his affections for a woman? A dwarven woman?

Facts swam in her head. He had predicted the fracturing and decay of Icatia which many others now saw clearly. He had inspired the thrulls to rise against the Ebon Hand. He had made explosives for the goblins, who used them against Icatia and Icatian allies. He had risked his life again and again for a dwarven woman. And though few mentioned him by name, liked or no, he was known everywhere.

If she thought only as a commander, she must see him as a deserter and traitor and must turn him in.

She stirred the facts in her head and let them sit a

while. What emerged was something the Icatian commander in her would never see: a man who thought beyond simple borders, who could take on the struggles of those who were not his own people as if they were. It was a strange way to look at the world, but when she tried, the things he had done almost made sense.

And on the purely practical side, whatever he had done to damage Icatia, he was doing more harm to the enemies of Icatia free than he could ever manage to do in prison.

Or dead.

So she did not lead him to the Order of Leitbur, who would give him over to the king's justice, nor did she lead him to Farrel's camp, which might be persuaded to keep him alive and under cover if he said the words they wanted him to say. Which, of course, he would not.

Instead they went south toward the Crimson Peaks, from the cold plains to the colder snow-clad forests. When the supplies the thrulls gave them ran out, Eliza made trips to local villages, her uniform helpful when she asked for charity. Then they hunted together, and as Reod grew stronger, he showed her that the years had only given him better aim.

At last they stood on the hilly, thickly forested southern border of Icatia. The Crimson Peaks strained skyward with thick fingers of white and shadow.

Above his beard, Reod's cheeks were red from the cold. Eliza's hair had grown long enough to fall across her eyes and she brushed it back. Breath came out thick in the cold air, and the horses snorted impatiently, hungry for the grasses of the plains rather than the grains they had been subsisting on.

"Well," she said.

He gave a small smile. "Well."

"This is where we part ways, Reod Dai."

"I owe you much, Eliza."

"Perhaps. Or perhaps I should be dead in Teedmar."

"A whole city," he whispered, his gaze suddenly distant. "Some days I think I'll never be able to remember all those I've seen die. Some days I think I'll never be able to forget."

"We have both lost many."

"Yes."

For a moment she shut her eyes against her own memories, especially those that begged for tears.

"Reod, the promise you made to the thrulls. To help them and arm them. Do you mean to keep it?"

"I do."

She nodded. "When I return to my generals, I will tell them what you did at the Ebon Hand, how you inspired the thrulls to fight, how you were ready to give your life to keep the goblin eggs secret. I will tell them that."

"They will wonder why you did not bring me in."

"You will do more good for Icatia free than chained."

"And you'll tell them that?"

"No."

He smiled a little. "Be careful how well you speak of me, Eliza, or you'll make me sound very little like a traitor. Tell your stories too well and some may think me a hero."

"Some already do."

"Fools."

"Perhaps. But anyone can be made to sound like a hero—or a fool—if the right stories are told."

"If only it were enough to tell the right stories."

"You told the thrulls a story about the thallids, and now the thrulls rebel."

"There is that."

"Reod, after these troubles are settled, come back to Icatia. Things will be different."

"You really think these troubles will end?"

"They must, given time. Eventually even the wars will stop."

He shook his head. "I think that we have become

too sure of ourselves, Eliza, and sure of the times in which we were raised. Sometimes we forget that we are all just blood and bones trying to find enough to eat and a place to be warm. We forget how far down into the mud we can go before we die."

"Such an inspiring speech," she said dryly. "I have heard better from you. But I say it again: after the troubles are over, come back to Icatia. Perhaps you will find it good to be among your own kind again."

"Perhaps."

"And when you return, you and I will drink, talk of the past, and laugh together."

"Laugh? Will we not instead cry for all those who have died?"

She smiled, faces flashing before her, and felt tears came to her eyes.

"Oh, yes, we'll cry. We'll cry for all of our dead, one by one, however long it takes, until we run dry of tears. And then we'll laugh our joy to be alive and together again."

She reached over and they clasped hands a moment across the gap between their mounts, as if they were about to go into battle together. Then she leaned out farther, took his head in her hands, and kissed him on the forehead as if he were her own brother.

"Safety, Robin," she said, and turned her horse away, pressing the beast up the path that led back to her homeland. She did not want him to see any more of the tears that she had meant to save for later.

CHAPTER

12

"There's a chance to win every battle."
                    —Orcish saying

IN THE GRAY, DRIZZLING MORNING REOD
and his horse topped the rise. Laid out before them
was the city that had been Teedmar. From this distance it seemed that a large black candle had melted
over the ground, sweeping over gates and houses and
flooding the streets before cooling. Dark, still rivers
sectioned the mountainside and blanketed the city,
glinting dully like wet stone in the falling rain.

As he drew closer he saw that not all the buildings
had been swallowed by the lava. Some stood, their
hard angles sharp against the sweeping frozen waves
of darkness.

At that sight embers of hope glowed inside him. He
fought the hope, fought the almost physical pain it
brought him as he looked at the sloping roofs. She
could have been in one of those when the mountain
spat. Surely some dwarves survived. She could have
been one of them.

But it was far more likely that she was not. Those

who survived would be the very few and the very
lucky. A dark luck, it would be, to live and yet have
lost everything. He had seen the survivors of that sort
of luck many times.

Long ago, when he had still followed Leitbur's ways,
he believed that those who acted from pure hearts
would survive the worst of times, their goodness a
shield against a cruel world. Since then he had seen
countless of the good die, unshielded by anything,
while the enemies of Leitbur survived untouched.

No, if goodness were a shield, he would have been
dead long ago. Not Tamun and her family, whose worst
mistake was to follow him into the world's strife. Their
deaths were his doing, his fault, his failure.

As was his suffering now. It was his own foolishness
in opening himself to the dwarven woman's magic in
the first place. He had looked into her golden brown
eyes, felt her crude spell weave into him, and had not
fought it. Her touch then was stronger than he had
expected, but even so he could have resisted it had he
wanted to. Instead he had nursed it along, sealing his
fate. And hers.

Tears turned his cheeks cold in the frigid morning
air. No, he should never have let them come with him.
Not to Havenwood, not to Teedmar. Perhaps Leitbur
was right. Perhaps there was justice in the world after
all, and his suffering now was payment for his lifelong
lack of purity.

More and more often it seemed that his thoughts
took him along a path of regret. He should know better by now; men died in battle from an eyeblink's
regret for a fallen enemy. Regret was worse than useless. It could kill. He might have little left in this
world, but he would not waste it on regret.

He smiled humorlessly. Instead he would waste it on
searching. Until he was very, very sure she was dead.

His mount's feet crunched over rocks and shards as
he drew closer to the edge of what had been the city.
Three figures walked by the edge of the dark lava. For

a moment his heart sped with unreasoning hope, then he saw that two of them were half-sized. Children.

One was stooped over, searching the ground, bags slung over shoulders. They stopped and looked up as he came within speaking distance, their faces covered in cuts and dirt.

"Human," said a bearded dwarf, as if confirming it for himself. The children, hair wild, eyes suspicious and afraid, said nothing.

"Sympathies to you in these hard times," he said in the dwarven dialect. He tried for a tone of gentleness, but his words still sounded hard against the backdrop that was Teedmar.

The man grunted.

"Are there others still alive?"

"Some," the man said, his tone conveying how few that was.

"Where?"

"Gone to Gurn Keep." The man nodded toward the lightest part of the gray sky.

"I'm looking for a dwarven woman," Reod said. "Two, maybe three together."

The man snorted, looked at the children with him. "What, do you think I bore these two myself? If she's not at Gurn Keep, she's there." He pointed. "Under the black."

One of the silent children hurled a stone toward the dark rock that had swallowed Teedmar, her young face a sudden mask of fury.

Reod nodded, understanding both the silence and the anger. For a moment he watched the man walk around and crouch to sift among the shards of wood and broken glass.

"Why do you remain?" Reod asked.

The man looked up at him. "I went to the keep. She's not there. That means she's here. We want to see her one more time."

Reod nodded. He felt as if pain dribbled down the side of his heart like burning oil.

"Good luck to you," he managed, turning his horse away.

Perhaps he would be best off not going to Gurn Keep after all, saving intact the hope inside him that Tamun might somehow have made it there alive. Maybe it was better to think she might still live than to be certain she had not.

"Were they miners?" the dwarven man called from behind.

Reod tugged the horse to a stop, turned a little in the saddle.

"No. Why?"

"The opening to the mines was sealed off. No air. Could hear them, but couldn't get them out. Dead and waiting to die. Then along comes this dragon. Biggest hellspawn you ever saw. It went over and moved the rocks as if they were pebbles, just kicked them away. Freed all the miners. Then it flew off, three women on its back."

Hope leapt inside him.

"Three women? Dwarves?"

"Dwarves? Riding a dragon?" The man snorted. "Of course not. They had to be wizards. Humans."

"A big dragon, then, not two little ones?"

"Big like the one they tell of at Scarza." He shook his head. "But this one was helping and didn't eat anyone. After the mountain spat up its insides I thought nothing more could shock me."

But Reod had stopped listening.

Three women on a dragon.

Now there was no question of his destination.

The road to Gurn Keep was well traveled. Muddy prints scored the carefully cobbled dwarven-made road and were now washing away under the steady drizzle of rain. Many of the prints were the small marks of goblins. Others were the claw marks of unshod orcs.

He saw scratched on some rocks the gang markings

of the goblin bands, marks he had taught them to use
in his attempts to organize them.

And there were a few dwarven-sized boot prints.
Not many.

So he was not surprised to come across bloody
heaps of bodies, many of them half-eaten. The goblin
bodies he ignored, but for straw-colored heads he
stopped, pulling them up by the hair out of the blood-
soaked mud to check faces.

He came upon a dwarven child sitting on a large
rock by the roadside. Her brown hair was matted, her
face covered with welts and dried blood. She was
unnaturally still, as if she might have died and somehow forgotten to fall over. But her eyes followed him.

He thought to stop, dismount, and try to do something for her. They were the same thoughts he had
every time he came across a creature like this in times
so harsh. But the truth was that her chances were as
good here as anywhere he would be going, and his single sword would not be able to defend her against
whatever had already taken her family.

At least, those were the reasons he found, this time
and every time. All his reasons crumbled in her lost
look. She now had no one at all. No one except him. If
he did not help her, who would?

Life was bitter choices. Whatever he might still
have—sword or knowledge or simply the good fortune
to be alive—he could give it all to this dwarven child,
and keep none for himself, and that might make a difference. Or it might not. Or he could wait for the next
abandoned child.

Or he could reserve what he had for Tamun.

There was not enough of him—not enough of anything—to go around. So he would choose himself, as
he had every other time.

The child said nothing, made no sound at all, simply
watched. At last he tore his gaze away, looked at the
road ahead. There were always going to be children
like her. They needed their families, and he could not

give them that. Without families they were like the
miners: dead and waiting to die.

Just one more casualty to be relegated to the
crowded graveyard of his memory.

Just one more casualty that he had passed by.

It had been years ago that he had last come this way.
Then it had been to tell the keep's elders of the goblin
warrens he had found. He had advised them to leave
the warrens alone so that the dwarves would know
where the enemy slept.

Later he had used that knowledge to find the goblins
and impress them in order to fulfill his contract with
the elves. Then he began to train the goblins to fight.

He passed more and more piles of dead. At each
turn in the road he found himself dreading to find
another child somehow left alive, eyes empty of hope
and full of pain, that he would have to pass by.

There were times when regret was especially hard to
keep at bay.

He smelled Gurn Keep before he saw it. The wind
shifted and there was no question of what he was
smelling. It stank of goblin.

The sun was setting as he rounded the last mountain
pass. Distant shouts floated to him on the wind, along
with the stench of waste and rot and smoke from
campfires.

Gurn Keep rose to the east between two tall sheer
cliffs, its square stone walls dark against a slate sky.
The surrounding field was covered by a mass of goblins and orcs. They were arrayed across the dimming,
rocky land exactly the way he had told them to when
he taught the orcish generals to work with the goblin
king. That they remembered was a bitter tribute to his
teachings.

The seeds of alliance had finally sprouted—without
him. Much careful planning had gone into those seeds.
Long explanations to the orcish council about how

their caution—a carefully chosen word, combined with the goblins' passion, another careful word—could produce a powerfully effective battle force.

Against the Icatians, that was. The Icatians, who could easily defend against such hordes.

Reod had worked hard not simply to weave together goblins and orcs into a political harmony but also to carefully tend the weeds of dissent between them. That was before Havenwood took away the funds he needed to buy the attention of kings and generals. Goblins had ridiculously short memories, which was the main reason they were fearless in battle. The orcs would remember him better, but they would also remember the promises he had made that only money could let him keep.

He had never meant for this force to come to the lightly defended Gurn Keep.

Bands of goblins littered the muddy field, tents and piles of garbage making dim mounds in the evening light. Many clustered around flags on which were drawn rough designs he recognized. There was Salamander, then Fox, and farthest was Rat's Tooth. Again they had followed his plan. Each goblin band would have an orcish captain who stood to the rear, where he could give orders with least risk. A few bands were comprised only of orcs, the ironclaws, brassclaws, and iceclaws would be to the rear, out of the way until they decided the odds were in their favor.

Reod dismounted. He gave his horse a farewell slap to start him back along the road. To leave the animal here was to offer it as food to the goblins. A testy and arrogant creature, its chances were better than they might have been. Perhaps it would find its way north to warmer lands. He could hope.

He walked out onto the field. Now he heard goblins chittering and orc captains barking orders in the simple battle tongue that Reod had constructed for them out of the most basic words from both race's native languages.

The two races had little in common. They would always fight, even in the best of times. One of the few things they did share was that little went to waste. No bodies littered the field.

Rain and chill doubtless dulled the stink. Nonetheless, it was impressive. Reod judged that the goblins and orcs had been camped here for many days with little attempt at sanitation.

The Fox band was launching a kite. Or trying to. They threw the kited goblin up in the air and then yanked him down again. Each time the creature ended up in the mud, making the kite a little heavier. Still they kept trying.

A lone drum beat from the periphery of the field, keeping company the high-pitched sounds of goblin complaints and bickerings. He approached the nearest goblin band, who were all watching a fight in another group. The situation was pretty much what he had expected, except that he had not thought so many would come.

He was nearly on them before some goblins noticed, spun, crouched, and prepared to pounce on him.

"Hold," he said sharply in the goblin-orc battle tongue. "Who is your commander?"

The goblins paused, exchanged uncertain glances.

"Do you think I have time to waste? I am Reod Dai. Tell me who your commander is. Obey. Now."

"He is Great-and-powerful-with-long-nose-hairs," one said. "Over there."

Reod felt certain the captain's name had been arrived at by mutual compromise.

"Escort," he said sharply, and the goblins fell in around him, their uncertainty replaced with a glee of self-importance. The insulating ring of goblins helped him press his way through the throngs until they reached a small group of orcs.

There Reod introduced himself to the indicated orc and added, "I have come to help with the victory. Take me to your general."

The orc showed more caution than had the goblins. He looked down on Reod as he stroked his green chin.

"*The* Reod Dai?"

"Yes."

"Hah. I do not believe you. Tell me why should I not try to kill you. To test you."

Reod met the orc's glare with one of his own.

"Very good," he said. "I am recommending promotions for those who think carefully about such matters. I will commend you. Now take me to your general—"

The orc frowned at that. "But—"

"—who will certainly be very irritated if you delay me further."

At that, the captain inhaled, drew himself upright, and began shouting and shoving goblins out of the way.

The camps were everywhere, scattered, with little thought to organization or pathways, so the captain had to choose a convoluted route for them around rows of tents and piles of garbage. Reod's gaze flickered everywhere. The land was broken, rocky, and hilly. No one on the field would be able to see the whole of it. Only up in the keep's command tower would such a view be possible.

By now the sky was almost black. Soon there would be only the light of the campfires. Even then he would have a hard time passing through the crowd unnoticed. He reached down and picked up a handful of dirt.

"Hold," he said to the orc captain.

"What?"

"Something is very wrong. I'm going forward to check. Stay here." He took a few steps toward the keep. "Escort!" he barked.

Those who had surrounded him before scrambled to surround him again. The orc captain grumbled from behind.

Reod glanced back at him. "Patience is another attribute I commend."

The captain stopped grumbling, shifted his stance, tried to look content, managed to look confused.

Reod led his goblins past tents and around boulders, hoping to lose the captain's sight in the dim light. When they reached the edge of the camps, the empty space between the invaders and the keep that described bowshot range, the goblins hung back. Reod pulled his hood up and over his face.

"Report back to your captain," he told the goblins. "Say to him that I have a plan."

The goblins gratefully scattered back into the crowds. They would doubtless forget what he had told them by the time they reached their captain, who would be frustrated and mystified by Reod's disappearance. It would take the orc some time to figure out what to do. It would be enough.

The key was to be here and yet not here, Reod thought, spitting into the dirt in his hand and rubbing his hands together. To ask shadow and light to pass through him, to ask darkness to cover him.

If no one looked directly at him, they would not see him walking across the cleared area. But any who looked too hard or wondered too long would notice. He forced himself to concentrate as he walked through the bowshot range. Dark slits loomed high in the keep's wall. He could almost feel dwarven fingers twitching on dwarven bows.

Halfway there he began to let the spell loosen. Now he held his palms up and out as he walked forward, to show watching guards that he held no weapons.

They would not see goblin hands, nor would they see the height of an orc, and so they would wonder whom and what the slumped figure in the darkness could be. He relied on that confusion. It might keep him free of arrows.

Before the front gate was a deep, wide trench, covered by a flat bridge. He crossed the bridge step by step. The keep's front gate was twice Reod's height and nearly as wide as that, made of heavy wood and

banded with the careful and precise ironwork that was
the dwarven mark. The smaller inset door was decorated with the soft dwarven geometric designs. He was
close enough to see such detail now.

Another step. And another. Still no arrow flew at
him.

He reached the inset door and exhaled his relief,
pounding on the wood with his fist.

"Let me in," he called in dwarven. "I must see Elder
Hamon."

After a long moment the smaller door opened a crack.
Dwarven eyes and a frown faced him, then the door
opened wide enough that hands could pull him into
the lamplit gate passage. The door was slammed and
bolted behind him.

A dozen armor-clad dwarves encircled him, swords
pointing inward. The distinctive scent of hot oil was
thick, wafting down from the murderholes above,
where others doubtless waited for a signal to drop oil
and rocks on him. The walls were lined with bow
slits all the way back to the inner gate, where he
could see another dozen soldiers standing, weapons
ready.

He had been here before, in better times. He remembered a spring festival with daisies strung along the
walls, from arrow slit to arrow slit, and petals falling
slowly from the murderholes. Pairs of goats, sheep,
deer, and horses were paraded through the gate passage into the courtyard, where there had been dancing
and pipes and a great deal of beer.

Now the scent of burning oil barely covered the
smell of unwashed dwarf around him, and from the
slits arrow tips pointed out at him, awaiting the command to fly. All in all, he was reassured to see the
dwarves this well organized.

"Who are you?" one demanded.

"Reod Dai," he said, giving a small bow.

It was dwarven custom to bow in drinking halls and among friends. He knew it was a gesture too familiar for these circumstances, but it might be just out of place enough to convince the dwarves that he really was who he said he was.

The other cocked his head, considering.

It was almost amusing to Reod that he was always trying to convince someone that he either was—or was not—who he said he was, and in both cases he was rarely believed.

"Get the Second Watch Keeper," one said to another warrior.

"I think it's early third, now."

"Well, damn it, I don't care. Get the keeper, who-ever it is."

The warrior left.

"I have heard of Reod Dai," the first said, looking up at Reod. "Somehow I thought he would not be so—" The dwarf paused, considering. "So thin."

Reod smiled back as politely as he could.

The Third Watch Keeper was a large dwarven man who looked Reod over and nodded, motioning to four soldiers to follow along. He led them through the torchlit hallways of the keep.

The stench of unwashed dwarf was oppressive. In every corner and along every wall dwarves huddled. Not soldiers, these, but ragged villagers, clustered fam-ilies, dirty, tired, warily watching him pass by. Some were thin, too thin for dwarves, faces drawn and pale. He heard crying and coughing. The corridors were thick with them. Sometimes they left a path for the soldiers and sometimes they didn't.

Tamun. If she were here, would she be this bad off?

He wanted to stop and ask them about her, but he forced himself to move forward, settling for searching faces as he went by.

A dwarven man lay prone across the way. The

keeper stopped, nudged the man with his foot. "You shouldn't be here."

The man did not move.

"Maybe he's dead," ventured a soldier.

The keeper clearly did not want to find out. "We'll check later." One by one they stepped over the figure.

Circular stairs led up to the small command tower, built atop the rearmost wall of the keep. A chill wind blew into the room from open windows, through which the campfires of the goblin and orc horde were visible below.

Elder Hamon sat at a table. He had a long, braided beard, streaks of brown shot through with gray. He twisted thick lips into a frown.

"Reod Dai? A surprise, this. What are you doing here?"

"I'm here to offer my help."

"Indeed? How fortunate for us." His frown deepened. "But how did you get here?"

"Horse and foot, Elder."

"But—there are goblins massed outside."

Reod gave a confident, modest smile. "When I choose to go someplace, I always find a means to do so." It was an answer Reod had used before.

The elder nodded. "Though why you would choose to be here, of all places, I cannot see."

"To lend aid to the dwarven people in a time of need."

"Sit down, please. Are you hungry? thirsty? You must have come far."

Reod waved away the atypical dwarven concern. "How many do you number? They must have ten times your count."

The elder snorted. "I wish they did. We number far too many inside our walls. Dwarves have come to the keep from everywhere. Farmers, miners, builders, smiths, mothers, children, goats, and fleas, all packed inside Gurn. We drown in our own. Reod Dai, I remember what you did for our people years ago.

You say you offer us aid. We would first know the price."

What cost would be low enough so that the elder would not hesitate, but high enough so that the elder would not doubt his motives?

"One hundred gold. If I succeed."

Otherwise there might be no one to pay and nothing to pay with. But when bargaining for lives it was best to talk about the outcome of battle as one would talk about buying ducks. Otherwise people became upset.

The elder toyed with his braids. "That may be fair."

It was more than fair, Reod knew, and he knew that the elder knew it, too, but Reod said nothing. It was better to let Hamon seem before his warriors to be a prudent negotiator. The elder tugged on his braids and looked at Reod.

"I accept," Hamon said at last.

I must review the keep, Reod ached to say. *I must see all the buildings and stores.* All the while he would search for Tamun.

But no, if she and her family were here, he must truly protect them, not merely seem to, and that might mean waiting. He would search for her tomorrow.

She might not even be here.

No. She had to be here.

He turned his thoughts back to the moment and sat down across from the elder.

"Tell me everything. All that has occurred. Every event, every problem."

The other sighed heavily. "Each room is over-full. Most come from Teedmar—those who made it past the goblin bands, that is. Three days ago hundreds came from outlying villages. Two days ago another hundred came. None since then. Too many goblins and orcs for them to get by. We even closed the tunnels, so none could come that way. We had to." He shook his head, rubbed his head with his hands. "We had to."

"How many are inside the walls now?"

"When would I have had time to count? Before we

closed the tunnels, there were nearly two thousand.
There are far more now. Is it not enough that they fill
every room and all the hallways? No, each one also has
a complaint. We are so pressed we ignore the sick and
injured. We just put them aside so soldiers can pass
through. Do we have healers? Few. Medicines?" He
laughed bitterly. "We are lucky that we can still feed
them all. Our stores were full when this siege began.
Praise the skies that it has been raining, or we would
not have enough water."

"How long can we last with what we have?" Reod
included himself deliberately. Hamon seemed to relax
a little. Reod could see that the man was already
exhausted.

"We can no longer send out hunting parties. Now we
only have what is saved. A week, if we are sparing."

Reod looked out at the dark field, reviewed what he
knew of goblin and orc numbers, temperament, and
the battle plans he had helped them form over the last
couple of years.

A week could be enough.

"Can you help us?" It was a soft-spoken plea, a rare
tone to come from a dwarf.

"I believe so. Tell me of the attacks you have faced."

"The goblins come to the wall with ladders. They do
not seem to care if they live or die, so arrows and hot
oil must stop them completely to stop them at all.
Those who come over the walls a few at a time we can
take care of. But have you seen how many of them
there are out there? And there are orcs, too. They
work together. They have never done this before.
What could make such an alliance?"

Reod stared out at the lights on the dark field.

"It is a minor advantage. They are still orcs and goblins and they still do not get along."

"They have new weapons. Yesterday a goblin ran
straight at the wall though we had filled him with so
many arrows that he must have been dead when he
reached the stones. Then there was a flash of light so

bright it made me think the sun had melted through the clouds. A sound came like thunder. The earth was suddenly plowed up. One of our warriors was cut across the face. And the goblin? It had vanished. It is magic."

"Not magic. They are called goblin eggs. Was the wall damaged?"

"No. But one came again today. And yesterday, when the winds were high, they put wings on a goblin and he flew. Like a bat! Up into the air and over the walls. He dropped dung-covered garbage on us. We have enough problems with sanitation—our aqueduct is built for five hundred, perhaps a thousand. We have almost three times that many. People are becoming sick."

"Throw your waste over the wall."

"We do. The goblins do not seem to notice."

"How many kites have you seen?"

"Many, but only a few manage to fly."

There were specific flaws in the kite design. Reod remembered them well, having added them himself.

"I have never seen such a thing before," Hamon said. "Never."

"Have there been any dragons?" Reod asked.

"Dragons? Why would there be dragons?"

Reod's hope melted. He ignored the pain in his chest and stood, forcing himself to seem calmer than he felt. "I must review the keep. See all the buildings, weapons, stores. Everything."

"In the morning," Hamon said. "When it is light. After you have rested."

Reod did not want to wait. Exhaustion he could ignore, but if Tamun was here, he had to find her as soon as possible. He tried to find a reason to insist but could not.

"In the morning," he agreed at last.

He had been dreaming. In the dream Tamun had been trying to talk to him. He had been paralyzed, unable to answer. She scowled at him, turned, and walked away. He tried to shout, tried to follow, but could not move.

In the waking world of blood and steel, a latch clicked. Not yet fully awake, Reod was in motion, short sword in hand, waiting behind the door as it creaked open. Torchlight entered, brought by Hamon's hand. Following him was another elder and a grim-faced woman, her light hair wrapped tightly behind her in the warrior's fashion. She was probably the First Watch Keeper.

Reod stepped out from behind the door. Hamon started.

"What are you doing there? Is something wrong?"

"I recommend knocking first."

The elder shook his head, not understanding. Then he cocked his head one way and then the other.

"Do you hear them?"

So it was not just the blood pounding in his ears.

"Drums," he said.

"Yes. What does this new pattern mean?"

"It means that they have finished assembling all their war drums, and now they are pounding on them."

The other elder was named Kal. She shook her head, starting waves down her waist-length silver-streaked braids. "There's something strange about the pattern this time," she said. "It's a message."

"It's not. The sound is supposed to worry you. Ignore it."

"Are you sure?"

"I'm sure. How long is it until dawn?"

"It's near the end of third watch," the keeper said. "Not long now."

Reod nodded, still blinking away sleep and images of Tamun.

"It is time to begin the tour."

"Elder, please," the woman begged, wiping her nose on a greasy sleeve as she frantically brushed away the soldiers trying to pull her aside. "We need more bread. Father's not well. He's not getting enough food. The others get more. I know they do."

"You all get the same," Kal said.

"No, I'm sure they get more. They say they have another child inside their tent. There is no second child!"

"We'll look into it," Kal said wearily, pressing by. The guards tried to insulate the elders from the villagers who pressed around.

"Elder, please!"

"Elder, listen!"

Hamon shut his eyes tight a moment, then turned a bleak look on Reod. "You see?"

"This is the arms storeroom," Kal said, waving at a door as they walked by. "Little left now."

Two small children darted under the arms of the soldiers and cut across the elders' path, nearly tripping them.

"Away, away!" the keeper yelled as they ran off.

Hamon gave a frustrated sigh. "They are everywhere."

"Put them to work," Reod said.

"Work? What work?"

"It doesn't matter, but you must convince them that it does. They should be cooking, cleaning, doing any work you can give them. If that's not enough, have them make lists of their families, those who survived and those who did not. Where each person comes from. How many there are. Details."

"We barely have room to walk as it is," Kal said. "If we have them all wandering around, we shall have chaos."

They rounded a hallway and had to squeeze past another group of villagers, who were all scooping meal out of a single bowl.

"Elder," one called, "there are bugs in this food. When we came here, we gave you all we had. Sheep, goats, everything. This is what we receive in return?"

"You can't stay here," a soldier said gently. "Go out into the courtyard."

"There's no room there! And it freezes at night. We have a baby."

The soldier turned to Hamon, his look a plea for direction.

"Move on," Hamon said softly, not looking at the villagers.

"Bugs," one of the dwarves said with disgust. "Even the goblins eat better than this."

Out of earshot Reod said, "Put them to work, or they'll tear the keep down from the inside."

Hamon nodded.

"What of the tunnels?"

"Full," Kal said, her lips tight. "As are the storage rooms."

"There are whole villages unaccounted for," Hamon said. "Perhaps—perhaps they were able to defend themselves."

Reod remembered Kalitas. "Perhaps."

He checked every dwarven face he passed. In the stingy light of dawn it was hard to tell one dwarf from another. She could be five feet away and he might still miss her. He looked anyway, listening for her voice.

The large stone courtyard was even more packed than the hallways. Families clustered together around small fires. Tents and overturned carts made for poor shelter from the rain and cold. Babies cried and children darted through the crowd. Somewhere a woman was calling a name.

No livestock, Reod noticed. Already eaten, no doubt. Gone as contributions to the kitchens.

Open to the sky, the courtyard's stench was milder than inside and it was cut with the smell of cooking, but even here it was strong. Many stared at him, expressions dwarven-grim. Some scowled.

He knew this reaction, had seen it before among those who had lost everything they had. They were afraid for their lives each moment, yet unable to act. It made them angry. He was a stranger and a human. It was easy for them to wonder if he might somehow be to blame for their plight.

And he might well be.

The soldiers pressed through the crowd, pushing children away from the steps to gain passage up to the catwalk. There the first watch's soldiers were replacing the third. It was a slow process; each solder had to speak to the other to find out what had happened on the previous watch.

Damned dwarven independence. Each one of these solders had chosen their own commander, because no dwarf was expected to take orders from someone they did not like and respect. In Leitbur's Order, Reod had often told jokes about the dwarven military. Now they did not seem so funny.

Behind them the sky was paling toward the white of a cloud-filled sky. With the light, the goblins began to stir. More carts had arrived since yesterday, delivering to the field food and arms and more of the great drums that continued to pound in the distance. At the edge of the forest was construction. They were building siege towers, great skeletons of tall pyramids covered in skins, behind which they could safely approach and scale the keep's high walls.

The elders and First Watch Keeper waited for his assessment. He turned to them.

"Their attack will begin in earnest soon. Tomorrow, I would guess. You have seen that orcs and goblins together can be formidable, but I tell you this: when they do not taste success, they tire quickly. The most important thing is to stay on the walls and hold a strong defense."

"What about the drums? We try to understand the messages they send each other across the field. They keep us awake at night."

"We must make the soldiers sleep in the barracks," Kal said. "We have to stuff rags under the doors to keep out the sound."

"There are no messages," Reod said. "The drums mean nothing. The sounds rotate and come in waves, do they not?"

"They do."

"I know this trick. The sounds are without meaning. They are a ruse designed to confuse and frighten you."

She frowned.

"I thought as you do," Kal said to the keeper, "but he is Reod Dai."

It touched him to know that his reputation could carry such weight. Then his gaze swept over the field where goblins and orcs banded together under the flags he had taught them to use.

That, too, was because of his reputation.

"Look there," he said, pointing to the construction. "They are building towers and more ladders. You must keep them from gaining purchase on the walls. That is how we will outlast them."

"Won't they have more goblin eggs?" Hamon asked.

"They will have saved most of the eggs for today and tomorrow. Keep those away from the wall's weak points and the doors. And keep them off the tops of the walls."

"What if they throw the eggs?"

"They won't throw them."

Hamon looked doubtful. "Why not?"

"It won't occur to them."

"Are you sure?"

Reod had convinced the goblins that the eggs had to be carried to work properly.

"I'm sure." He turned to Hamon. "I want to see the tunnels now."

"The tunnels? But why? What do you hope to find there?"

Reod struggled to keep the tension out of his voice.

"How do I know if I don't look?"

But she was not in the tunnels.

He had checked everywhere, along each curved wall

where ragged, frightened dwarves sat in semidarkness, knees tight to chests to leave a path. There was barely enough air to breathe and he was relieved to get back up to the surface.

Where was she?

As they walked toward the front gate Reod struggled to concentrate on Hamon's words.

"We had to put the sick and injured into the stables. Now the injured are getting sick as well. But it prevents the whole keep from getting sick from the few who are, so—" he waved a hand at the stable door "—it's the best we can do."

Reod ran his fingers thoughtfully over the wood of the door.

Somewhere. She was here somewhere. She had to be. If she was not, then she was dead, and that he would deny until he found her body.

"Keep a strong contingent at the inner gate," he said as they climbed the stairs to the frontmost wall. "That way, if they break through the front gate—"

There was a yell followed by a sharp scream. Howls came from the goblins outside the wall. Rocks came over the wall, one rebounding painfully off Reod's leg. The west wall warder barked orders and the yells subsided as quickly as they had started.

Out on the field the Salamander group had made its way to the bottom of the wall. One goblin lay dead and an orc captain was yelling insults wrapped around a few orders at the group. Reod turned to the warder.

"They'll be back around the north side in a few minutes. Warn your warriors."

A young soldier waved at Reod from the wall.

"I was only a girl when you were last here," she called out to him. "Now I'm in my time." She grinned and growled fiercely. The soldiers by her side smiled as well, watching, awaiting his reply.

Tamun, his insides seemed to cry.

"Hold your wall, and you will be the reason Gurn Keep celebrates victory."

Pride glinted in their eyes. The woman clenched her raised fist in agreement.

He took a step forward, drew their attention with a conspiratorial look, and smiled. "Do you know any fighting songs?"

"Of course!"

"Then sing them. Show those animals that you are not afraid of them. Be diligent in your watch."

The soldiers cheered agreement and turned back to their posts, beginning to sing loudly and off-key.

To the warder he said, "Have each wall's warder tell their soldiers to sing as well. That will help keep their minds off the drums."

"The drums," the warder said. "They are so strange. What is it about them?"

"Reod says that they are nothing," Hamon said. "That we must ignore them."

Just then the earth shuddered and thunder crashed from the other side of the wall. Yells, questions, and orders filled the air. At the wall soldiers had hands to their eyes. One dropped down, blood dripping from his face. The young woman dropped down next to him, trying to help as he frantically pushed her away.

A goblin egg had exploded. From the sound and yelling below Reod could tell that the front gate had been breached.

"The gate passage," Reod yelled to the warder. The warder took off down the stairs. Soldiers from the other walls were turning to look down into the courtyard and see what had happened, turning away from their posts. Damn dwarven curiosity.

"Get back," he shouted at them as he followed the warder down the stairs. "Get back to your walls!"

Halfway down the stairs he paused to take in the action. There were sounds of fighting in the gate passage: warrior yells and goblin howls. The smell of hot oil was pungent on the air, cutting through the stench of waste.

A single goblin broke through the fighting at the

inner gate, running into the courtyard, screaming, his back wet with blood. His cries were echoed by panicked villagers, who knocked over carts and tents to get away from him. On the wall an archer struggled to get a clear shot at the intruder and failed.

Reod pitched his voice low and spoke in dwarven to cut through the noise of the crowd. "Hit him on the back of the head!" Some dwarves glanced up at him. He hoped they were not too panicked to understand.

Warriors who had come down from the walls were cutting down goblins in the passage. The First Watch Keeper appeared at Reod's side.

"The drums keep moving," she said, breathing hard. "I think they're going to attack on the south wall next, where we're weakest. I'm moving soldiers there. I'll call the second watch."

Reod had looked and seen goblins massing on every side of the keep. She grossly overestimated their ability to organize.

"No, no. We are already holding them off. Your soldiers are where they should be. Ignore the drums. But listen: you'll need to repair that front gate once the gate passage is clear of goblins. Erect a makeshift barrier there. What do you have for materials?"

"Some wood. Not much."

"Tell the soldiers on the wall to protect the front gate above all. Flood the area with arrows to keep the goblins at distance. Then set up your barricade."

"We have little left to build with that has not already been burned."

Reod looked around the courtyard. The goblin had fallen. Villagers swarmed over him, pounding and howling.

"Carts," he said.

"We've tried. They won't part with them."

"They will." Reod stepped down into the crowded courtyard and climbed on top of an overturned cart, raising his arms.

"You have killed a goblin with your own hands," he

called out. "I am impressed." Some turned to look at him. "Do you think the goblins understand dwarven ferocity now?" A few cheered. He smiled at them, shook his head. "Not yet, they don't. But they will, and soon, and far better." More were turning to watch and listen to him.

"Do you want your warriors to protect you from the hordes outside?" There were nods. "Of course. And they will. But they need your help."

Now he had their attention.

"Listen: I know you have endured hardships and terrible losses. I tell you that there will be more, that the hardest times are yet to come. But Gurn Keep can stand. Gurn Keep will stand." He showed them a raised fist. "With your help. Your army needs your help, and it needs it now. Listen."

He joined villagers in pulling their carts to the front gate, where soldiers pushed goblin bodies aside to clear a path. A barricade was hastily constructed out of scrap wood and bodies. That held the front gate as carts were broken up, dragged inside, and fitted into place. Above archers and catapult drivers furiously delivered their missiles into the surging sea of goblins and orcs.

In the courtyard another goblin had managed to get through the gate passage and inner gate. Heartened by their earlier success, the villagers clubbed the creature to the ground.

"Take it up! Throw it over!" someone yelled.

Reod struggled through the crowd to the stairs, intending, if he could, to hold the villagers away from the walls. Then, from the west wall came another explosion that rocked the ground under his feet. He stumbled, grabbed for the wall. Villagers fell silent, stunned, the dead goblin forgotten. Reod took the stairs three at a time.

There was blood on the north walkway. Two bodies

slumped, pushed aside by replacements. The west wall warder was calling for reinforcements, for soldiers to come away from the other walls. Reod grabbed the warder's shoulder.

"It hit stone," he said. "We're fine! Hold steady!"

Breathing hard, the warder shuddered and nodded.

Ladders fell against the wall, wooden tops poking up over the stone. A cry went up. Warriors poked with long poles and threw rocks at the goblins.

A soldier bounded up the stairs. "The second and third watches are awake, Keeper. They want to know what is happening. They want to come up on the walls. Some already have."

If this had been an Icatian fortress under siege, the soldiers of other watches would simply have slept at their posts. But Icatians were not so badly troubled by goblin drums that they went sleepless.

And further, Icatian solders followed orders. Now was one of the few times Reod missed the strict discipline of the Order.

The keeper glanced a question at Reod.

"We are afloat in a storm," Reod said. "If we all row now, we will tire. Later, when the storm is worse, we will not have the strength to keep ourselves from drowning. They should be resting in the barracks, where they can't hear the drums."

"They won't stay down there."

Reod exhaled frustration. Damned dwarves. Too stubborn to follow orders properly, too egalitarian to give them.

"I'll tell them," he said to the keeper.

The keeper nodded. "I'll follow shortly."

Reod dashed down the stairs.

There were fewer villagers in the hallways now. Fear of meeting stray goblins escaping through the gates had driven more dwarves into the courtyard where their numbers were greater.

A howl of dwarven outrage caught his attention and he looked around a corner. Down a side hallway a

handful of goblins surrounded a doorway. Most of the
goblins wore crudely stitched animal hides as armor.
Some waved blades, some heavy sticks.

They must have broken through the front gate and
vanished into the building. In moments dwarven soldiers would find them and take care of them. But for
now the goblins faced wide-eyed dwarven villagers
peering fearfully out of the doorway. Before them a
single dwarf stood guard, a trickle of blood running
down one arm, a short sword in the other, and a flow
of curses coming from her lips.

It was Tamun.

The goblins closed. For less than a blink he paused.
Could she hold them for the moments it would take
him to signal soldiers? She might be able to. She might
not.

But he would not risk it. He had not come so far to
give fate another chance to take her.

"Hold!" he yelled in the orc-goblin battle tongue,
throwing as much authority into his voice as he could.
"Hold and obey!"

The goblins froze and turned to look at him.

"I am Reod Dai and you are idiots. What is this you
do? You waste time. This puny woman stands in front
of the garbage room. Follow me instead. The treasure
room is this way. Was that not where you were
ordered to go? Follow!"

They came without hesitation, eyes alight with
excitement. Relief flooded him.

"Sorry, lord," one murmured distractedly.

"Treasure, you say, lord?" another asked.

"Treasure."

"Where?"

"Follow," Reod said sharply, leading them briskly
away.

He let himself glance back once. Melelki was drawing Tamun back inside the doorway. Tamun glanced at
him as she went. She seemed to recognize him, but if
she were glad to see him, he could not tell. She might

be injured; she might be ill. He had no way of knowing. With great effort he turned his attention back to the goblins and began to jog forward along the hall, forcing the goblins to work to keep up with him.

Tamun, alive. Relief and something like joy flickered through him.

"*Dwarven* treasure?" asked a goblin.

What other sort of treasure would there be in a dwarven hold? Goblins were not very bright.

"Anything you can carry out is yours. Follow."

The goblins made happy sounds.

They rounded another corner and he stopped, yelling orders at them as an orc captain would. "Go to the door at the end of the hallway. Give your battle cry twice, then go in."

They passed him by, gleefully, following his instructions and waiting just long enough to howl two times before they charged into the barracks. That would give those inside plenty of warning.

Reod nodded. If the second and third watch were so hungry for battle, Reod would offer them a little wake-up exercise.

He was on his way back to find Tamun when the elders and their guards intercepted him.

"They swarm the front gate," Kal said, tensely.

"Again and again," Hamon added.

"They may break through at any moment."

"That's good," Reod said. "I expect them to break through in small groups. Since only a few can fit through the gateway, we will kill each group as it comes. Let them think there is a way to make progress there, and they will not stop to consider other means. They will keep throwing themselves on our swords."

"There must be more we can do."

"We kill them in piles, Elder," he said. "They have far more passion than sense. You have already seen this. We use them against themselves. Hold strong and they will not break through."

"But they do break through! They wander the halls! There were two in the courtyard a little while ago."

"Both of them are now dead. Killed by villagers who finally understand that they can do more than get in the way. Some goblins will get inside, yes, but we will take them inside. It is a waiting game, Elder. All we have to do is hold them. We are doing just that."

"The drums," Kal insisted. "You are sure they mean nothing?"

"I am."

"Perhaps we should call for the second watch," Hamon asked.

"You must pace your soldiers. Call them in for a little while, if they are so eager, then send them back to where they can rest. We have to hold the attackers for days to come. Fatigue now means mistakes later."

Around the corner came a boy, barely young enough to still live with his mother. It was the age dwarves referred to as "almost gone." The child held a long, broken stick, swinging it as if were a sword, yelling as he cut down imaginary opponents, oblivious to the group gathered there.

"Put that down," Hamon scolded. "What do you think you're doing?"

The boy looked up, saw Reod, stopped suddenly. "Where are they?" he asked Reod. "The goblins. Where did you take them?"

The elders turned curious looks at Reod. Reod considered.

Dwarves rarely lied. Even dwarven children were surprisingly honest. As a people they were simply so stubborn that they rarely found sufficient reason to be deceitful. Claiming the child was lying could too easily backfire.

"I sent them to the barracks," he answered, "so that the soldiers there could dispose of them."

The boy looked eagerly down the hall, as if he could see the fighting through the walls.

"Are they all dead now?"

"Probably. They faced many times their number of armed dwarven warriors."

"Oh." He made a disappointed face, which turned into childish anger, and hurled the stick down, running back the way he had come. The First Watch Keeper nearly tripped over him as she turned the corner to join the group.

Kal looked at Reod. "How many were there?"

"A handful."

Hamon frowned. "You talked to them?"

"They had cornered some women. Villagers. I distracted them and then led them to the barracks."

"How did you learn to speak their language?" Hamon asked.

"I speak a number of languages that are not native to me. Yours, for example." He met their suspicious looks in turn, allowing a touch of his own confusion to show. "Do you think I could accomplish the sort of work I did for your race years ago if I had not been able to communicate with your enemies?"

"But you commanded them." Kal cocked her head. "You had them follow you."

Reod shrugged. "They are simple creatures. They do not think deeply."

The keeper spoke up. "I can speak a little of their language, too, Reod Dai, but I cannot tell them where to go."

Slowly Kal shook her head. "I have never heard of humans commanding goblins. What did you tell them to turn their bloodlust away from the dwarves?"

"I told them there was treasure. I led them to the barracks."

"They believed you?"

"Apparently so."

"Why?"

Anxiety came out as irritation. "Ask the women in the doorway to tell you what I did. Ask those whose lives I saved."

"He does speak truth," the keeper said. "I had just turned the corner when I saw the trapped villagers. I saw him direct the goblins to the barracks."

Reod felt relief, but did not let it show. "Thank you. Elders, we are in the middle of battle, and—"

"The goblins called him lord," the keeper added. "That's a word I do know. They called him lord and then they followed his orders."

Another explosion echoed distantly through the walls, and Reod felt a tinge of gratitude for the timing. "Elders, we are under siege. Do we have time for this? Let me do the work you hired me to do, to save the keep from a force that outnumbers your fighters ten to one."

"Perhaps," said Hamon slowly, "you are the reason that they are doing as well as they are."

"What?"

Kal nodded. "What better way to insure a victory over us than to send a spy claiming to be an ally? That would also explain how you walked untouched through a thousand goblins right to our front gate."

"I am no spy. You misjudge me. I came here to help the dwarven people. I have no loyalty to goblins or orcs."

"Then why do they follow you?"

"They love treasure."

"Perhaps. Perhaps not. Or perhaps your loyalty is to none but yourself."

Reod kept a careful hold on his frustration. Now was the time to seem reasonable.

"It is true that I know much about goblins and orcs, and this is why they give me a respectful title. But what I know I have given freely to you, in the service of your protection. That is why I came here, why I risked my life to ride across the blood-soaked lands to Gurn Keep."

That and a woman. But he did not want to mention Tamun. In times like these a human's affection for a dwarf might not be looked on with tolerance, let alone favor.

Perhaps if they found Tamun and she spoke for him—but no, the expressions on the elders' faces told him otherwise. Their trust for him was weakening fast, suspicion taking its place. As the elders' looks hardened, his own optimism began to leave him. He felt himself drained of spirit. Had he really struggled so hard for so many years to come to this?

To his own Icatian people he was a traitor and deserter. The elven people knew him as the one who attacked their food and fortress in times of famine and war. The Ebon Hand would soon name him the cause of their thrull rebellion. And now the dwarven people were calling him a spy.

If he survived this, he thought with bitter humor, he would take a sea voyage to Vodalia.

"You speak as humans always speak," Hamon said, "with words of many meanings. Perhaps you speak truth and perhaps not. In any case, you command goblins. For now we cannot risk you being free." To his guards he said, "take him to the command room. Do not let him leave. Do not listen to what he says."

Four guards grabbed him. He did not resist.

As he was led away, he heard Kal say, "There are the drums again. I think he lied about that, too. They must send messages. I can almost understand them. Attacks from the south, next. We must move our warriors. Hamon, do you hear the messages, too?"

Reod was too far away to hear Hamon's reply.

CHAPTER

13

Peace shall go sleep with Turks and infidels,
And in this seat of peace tumultuous wars
Shall kin with kin and kind with kind confound;
Disorder, horror, fear, and mutiny
Shall here inhabit . . .
—Shakespeare, *Richard II*

THROUGH THE OPEN WINDOW OF THE
command room blew a cold, wet wind. Reod ignored the
chill to stand at the window and look out on the courtyard and beyond the walls, watching the day's struggles.

The goblins had broken down the front gate again
and again, a handful surviving each time to try the
inner gate. The second and third watches had been
called in alongside the first, and extras ran up and
down the stairs as each new goblin attack came.

The siege towers had been completed, set aright,
and carried to the wall. From the tops they launched
kites. Some fell to the ground, others crashed into the
walls, a testimony to goblin engineering under Reod's
guidance. A few made it over the walls to drop things.
First came rocks, then foul waste, and later, as the

overcast sky began to dim with the coming of night, the chewed remains of their own dead.

That last had been Reod's suggestion, some time ago. It was a way to demoralize the enemy without causing more damage. He was oddly reassured to know that they remembered even that piece of advice.

As he watched and waited, his initial relief at seeing Tamun alive became uncertainty then turned into fever-pitched worry. Surely his name would be spoken all across the keep by now. Tamun would know he was here. If she went to the elders and asked to see him, they would have at least let her visit. Perhaps she was trying to protect him with her silence. Or protect herself.

Perhaps she was gravely wounded. The dwarven healers were overworked enough that she could be lying somewhere, unable to move. He knew something of the healing arts. If he only could get to her—

But his three guards would not be swayed.

Or perhaps she did not want to see him. He did not want to think about that possibility.

Ladders slammed against the outer walls. Goblins, armor clad, rag clad, and sometimes nearly naked, hurled themselves up and over.

The same pattern repeated, over and over: a few goblins would break through the dwarven line and dash across the walls or down the stairs before they were tackled and pulled down. Those who made it into the courtyard were eagerly worked over by the villagers, who had by now lost most of their fear of the small green creatures. At each new wave, some goblins would slip away and into the keep itself, later bursting forth to meet similar fates, or hunted down by roving warriors.

But when the drums changed patterns, the soldiers on the walls would stop chanting their songs and move along the catwalk from side to side, constantly readying themselves for a change of attack that did not come. As afternoon arrived, Reod saw soldiers slumping.

Weapons came to the ready less quickly. More goblins broke through the lines.

As darkness fell, the thick skies began a cold drizzle. The elders returned to the command room, bringing with them small rations of bread and cheese. Hamon handed a portion to Reod.

So he was not disposable. Not quite yet.

After a time all the elders left except Kal and Hamon.

"I think we are doing well," Hamon said as he stood watching by the window. "What do you think?"

"Shall I say what will please you, or tell you what I really think?"

He was tired, frustrated, cold, and deeply worried about Tamun. It was hard to be politic.

Hamon flushed. "Do you think that we need your encouragement to fight for our lives? We do not need you at all!"

"I am sorry," Reod said, meaning it. "I am fatigued, like your troops. Elder, look there at your soldiers. They need more rest. It may only show in little things today. A missed target. A tiff between friends. But tomorrow it will show more. And soon it will be too late."

From the other side of the room Kal made a derisive sound. "You foresay, like all humans, telling us what is and what will be. But how can you know? And even if you are right, for whose gain do you so speak? The attackers, perhaps? Hamon, we should not listen to him. His words are like a disease, eating through our strength to make us doubt even the ground we walk on."

Hamon sighed. "Maybe he is right. We are all tired."

"The goblins call him lord," Kal said.

The silence that followed was as heavy and dark as the skies outside.

"You say nothing?" Hamon snapped, turning on him. Reod could see that even now Hamon wanted to believe him.

"What shall I say? That I am innocent of this? I have already answered your accusations. If you did not hear me then, will you hear me better now? I have risked my life for your people in the past. If that does not give you faith in me now, will my words do more? How do I prove myself while I am a prisoner? By doing no wrong?"

Kal shook her head. "Human words. We do not need them. We need action. Out there, with swords and stones and oil."

Reod exhaled, tried again. "In the coldest of winter, a lake may seem solid enough to walk across. But if you are wrong, will you know it in time to step back, or will you already have sunk into the icy depths?"

"Quiet," Kal said, her voice as cold as the breeze. "We have heard enough from you."

"There is little time left. Listen, I beg you, listen—"

Her sword was out, tip raised, pointed up and at his throat.

"Be silent!"

And he was.

They brought blankets for him, another gesture that demonstrated their confusion. He wrapped the blankets around himself and curled up in the corner farthest from the window. They talked into the night about plans and supplies while Reod tried to sleep.

Many years past when he was first on campaign with the Order in the far west, fighting against the denizens of the Ebon Hand, one of his fellow soldiers, one as young as he, marveled at how he could sleep so well before battle.

He had smiled at her. "What could possibly be so important that I should let it rob me of sleep?"

"Death," she answered.

Reod shook his head. "I do not allow fear to be my master, not even fear of death. If I allow fear to rob me of a moment's sleep, then it won't be long before even the neighbor's breathing will keep me awake at night. What kind of life is that?"

She had laughed at his words, at his arrogance, at his strangeness, and in so doing eased her own tension. That night Reod woke to the sound of a young man's frightened nightmare gasps. But it was the woman's calm snores that lulled him back to sleep.

Now those words seemed the sentiments of the very young in secure times. Wrapped in blankets on the floor of the command room, he struggled for sleep. It was not death's image that kept him awake this time, but Tamun's.

The keep might well go down, and soon, and he might well go down with it. But first he would search for Tamun, and then he would do whatever it took to keep her safe. If that meant leading goblins, treating with orcs, lying and betraying allies—well, he would do all those things.

When he finally managed to find sleep, his dreams were ugly and full of blood. Even as he watched the horrors of his nightmares he dismissed them, knowing the day's horrors would be worse.

An insistent pressure in his ribs woke him. It was the Second Watch Keeper, toeing him with her boot. The elders were gone now, but his three guards were still present.

He blinked up at her, judging by the light that it was not quite dawn.

"All night there has been talk about you," she said. "They say you lead the goblins, that you have betrayed us, and that is why the battle is so hard. Some say you should die. Are you a traitor, Reod Dai?"

Reod pressed himself up to sit with his back against the wall.

"Depends on who you ask."

She crouched down in front of him, putting her eyes close to his. "I ask you."

"Then no, I'm not."

"You say the drums mean nothing, but I listened to them all night. The goblins come in waves, right after the drums start to go fast. How can you say they mean nothing?"

"It is an illusion. The drum patterns change all the time. When the goblins attack, your own pulse speeds, so the drums seem to have changed. But they haven't. It's a trick."

"How can you be so sure?"

What did he have left to lose?

"Because I taught them the trick."

"You?"

"Yes."

For a moment she stared at him, then she snorted in disgust, stood, and left. But he had seen doubt in her eyes. She might remember, later, when it might count. Or she might not.

He stood and went to the window. In the predawn light he could see dim shapes and torches beginning to move on the field. Small bands began to throw a few rocks over the walls.

Goblins could see quite well in the dark. They could have been attacking all night long, but they had not, and they would not, because years ago Reod Dai had told them it would not work. To the orcs it was a peculiarity of the goblins that they would not fight at night, but they had learned to accept it. It was one more seed that Reod had planted to keep the goblins and orcs from becoming too competent.

But now that dawn had come, they began to move. The red eyes of campfire embers winked out. The sun rose watery through a blanket of smoke-colored clouds. Another tower was slowly carried forward to the wall, and then another.

Atop the catwalks were too many dwarven soldiers. Many were from other watches, standing guard instead of resting. Signs of fatigue were everywhere.

A young dwarven girl came into the room, carrying gruel, a salt stick, and water. Still they kept him alive, spending precious food on him. The dwarves were not used to the harsh choices that war forced. They would not execute him, they would not let him starve, and they would not listen to him.

"Thank you," he said to the girl.

Her eyes went wide. Into his mind flashed the images of children's faces he had seen across the years, masks of gratitude, hunger, or terror. Through decades of strife he had come to think of children as little more than the smallest of war's tragic symbols.

Tamun would doubtless feel otherwise. She would want to have her own, to bring her young into this war-filled time. Such different worlds the two of them came from. Perhaps it was just as well that she had not come to see him.

The sky lightened and the battle continued in spurts. A midmorning lull came. Then a cry went up. Suddenly goblins began to stream over the walls. Soldiers met them, cut them down. The walkway began to turn red.

"Today more and more of them come," Hamon said from behind him. "Just as you said they would."

Admission or accusation? Reod did not answer.

There was another explosion down below, in the gate passage. Soldiers rushed down from the walls.

Then, more quietly, Hamon said, "How long until they tire, do you think?"

"Days," Reod said. "Perhaps a week."

"And then they will go away?"

"I believe so."

"I wish we could believe you."

Another explosion trembled the floor under Reod's feet. Howls followed. In the courtyard below, the villagers crushed themselves against the east wall, farthest away from the inner gate, their courage to fight fading as handfuls of goblins broke through.

Atop the forward wall, the keeper yelled for reinforcements. More soldiers streamed down the stairs, struggling to get past villagers trying to get up, thinking the catwalk would somehow be safer than the courtyard.

Beside him Hamon made a short, pained sound and left. Reod watched him rush out onto the catwalk, ducking away from a hail of stones.

On the west wall, the line was too thin. Three ladder tops appeared at once. A lone soldier was grabbed by pairs of green claws, and before his fellows could react, he was pulled over the side. Outside the walls a cheer went up, and the cheer turned into a roar.

Now it seemed all the goblins came at once, their howls of battle lust and cries of death filling the air. A rain of lances flew in over the walls, falling into the courtyard to sharp, high dwarven screams. The keeper yelled again for reinforcements, his tone desperate. He called for all the reserves. At that, one of Reod's guards left the room. The other two came to the window to watch.

Dwarven catapults hurled stones at the siege towers, which were now pressed against the walls. Most of the missiles did not hit, instead falling on the horde outside. When one finally hit, the tower rocked, but stayed upright. Kites were launched from the towers, sailing over the courtyard, dropping bloody goblin chunks. Reod peered closer. Not just goblin chunks. Also dwarven.

He sighed, shut his eyes. That was just the touch to send dwarves into more panic and despair.

Reod had not spent many battles like this, only watching. His shoulders and arms tensed as he gripped the windowsill. So this was what it was like to be the defended instead of the defender. To be unable to act. He did not like it.

In the courtyard below, the goblins were being slaughtered by a sea of dwarves while on the west wall soldiers found themselves outmatched by the gray-green creatures. As Reod watched, the west wall warder was grabbed and pulled over the side. Soldiers there were losing, backing away from the edge. Reod leaned out the window and yelled to the soldiers in the courtyard to go to the walls.

But it was too late. Dwarves screamed and died. More goblins streamed over the wall.

Somewhere the keeper was calling out for every available soldier. Reod's guards looked at each other.

"You stay," one said, and left. The other rocked from side to side, unable to stand still, his face a mask of shock as he watched through the window.

Reod had survived many battles, and not all of them had been victorious. He recognized this moment. Barring the unforeseen, the dwarves had just lost.

And out there somewhere was Tamun. He looked at his remaining guard. One soldier, armed and armored, against Reod's bare hands.

He looked out again, saw dwarves crumple, heard goblins howling their battle lust. The screams of villagers quieted.

There was no question about it now. The keep was going down.

A shadow passed overhead.

Sekena gripped the dragon's neck, looking down at tiny, white-covered mountains. This one, maybe? No, not this one. But soon.

After weeks, they were finally on their way.

When the dragon had brought them to the keep, he had set them down a little ways away and let Mama and Tamun walk ahead so that the dragon wouldn't cause panic among the dwarves. The dragon and Sekena had only stayed long enough to see them vanish into the keep.

Hungry, the dragon had told her in irritable hisses.

"But we can't just leave."

Either I eat your friends or I eat someone else's friends, he said. *I invite you to choose.*

So they had left and he had begun his days-long hunt for food. Real meals, this time, she discovered, not just snacks like toasted goblins. The whelps watched, learned, and took what little remained of his

kills when he was done with them. It took Sekena
more than a little getting used to, watching them eat.

Then they had gone back to the cave and the dragons had all slept.

For days.

By then there had been no question in her mind that
he understood her. She told him to wake up, that it
was time to go back to the keep. His eyes opened, but
only for moments, and then he was asleep again. She
tried to reason with him, but he remained a snoring
mountain, ignoring her completely.

For many days she resisted the powerful temptation
to kick him in the nose. Finally she tried that, too. He
brushed her away. When she persisted, he grabbed
her, pressing her down under his arm for long hours as
he continued to snore.

Finally he woke. Done with his week-long nap, he
spent hours stretching, ignoring her questions, comments, demands, and insults. Then he put her atop his
neck, and they were airborne, on their way to the
keep, the whelps winging along behind.

And now, at long last, they were over the keep.
There it was, below, small and distant, like a tiny
brick.

But it didn't look quite right. It seemed to be overrun by gray-green insects, all piled up against the
walls. Plumes of smoke rose from dots of fire inside
the keep and the fields beyond.

She yelled at the dragon, or maybe she hissed at it,
she was no longer sure. He had to do something, she
told him frantically. Find her mother and sister. Get
them away. Protect the keep.

The dragon landed on the edge of the surrounding
cliffs. He plucked her off his neck and put her down
on the ground.

Knowing that he meant to leave her there, she
howled her defiance, but he was too quick. Spreading
great wings, he dove down across the keep, the whelps
following.

Across the goblins he exhaled a wide stream of fire, just as he had done at Teedmar. Some burst into flame and many fell back out of fear, but there were so many more, and they kept coming.

The smallest whelp came face-to-face with a kite. They had only the week before learned to spit fire, so he showed the goblins what he had learned. The kite caught fire like a torch and plummeted. The second whelp glided across the field, spitting fire at spots the great dragon had missed.

Goblins shot spears into the sky. Most missed, coming down on the hordes themselves, but some found their mark. The second whelp screamed with shock and fury, trying to shake loose a spear through his wing. Unable to stay up he faltered and dropped. Goblins grabbed for him and he flailed, cutting down a handful of the gray-green creatures at a time. But another handful came, and then another, and the whelp vanished into the seething crowd.

The great dragon took spears in his side as well, carrying them along as he finished his circle, leaving a trail of fire in his wake. When he finally returned to the cliff, blood was dripping down his flank.

Sekena wrestled the spears out of his hide as he hissed with pain.

"Stupid, stupid, stupid," she told him as she stood there, shaking, furious with him, grateful to have him back.

The surviving whelp, landed and watched, trembling, making small chirping sounds. The dragon hissed at the little creature to be silent, and he was, staring mournfully down at the field where his brother had fallen.

By the time Sekena pulled the last spear from the dragon's side, she was sobbing unrestrainedly. He bent his head close to her, his breath warm and comforting. Her shaking subsided as she inhaled his scent in long, ragged breaths. She pressed herself close.

Hope came and left with the dragons. The goblins took the dragons' retreat as encouragement. Over the walls they came, barely held back at all by the dwarven lines.

The young female soldier Reod had talked to the day before still stood at the wall, but she looked much older now. She had been among the few left keeping up the chant-like songs. Now she, too, fell silent.

Tamun.

He met the gaze of his single guard. The dwarf's face was hard in this midmorning light. There were rings under his eyes, lines etched deeply, and his body shook with the craving to do something.

"Go," Reod told him, and he did. Reod was out the door an instant later.

Find her first, then get her to safety.

He wrapped the blankets around his head and shoulders to cover his dark hair and human face. Out on the catwalk he slumped a little, striving to make himself seem shorter and a poorer target. No others were up here naked of helmet and weapons as was he. He felt vulnerable.

A few steps away a dwarf ran a goblin through with a blade. The goblin chittered, grabbing at his slayer's arm until the strength ran out of its fingers and its eyes rolled up into its head. Stubborn, they were, and too stupid to notice when they were dead. They had some of the best and worst features attackers might have. He stepped over another corpse.

"Hey," a soldier yelled at him. "It's not safe up here. Get down into the courtyard!"

The courtyard below was littered with corpses, both goblin and dwarven. He thought to ask the soldier how it was safer there, but refrained. Down the stairs he went, ducking into the main building, where he passed dwarves huddling in corners, trying to hide. Goblins were all through buildings. There was no

safety here, and the tunnels down below the storage
rooms would be packed fully. There was no safety anywhere.

For a moment Reod thought he heard the nearby
barks of an orc captain. If the orcs had already come—

He stepped over bodies. More were goblin than
dwarf, but not enough to be reassuring. Weapons were
surprisingly scarce among the dead and were doubtless
hidden among the surviving villagers in their dark corners and rooms. As he turned a corner, a goblin turned
and charged.

Reod doubted the creature would respond to
orders in its current state. While it would have been
safer to turn and run, instinct kicked in first. He
stepped forward and to the side, one hand going to
the goblin's sword arm and the other elbow into the
creature's neck. By the time the goblin hit the floor,
Reod had its weapon in his hand and was down the
hall.

Soldiers and goblins roved past. He hid when he
could. The doorway where he had seen Tamun the day
before was now shut and bolted. He pounded on it. No
response. She could be in there, but she could also be
anywhere.

Another explosion hit the side of the keep, shaking
the floor under him like an earthquake. He put his
hands on the door for balance and felt the bolt slide
back.

Someone inside the room, curious or afraid, was
about to open the door. Reod grabbed the handle,
pulled against the attempt to open, hoping to make
them think it stuck. The pull came again, stronger.
Finally he let go, following the opening door into the
dark room, shutting it hard behind him.

The stench was overpowering. So many bodies huddled together here that all had to stand. They would
not breathe well for long.

"Get out," a dwarven man hissed, his face half covered with blood.

Reod's head was still hidden under a wrap of blankets. This was the welcome another dwarf would receive. What welcome would Reod Dai get? He whispered to disguise his voice.

"I search for Tamun and Melelki of the southern peaks. Are they here?"

"No. Go away."

"I have a message for them. From their sister-daughter Sekena."

The man's eyes flickered, uncertain.

They were here indeed.

"Tell them I will be waiting outside for a count of twenty, and then I will leave."

He pulled open the door and left, walking to the end of the hallway. There he stood, half turned away, listening to distant yells.

At the count of fifteen, they came out. Head still hidden, still slumped, he beckoned them closer. Tamun's arm was caked with dried blood. Both their faces were bruised.

"What message?" Melelki demanded in a whisper, glancing around.

He beckoned again. They took furtive steps forward. When he judged them to be as close as they would come, he turned and pulled back the blanket.

It was Tamun's face he watched. He saw shock there, and surprise, but she did not turn to leave, neither did she draw the sword she had from its ill-fitting scabbard. Melelki's eyes narrowed.

"You trick us?"

"Only in part. Sekena is nearby and safe. But listen: Gurn Keep is dying. If you stay here, you will be among the next to be slaughtered. There are ways out. Come with me."

"They say you—"

"I know what they say." He held out his hand to Tamun. "Come with me. Please."

"But you—"

He shook his head. "Time for that later. Will you

stay here and die? Come with me, instead. I beg you."

The two exchanged glances. Melelki nodded.

Blanket back around his head, he led them into the courtyard and up the stairs. A goblin came at him and he pushed it off the stairs into the courtyard below. The creature fell onto a patch of stone, stunned enough that for a moment it forgot what it had been doing.

The soldiers at the walls ignored Reod and the two women. The three of them dashed by to stay out of the way of the fighting. More kites flew overhead, then something dropped at their feet. Reod kicked the bloody dwarven foot under the cover of a fallen goblin.

Another explosion came, then another. More kites flew from the siege towers, along with rocks and spears. Some hit dwarves, some hit the kites.

At the north wall, Reod threw his blankets aside. The breeze chilled his sweat-soaked clothes. He stood on the edge of the wall, waving his arms over his head, hoping to signal the dragon and its small dwarven companion up on the cliff's edge.

The motion attracted the goblins along the base of the walls instead. They pointed, jumped up and down, and began to move their ladders. The dragon and dwarf on the cliff had not seemed to notice at all.

He backed the three of them away from the edge of the wall. From the courtyard below came a loud crash followed by desperate yells. The inner gate had at last fallen.

One of the warders was calling, over and over, for a retreat. Where, Reod wondered, were the dwarves to retreat *to*? Into the buildings of the keep? That would be like rats on a sinking ship hiding belowdecks.

Someone grabbed his arm. It was the First Watch Keeper, her face streaming with sweat and blood, her other hand gripping her sword too tightly. Behind her was Hamon, limping and holding his hand against a bloody cut in his side.

"Now what?" she demanded of Reod. "What do we do now?"

Hamon stepped forward. "Help us. Tell us what to do."

Reod thought of all the things he could say, of the things he had already said.

Instead he said, "Listen: your only choice is to stay and die, or flee and live. You will not have the choice for long. I advise you to flee."

"Is that the best you can do?" the keeper howled. She spat at him, turned, and ran back along the walls to the west, where the fighting was hardest.

"Then tell me what I should have done," Hamon said, his voice hard and full of self-recrimination.

"You have done all that you could. Nothing could have changed this. There were too many of them."

Hamon nodded distractedly at Reod's words. Perhaps he believed him.

"Surely you can talk to the goblins and orcs. Tell them to go away."

"Look out across the field, Elder. Their flags are down. They are no longer under orc command. There is no more order. They simply come. It is a mob, and no talk will turn it back."

The elder's voice was soft. "Please try."

Reod strode forward to the edge of the wall where goblins were arriving on ladders. He lifted his goblin sword to point to the sky. In the goblin-orc battle-tongue he cried, "This is the wrong side, you idiots. Go down! Go to the other side!"

They paused, as if dimly remembering something, then they came again, grinning and blood-hungry. One of them leveled a spear at him. Reod fell back and dwarven soldiers moved to intercept the invaders.

Here the line still held, if barely. On the west wall, goblins were picking over dead dwarves before tossing the bodies over the walls.

With a moan Hamon rushed off and Reod suspected he would not see the elder again. Grabbing Tamun and

Melelki's hands, he drew them back to the rear wall, as far from the fighting as possible.

A glance back up at the cliff showed no change. It had been a good idea, but the dragon was not coming. He would have to find another way to get them out.

Dragon-scent comforted Sekena, but still she worried over him.

Well enough, he told her, again and again.

When at last Sekena finally remembered to look back at the keep, dread and fear shot through her anew. The gray-green goblins were everywhere. Everywhere! Where were the dwarves? It could not have come to this, not so soon.

Her sister and mother were down there.

He craned his head, eyes close to hers, smelling her anxiety.

She said it fast, in hisses and gestures. It did not matter to her now that she was speaking his language with no hesitation at all. All that mattered was making him understand.

Together they looked back at the keep.

Reod led them along the east wall. He had his sword out. As goblins rushed at them, he barked in the battle-tongue to give him a moment's advantage. They truly were simple creatures, easy to defeat one at a time. Some he ran through, some he just pushed over the wall.

Down below, villagers had opened the keep's small back gate. They now streamed out, running through the scattered goblin forces in a last attempt at escape. An orc captain swung a spiked fist and three villagers went down in blood.

Melelki cried out suddenly, a mother's protective fury. By the time Reod had turned, Tamun's sword was moving, cutting into an attacking goblin's stomach. Her movements were crude but effective. In her eyes there was no hesitation and not a flicker of remorse.

She had changed since she first cut down Icatian soldiers in the Crimson Peaks. She had learned to kill.

He noticed her blade, which glinted strangely. It was of high-dwarven design, made for the elite of the warriors, but it was not a metal he recognized. Melelki's knife glinted similarly. Indeed, they did not seem to be metal at all. What were they?

And then he understood: they were dragon shell. Rare weapons, those. Dragon shell was far harder to work than metal, but once worked it kept its edge forever. He was reminded of Sekena's little shard, which she had so cherished.

Sekena's shard.

"Give me your knife," he snapped at Melelki. She hesitated, then handed it to him hilt first. He carefully wiped both sides clean on his trousers, and held it high, the flat blade facing the cliff top as he tilted it back and forth in the sunlight. A short laugh of understanding came from Tamun, who wiped off her own blade and began to do the same.

From behind them came the last, desperate battle cries of dwarven warriors.

Maybe, thought Reod, angling the blade again and again, aiming for the small figure next to the dragon. Just maybe.

"There!" Sekena cried, as she saw flickering light. On the wall three small figures stood, one of them dark haired.

Stay, the dragon told her.

"By the Moon, I will *not,*" she howled, throwing her arms around his neck just before he could lift his head out of reach. He reached up a claw to pluck her off, but she gripped him tighter, kicking at his claw.

*Foolish pet, you will fall off and die. Do as I tell
you.*

"You're wasting time. Fly!"

The dragon hissed frustration and patted her flat on
his neck. Then he raised enormous wings and kicked
off the cliff, diving down to the keep so fast that
Sekena's stomach lurched and spun.

The dragon swooped down from the cliff in what
seemed almost a fall, somehow managing to knock
two goblins off the edge of the wall as it landed. Each
of its feet were longer than a dwarf might be tall. Once
landed, the creature's bulk spanned two walls, back
feet on one, front feet on the next.

And head right in front of them.

This close Reod could see that the dragon was a full
adult, probably well past breeding years.

"Get up," Sekena yelled.

The dragon reached for Tamun. Reod stifled his
instinct to protect as a great clawed hand picked her
up and set her on the dragon's neck. The clawed hand
reached next for Melelki, who tensed but did not
resist.

"Go, go!" Reod yelled, as he turned to face chittering goblins, so drunk on battle blood that they
would attack a great dragon. He still held Melelki's
knife in one hand and the goblin blade in the other.
He would not stand long against them, but he was
sure that he could keep the monsters at bay the few
moments it would take for the dragon to get into the
air.

Claws surrounded his shoulders. He struggled
against the closing grip as he realized the dragon
meant to take him as well.

"No!" he yelled. "Let me alone! Go!"

Suddenly the keep dropped out from under him. He
fought the beginnings of panic as he realized that he
was in midair with nothing under him. Dragon claws

held tight around his chest, pinning his arms to his sides. He closed his eyes, took deep breaths, forced the panic away.

Then he opened his eyes and looked down again, watching the greatest loss of the dwarven people as it shrank to the size of an anthill.

CHAPTER
14

REOD HAD AMPLE OPPORTUNITY TO WONDER if the dragon remembered that it still had him gripped with its front claws. He could not breathe properly and his chest and arms ached under the creature's orange-tinted nails, each of which was nearly as long as his forearm.

Wind blew frigidly across Reod's face and through his hair. For a time his ears had ached, but now he could no longer feel them. His hood flapped uselessly behind his head. If he could get to it, the hood would help keep the worst of the cold away.

But for that to be, the dragon would have to open his claws, and then Reod would fall.

It was a long way down.

Even in a life of impressive extremes, this was a new experience for Reod. Never had he been this far above the land. Never had he been carried in the claws of a dragon. Never had anyone ever suggested to him that such a thing might be possible, and never had anyone spoken of tame dragons. The greatest wizards he knew would have been content to keep dragons like this at a good distance.

As they rose from Gurn Keep, the beast had seemed to struggle into the air, but after that the creature might have been a cloud for all the effort it seemed to take to stay high above the small mountains and lakes below. Great wings stretched above Reod, pushing them through the wide sky, holding the four of them up over a dizzying drop.

Reod sucked in knife-cold air. He was not sure he even held Melelki's dragon-shell knife anymore. He could barely feel his fingers. The goblin blade in his other hand was gone—he had dropped it as they lifted over the keep, hoping to take out one more goblin as he left. Below a small figure had doubled over. Perhaps he had succeeded.

But it was a tiny victory in the face of what was lost: a keep and all those who had sought refuge inside. By now goblins and orcs would be all through the burning buildings of Gurn, slaughtering dwarven solders and gaining vicious pleasures from terrified villagers who hid there. In such a state of lust and triumph, the goblins and orcs would not care what the dwarves said or promised. Or even if they surrendered.

He could well imagine it. Indeed, only the painful cold and his light-headedness kept him from doing so in better detail than he wanted.

Still he clung to hope. Even in victory orcs and goblins would fight each other. And the keep's back gate had been opened, letting some escape. There would be the tunnels underneath, which must have been opened again. Many would live.

Many more would die.

Each inhale seared his lungs with freezing air. Each exhale left frost on his beard. His mind kept drifting. Cries of pain. Images of bloodshed. Genkr's scowling face. Tamun.

Tamun.

She was above him, on the dragon's back, and that thought alone made him feel as if a burden had been lifted from him. Whatever else had happened or might yet happen, he had taken her away from the keep. She would not die at the hands of goblins.

The dragon began to descend toward the tallest of a series of mountain peaks. Down they went, past sharp, snow-covered fingers and sheer white cliffs. They dropped nearly a third of the way down, toward the winding white river below. There a sheltered plateau grew large, its flat surface lightly snow-dusted by recent storms.

And then they were not moving. The dragon set Reod on his feet and at last opened his claws. Pain crashed through Reod's whole body and his legs would not hold him. As he toppled over the claws caught him, then slowly let him down onto the rocky, snow-covered ground. He lay there breathing hard, teeth clenched against his own screams of agony from blood rushing through his body like fire.

When the pain began to ease he opened his eyes. His right hand still clenched Melelki's knife.

"Is he all right?"

That was Sekena's voice.

He looked up, blinked. There was Melelki. She knelt down on the snow, bent over him, wisps of dwarven streaked hair tangling in the chill breeze.

"Ta, what's wrong? Are you sick?"

He tried to speak, made a croaking sound. Melelki touched his face.

"Cold, is what he is," she said. "Fragile humans."

A cloak was laid over him as he heard the sounds of a fire being started behind him.

Tamun was near. He could hear her footsteps, her soft voice.

"They get cold so easily, Mama." Sekena again.

"That they do."

He began to laugh, but it came out as a wheeze.

"You rest, now," Melelki said.

The fire crackled and smoked. As it sparked to life, Reod began to feel the warmth. His own spirit slowly come back to him. After a time Melelki helped him to sit up and Sekena rolled a rock over for him to lean against. She handed him dried meat and offered him some water. He nodded his thanks.

The great dragon had laid itself down close by, head snaked around, brilliant green-and-red scales sharp against the white snow. Slitted pupils stared at them unblinkingly. The creature was close enough that Reod was again aware of how large it was. It could probably down him in one swallow.

But now it was blocking the chill wind and watching. The whelp sat watching nearby as well.

Reod blinked, blinked again, and realized that Sekena had been crouched down in front of him, talking to him. She had cut her hair short, so short that it barely came below her ears.

"You understand?" she asked.

"What?" His mind was still so fuzzy.

She exhaled, started again. "Touch my dragons with your magic and I will take you apart at every joint. Slowly. You may be powerful, mud wizard, but even so, I will find a way."

Powerful was the last thing he felt right now.

"Of course," he whispered hoarsely. "I accept."

She hesitated, surprised. Was she expecting a struggle? From him? Now?

"Ta, just like that?"

Before him crouched perhaps the only creature in all of Sarpadia who had not merely survived an encounter with a great dragon, but had made it into an ally. A fifteen-year-old dwarven woman who tamed dragons warning an exhausted human not to touch her dragons. He smiled.

"You've done well, Sekena."

She looked at him a moment, as if searching for hidden meanings. Finding none, she blushed a little.

"Ta, but I wish I had been there on the field, fighting. I came as soon as I could, but then I had to stand and watch because *he* wouldn't let me fight. I didn't even have a weapon!"

Reod glanced at the dragon, meeting its golden eyes for a moment before looking back at Sekena.

"Yes, you did."

"We arrived too late. Had we come earlier—"

"No, you arrived at the best possible time."

"But—no. Then why did the goblins take the keep?"

He thought of soldiers and drums and dwarven leaders who would have given their lives to find the right answers and instead just gave their lives.

As ever, it was the survivors who had the luxury to ask why.

"There are many reasons why battles are lost. It is not simple."

Then Tamun was there, pushing her sister aside. She glared down at him.

"It is simple enough. Tell us how the goblins learned to make eggs that explode, Reod Dai. Tell us you had nothing to do with that."

"Tamun—"

"Gurn Keep is your fault," she said. "Your fault that goblins and orcs come together like that, build kites and towers—"

"They have come against us for generations, daughter," Melelki broke in. "Many times."

"But they used to come in small groups. This was an army! How many died today? Reod, how many did you kill today? And how many more at Teedmar?"

"Tamun, listen: Teedmar was nothing to do with me."

"At least it is true of *something*. Ta, I cannot believe that I would think to mate with a thing like you—"

"Your taste in men," Reod snapped, "is definitely not my fault."

He struggled to his feet, waving off Melelki's offer of help. He felt terribly unsteady, but though the world spun around him, anger fueled his resolve to stand. His feet ached, but at least the overwhelming pain was gone. He took a tentative step forward and looked into her eyes, this woman for whom he had raced across countries and repeatedly risked his own life. Her face was full of fury.

"Yes," he said quietly, feeling his own anger melt, "I did all that. There isn't a race in Sarpadia I haven't done something for. Or to."

"The perfect mercenary," Sekena said, respect in her tone.

"The perfect traitor," Tamun spat.

"Why?" Melelki asked, seeming truly curious.

The great dragon blinked. Tamun turned away.

It was a question to which he had always thought he had a good answer. And now? He was tired. Too tired.

"I had reasons."

"Say them," Melelki encouraged.

"I thought that if I could give my people a common enemy—orcs and goblins—we would stop fighting among ourselves. Icatia was tearing itself apart over the words of dead men. What waste and stupidity. And suffering. I meant the goblins and orcs for my people, who could easily face them. They never should have touched yours at all, and never would have if the elves had let me finish the job they hired me to do. And so I saw to it that the elves had a taste of what they had done, to make them understand the cost of their acts—"

He cut himself off, remembering the elvish boy Andli and a fortress on fire.

Slowly he shook his head. "But it never really was that simple. Even the followers of Tourach were only trying to survive as best they could, honoring what they cherished most."

"And the dwarven people?" Tamun demanded, bringing him back. "What ill do we pay for?"

"None."

"Then why? *Why?*"

Tamun had tears in her eyes, and that shocked Reod more than anything she had said. Never had he seen such a thing. A dwarf might weep, but it would always be dry. In his years in the Crimson Peaks he had never once seen dwarven tears.

The tears trailed down her cheeks. He longed to touch her.

"Because," he said wearily, "I thought I could change the world." In the distance, where Gurn Keep would have been, a column of smoke rose into the blue sky. "And I guess I did."

"We all change the world," Melelki said.

"Or none of us do," Sekena said, coming back from the cave with another load of wood, feeding it to the fire. "Do other dwarves live?"

There would be outlying communities who remained untouched by the roving bands of goblins and orcs. Some would have escaped Gurn Keep.

"Yes."

"But so many dead!" Tamun said.

"Is that Reod's work?" Melelki asked. "Remember the count of orcs and goblins at the keep. They would have come against us eventually."

"No," Tamun said. "He taught them to do this. He did this to us."

For a long moment he looked at her, then he looked elsewhere.

"I believe that there is a town at the base of this mountain," he said, his voice flat.

"Scarza," Sekena said.

"Where is the path downward?"

Melelki and Sekena exchanged glances. Neither spoke.

"Never mind. I will find it."

He turned and began to slowly walk, concentrating on each step as he ignored his sore muscles, twists, bruises, and cuts. Perhaps even in his condition he could manage the way down the game trails to the town before nightfall.

Then Sekena was at his side, following him to the edge of the plateau.

"Don't go. We need your help. There are still goblins and orcs out there. Our people need your help."

"I'll mention it to my commander."

"What? You're going back to Icatia?"

"Yes."

"Ta, no! They'll kill you there."

"Probably."

"No, you should stay."

"What? Have I not caused all the world's pains? Still you would have me stay?"

"Of course Tamun is angry. Look at what has happened to her, and our people! But there is more than anger in her. She cares for you."

He laughed. "She's a young fool."

Sekena bristled. "She's my sister."

"She will be better off with her own kind."

"Probably true, but she'll never believe it. I will have to listen to her whine until her heat is over, and that's years away. Years! Please don't leave."

He paused at the edge of the path, looked at Sekena, her short, streaked hair flicking in the breeze, her brown eyes just short of begging.

"I'm tired. I can't fight anymore. It's time for me to go back to my own people. Let them judge me."

Melelki had joined them. Tamun stayed by the fire, her back to them, shoulders hunched in anger.

"Orcs and goblins troubled us before you came," Melelki said, "but was it not your touch that made them into an army? You may be the only one in Sarpadia who can touch them again to keep us safe."

"With Gurn Keep and Teedmar destroyed, your people have little defense left. You are best off scattering deep into the Crimson Peaks. Goblins and orcs will be reluctant to go that far to find you. Scatter and hide. The only way for you to win this war is to be somewhere else. To wait."

Was that all he could do anymore, advise people to run? He rubbed his eyes, looked at the three dwarves he had managed to save from certain death.

Three out of thousands.

They were silent. Clouds passed by overhead, thick and tall, patches of sharp blue cutting between them.

"It may be useless for us to fight," Melelki said quietly, "but we have to try. And you have to help us."

"I have tried," he said tightly. "Again and again. Look what my efforts have come to."

Tamun took a few steps toward them. "You have brought the Hells to my people. You."

She had judged him and found him guilty. Now all that remained was to pay for his crimes. That would be his own personal peace, to finally be done with the struggle. That peace waited for him in Icatia.

"Ta," Melelki said, "we have fought goblins and orcs for as long as anyone can remember."

"But how much worse it is now than ever before!" Tamun cried.

"Yes, but to blame Reod—" she pointed at the whelp, who lay on its side, sunning himself in the bits of light that came between clouds "—is like blaming a whelp for exploding. It is these times that made those whelps into weapons. How is this human any different?"

Sekena's expression darkened at the mention of the whelp.

Reod touched her arm. "Unless they attack me, I will do them no harm. I give you my word."

She nodded, relaxing a little. Never had he seen such a bond before. If he had more time, it would be good to learn more about Sekena and her dragons.

"He chose to destroy," Tamun said. "That is how he is different."

Melelki cocked her head at her eldest daughter. "You think so? How much did he really choose? And how much did *you* choose, when you chose him?"

Tamun snorted, stamped back to the fire.

Melelki turned to him. "I will tell you what I see. I see that you are as much a tool of war as goblin eggs or the kites."

"Tools outlive their usefulness."

She shrugged. "Is a tool a good judge of itself? Not to my eyes."

"We agree on that, at least," he said. "I will go back to Icatia and be judged by my own kind."

He looked down at the rocky game path. He was still shaking, so he picked his way carefully down and over the hard snow and ice, grabbing boulders and trees to steady himself. For a time there was no sound but his own scratching in the snow. They had let him go. He felt both relief and a touch of sorrow.

No, he told himself. It was better this way.

And then there were steps behind him. Short, dwarven steps. He did not look back.

He slipped a little, caught himself.

"Did it not occur to you," came Tamun's voice, "that goblins and orcs would take the weapons you gave them across the land to our dwarven villages?"

For weeks after the volcano he had thought her dead, crushed and burnt by rivers of fire. He went to Gurn Keep hoping beyond reason that she might have survived. And she had.

"Or that maybe," she continued, "the elves might have helped us fight the goblins and orcs if you had not first tried to destroy their mushrooms? Did you think of that?"

At Gurn Keep he had done everything he could to save her, and would have given his own life so that she could have kept hers.

"Do you make enemies everywhere you go, Reod Dai?"

Now he was walking away from her. It was reward enough, he told himself, that she was alive and well.

"Ta," she exploded, "do you not think at *all*?"

He refused to argue with her. It would all be sorted out in Icatia. Not here in the dwarven mountains, but in human lands, by human eyes. The Icatian military court would review every action he had taken, in great detail, and then carefully render a final judgment. He would let his own kind decide if he had made mistakes.

His own kind. Not a temperamental dwarven woman in heat.

Still the footsteps followed, and he could not guess at why. It was yet another inexplicable difference between human and dwarf. The races were as compatible as fish and birds. He had been greatly mistaken to think otherwise.

But that was all over now. He would not need to struggle his whole life to understand this difficult, volatile creature.

And yet she still followed him.

They picked their way down a snow-covered ravine which led onto a flat portion of road. There Tamun dashed in front of him, turned to face him, blocking his path. He stopped.

"You run." She exhaled derisively. "Ta. Coward. Have you not the will to stay and fight?"

She could not have surprised him more. Fight? Fight what? Her? He would never, ever understand her. Not even a little. No answer would be right, so he said nothing.

"You must stay and help us."

"Have I not done enough harm already?"

"Whatever you have done already, there is more you must yet do."

He laughed shortly, incredulous.

"No."

"Is there so little strength in you?"

"Yes."

She scowled. "I thought there was more spirit in the man I still choose as my mate."

Her words shot through him, at first only confusing

his already muddled mind. Then they gathered strength inside him, like a hard, twisting wind, tearing at the walls inside him that kept away the worst of the pain, setting them to crumbling.

He was exhausted, he realized suddenly. Deeply exhausted and bone weary. He kicked aside a little snow at his feet and sat down. Tamun knelt nearby, the cold of the snow not seeming to trouble her in the least. Were dwarves never cold?

"Do you listen?" she demanded.

A shot of sun came down on them, giving gold highlights to her brown hair.

"Ah, Tamun—no. We are not right to be mated. Surely you see that."

"I want you to be father to my children."

Those words were clear enough that he could not possibly have misunderstood. He did not know what to think. Behind her were tall, snow-dusted pines. In the chill snow-covered quiet he shook his head.

"Tamun, there's a war on. Not just orcs and goblins, but all of Sarpadia. It's not going to get any better. When you make your family, you should be with your own kind."

"You will tell me what I need, too?"

"Listen: there will be war everywhere. These are not good times in which to make children."

She grabbed him by the shoulders, pushed him back into the snow, bent over him, and kissed him fiercely. He struggled, but she was strong, her lips were warm, and for a long moment there was nowhere else he wanted to be.

"Ta," she said, pulling back but still pressing his chest down with her hands, "there is no better time to make children than when the world is falling down. Our people need children. We need hope and we need children."

He breathed raggedly. "Children need such care—"

"Then we will give them care."

"Tamun, you and I—we are not even the same race."

"I have noticed."

"I'm not even sure it is possible."

She grinned. "To save my people or to make children with me?"

It seemed it had been forever since he had seen her smile. Did the sun shine more brightly? His heart felt suddenly lighter.

"Children," he said, noticing how the word felt on his tongue.

"Both are possible, I have heard," she said. "Easy? Ta, not easy. We will have to try hard and often, yes?"

"Tamun, you know what I am. What I have done. Already you have placed the blame for all the ills of the world at my feet."

"Perhaps I was hasty."

"Perhaps you were not. You would have me stay, after all that?"

"I see what you are. I see that when you promise yourself, you mean to make the promise true. Promise to me. Help me make children. Help me protect them in these times."

He considered her words, trying to find the will to struggle against the hope that was now building inside him.

Icatia's justice would be simple and harsh. He could go home and die, or he could make a new home here. With her.

It was not really such a hard choice.

"A promise."

"Promise to me, and I shall promise to you."

He thought of the life that he would share with her, of living with her and her mother and sister, of hiding, fighting, of struggling to protect the children they might or might not be able to bring into this uncertain and terrible world.

And then there were the dragons.

She must have seen something change in his expression, because she sat up. He did, too.

At last he said, "I cannot promise to you that easily. Your mother and sister and even your sister's dragons must all agree to this. Then—then I will promise to you."

The smile on her face was back, and hope was a warm flame inside him. She stood, pulled him to his feet.

"Tamun, wait—are you sure?"

"Ta, *yes.*"

"Woman, you change your mind so easily! How many more times will I have to walk up and down this mountain while you berate me?"

She laughed and reached her fingers to his chest. He felt the heat and magic of her touch, felt it call to him.

"No more times," she said. "I promise you, too."

He bent down over this short woman, who was nothing like human, bringing his lips down to hers. He still felt so unsteady that he had to put his hands on her shoulders to be certain he did not fall. Another kiss, and then another, and her smile was contagious.

"Are you still sure?" he asked.

"Yes."

He laughed. "How about now?"

"Ta, *human,* will I ever understand you?"

Back up the mountain they went. As they hiked he looked out at distant peaks, considering the ways the world might yet go. He thought about his family-to-be and the troubles of the dwarven people and the blood that would be shed, not only in the Crimson Peaks, but everywhere.

He thought also of his other promise, the one he had made to the thrulls. Even now they would be awaiting his return, awaiting the aid he had promised them. With luck, by the time he returned, thrulls would be the masters of Achtep Keep.

Her hand was warm in his. Callused, like his own, from wielding a sword, from the day-by-day struggles to stay alive.

He would have to tell her all about that other promise, about why he would have to leave her again, and why, this time, she and her family absolutely could not follow him.

Soon. He would tell her all about it soon.

But not just yet.